I0646688

TED TAYLER

DEADLY FORMULA

BOOKS

By Ted Tayler

The Freeman Files

Fatal Decision

Last Orders

Pressure Point

Deadly Formula

Final Deal

Barking Mad

Creature Discomforts

Silent Terror

Night Train

All Things Bright

Buried Secrets

A Genuine Mistake

Strange Beginnings

Dead Reckoning

A Normal November

Into the Sunlight

Tame the Storm

One True Friend

Whispered Truths

A Morning Murder

Quick to Anger

Vinci Books

vinci-books.com

Published by Vinci Books Ltd in 2025

1

Copyright © Ted Tayler 2020

The publisher and the author have made every effort to obtain permissions for any third party material used in this book and to comply with copyright law. Any queries in this respect should be brought to the attention of the publisher and any omissions will be corrected in future editions.

A CIP catalogue record for this book is available from the British Library.

Paperback ISBN: 9781036704902

Chapter One

"IS THE COAST CLEAR, MR FREEMAN?"

Gus hardly had time to unlock his shed door before the disembodied voice broke into his thoughts on how to spend his unexpected free time.

"What's the matter, Bert?" he asked, realising it was his friend from the neighbouring allotment.

"I can't come here without being pestered by the Reverend," said Bert, emerging from the dark recesses of his six-foot by four-foot hut.

Gus smiled.

Clemency Bentham, the celebrant from Frank North's funeral, had taken over the plot next to Gus. She was young and very keen to learn. Bert was the fount of knowledge in the village for everything related to gardening.

"You can't blame her for tapping into your wealth of experience, Bert," said Gus, "isn't that what I've been doing ever since I came to live here?"

"You keep to yourself, Mr Freeman. I never expect you

to discuss one of your cases with me while digging, hoeing or planting."

"Ah, she's trying to save your soul. Is that it?" laughed Gus.

"The Reverend keeps dropping hints. Why do I only see you here on the allotment, Mr Penman? Why don't you pop next door to the church on Sunday? Have you ever given produce for the Harvest Festival?"

"Were you ever a regular churchgoer, Bert?"

"Many years ago. Anyway, I don't see you going there, Mr Freeman."

"Not my thing, Bert. Tess and I got married in a registry office. We had no children to get christened. So I opted to go straight to the crematorium when she died, as we did with Frank North the other day."

"Cora and I got married in Devizes, at St Mary's; in 1955, I'd come home from Kowloon a month earlier. After my National Service stint ended."

"That tour of duty lasted eighteen months, didn't it?" asked Gus.

"Yes, I went to Oswestry for basic training, then travelled to Woolwich Barracks. That place had been home to the Royal Artillery since the latter part of the eighteenth century. We travelled to Southampton and then sailed out to Kowloon. It took us over four weeks. It was a different world, I can tell you. I missed the Wiltshire countryside, and I could have done without the sights I saw and the things I had to do."

Tonight was the first time Bert had ever mentioned his early life. Gus hadn't realised that he had ever travelled abroad. Let alone see action on the other side of the world. Gus had only just started school in Salisbury when National Service ended.

"Did you go straight into the butcher's shop after they demobbed you?" Gus asked.

"Cora and I spent the weekend in Sidmouth," said Bert, "no exotic honeymoons in those days. Then on Tuesday morning, I started back to work with my father. I'd been learning the butchery trade ever since I left school at fifteen. I took over the shop when he retired."

"Did you and Cora have children?" asked Gus, realising how little he knew, even after three years of seeing Bert several times a week.

"A boy and a girl," said Bert, "David and Margaret. They're both married with children. David lives in Canada. Margaret and her family are in New Zealand."

Bert had a faraway look in his eye.

"Are they able to visit you, Bert?" asked Gus.

"They're too busy. We talk on the phone from time to time. I couldn't travel that far, not with my aches and pains. It is what it is. We were never close after their mother died."

"When did you lose Cora?"

"My wife died in 2005. I lost her to dementia ten years before that. The children had already moved abroad. Neither wanted to return to England to help, so I battled on alone. It was a blessing when her pain ended.

"Had you both gone to church before Cora's illness?" asked Gus.

Bert nodded.

"I've not been through the door since her funeral."

"David and Margaret came home for that, I imagine?"

"They managed to get over for a few days. We have to count our blessings, Mr Freeman. They're fit and well, have excellent jobs, and the grandchildren get a good education. I'll be out of their hair soon enough. There won't be much to share between them when I'm gone. They aren't relying on it; that's a blessing. My little windfall might pay for a holiday or help with the kids' higher education. It won't change their lives."

"When I came here this evening, I wondered what to do with myself for the rest of the week. We cleared another case yesterday, and my bosses told me to take a break. All we've done so far is have a morbid conversation about death. Can we change the subject, Bert?"

"It's that Clemency woman's fault," replied Bert. "She keeps asking me how I'm feeling; and telling me to take it easy, not to overdo it at my age. Working this soil keeps me as fit as I've any right to be at eighty-five. I was here for two hours yesterday, and I distinctly heard her tutting when I passed the church gate and headed toward the pub. I earned a pint as a reward for my labour."

Bert fetched a seed tray from the shed and placed it on its side on the ground. He lowered himself to sit for a while.

"It catches up with you, doesn't it, Bert?" said Gus. "Are you sure you haven't been working too hard?"

"Don't start, Mr Freeman," said Bert, "it's a busy time of the year."

"I'll be helping you for the next few days, Bert. What do we need to do?"

"The sowing and planting are up together. See those rows of vegetable seedlings over yonder. You had better thin those out while they're still small. I put in the beetroots, carrots, onions, parsnips and turnips you love. Water along the rows to settle the disturbed seedlings back in after you've completed the hoeing. That teepee gadget of yours is ready for the runner beans. We'll hoe between the other crops to control the weeds if this weather stays fine. I always try to hold off watering until the evening if we haven't had a shower. It's cooler then, and I can make sure the root areas get a good soaking."

"It's a pity Clemency isn't around this evening. She would have learned so much."

Gus wasn't sure if Bert's noise qualified as a 'harumph', but it was close enough. Bert eased himself up from the wooden seed tray using his trusty walking stick and headed for the Lamb.

"See you in the morning then, Mr Freeman. Don't be late. There's plenty to do."

Gus watched Bert until he reached the entrance to the main bar. The older man was struggling with that arthritic hip. Gus revised his opinion on whether the stick was just for show. Then, with a sigh, he rooted in his shed for a book to read. There was plenty of time to work under supervision tomorrow.

Thursday, 10 May 2018

THE BINMEN AWAKENED Gus as they clattered along the lane. Good to know people still started work early in the morning to provide services for those who lived in rural England. He wondered how long it would last.

No doubt he would soon have to take his rubbish to a recycling centre unless he paid an exorbitant annual fee on top of the already eye-watering Council Tax for the pleasure.

Gus listened to the familiar sounds of the vehicle and the workers trotting in front to collect the villagers' bins. They seemed perfectly happy. One was whistling a popular tune; another lad called a cheery greeting to one of Gus's neighbours.

Gus knew where they were. The steady high-pitched beep told him the driver was reversing his lorry into the small cul-de-sac of council bungalows thirty yards up the lane.

Gus imagined that none of the workers woke this morning with a guilty conscience.

Last Friday afternoon, he had rushed home from work to attend to what he described to his team as a minor issue with a new security system. His cameras had been in place since that morning. Adam and Daryl, the fitters, had lunched in The Lamb pub.

DI Suzie Ferris was in the bar area, too, drowning her sorrows after a brief fling with an old flame ended in a midnight misunderstanding. Gus had arrived home, hoping he could sober her up and say something sensible. Something appropriate that helped her. That was before she told him what caused the misunderstanding and then stopped crying on his shoulder to kiss him.

No wonder he had a guilty conscience.

Saturday didn't bring any relief after Suzie stayed throughout the morning. Gus succumbed to her charms yet again.

Gus lay in bed and tried to hear the binmen. They had moved further along the lane, close to the pub. It was no good. He may as well get up and shower alone. The colder, the better, if he wished to erase the memory of Saturday morning.

He thought that no matter how terrible things got, he always had positives to remember from last weekend. The visit to Donna's house of ill-repute in the afternoon had yielded a new line of enquiry.

On Sunday, Neil Davis and Jake Latimer had trawled around massage parlours across two counties interviewing girls who worked with Laura Mallinder. Every scrap of information helped in a murder investigation. You never knew when a casual remark linked to an event you struggled to explain.

While Neil and Jake sought that elusive casual remark, Gus had fretted over Sunday lunch with Vera Jennings. Nobody could be lucky enough to keep their dark secrets hidden forever. He wouldn't mention what had happened, and safe topics of conversation were always plentiful with Vera.

Somehow, he'd cleared that hurdle and returned home the following morning unscathed. Suzie Ferris had maintained a discreet distance throughout the Bank Holiday. But, unfortunately, Gus knew it was only postponing the inevitable, which didn't help him sleep well at night.

When he had returned to work in the Old Police Station office on Tuesday, Gus found that the odd scraps he'd collected combined well with snippets Neil had gathered. As one after the other Gentle Touch clients told their stories, a viable solution emerged. Laura's ex-boyfriend, Ian Hewson, was firmly in the frame for her brutal murder.

It was typical of Gus that he retained a niggling doubt.

He'd seen it while sitting across the road from Maggie Monk's building, where a Turkish barber and a massage parlour carried on their very different trades.

Gus decided he needed a trip to Swindon to put his concerns to rest. He arranged to meet the two officers from Gablecross involved in the initial investigation into Laura's murder.

Gus didn't have time to pursue the niggle over whether the barber had access to the parlour. While he stood downstairs keeping watch on staff and customers in the nail bar, Theo Hickerton and Jake Latimer interviewed Ahmet Tekin.

Neil raced upstairs as soon as Jake shouted that Tekin had stabbed Theo Hickerton.

Jake and Neil had grappled with the assailant, and he was now facing a murder charge.

It didn't take Gus long to work out the sequence of events that fateful evening.

Hewson had burst into the parlour, and there was an almighty row between the former lovers. Tekin had waited until Hewson left and then gone upstairs to comfort the woman he loved. Laura had already rebuffed him on several occasions. This time, her reaction proved too much for Tekin to take. She laughed at him. He stabbed her to death.

It might have been a double murder if his make-shift weapon had struck Theo Hickerton's chest a few inches lower. Laura Mallinder's murder was solved. It was another cold case closed by Gus and his Crime Review Team.

Yesterday morning he'd driven straight to London Road and the Wiltshire Police HQ. Some meetings were more pleasant than others. Gus knew a warm welcome awaited him. ACC Kenneth Truelove stood by the window as he entered the room with Geoff Mercer. Geoff had been waiting at the top of the stairs when Gus signed in at Reception five minutes before ten.

"Excellent work, Gus," Geoff had enthused.

"We got there in the end," said Gus, "even if we arrived in Swindon thinking the lad Hewson was the guilty party. I imagined Tekin would give us information that confirmed Hewson was the only person upstairs with Laura Mallinder that evening."

"Ah, but you must have imagined another likely scenario?"

"All I had to go on was the distressed look of the fabric of the front of the building when Theo Hickerton took me to the murder site. You know, those old Victorian buildings. Hundreds of shops and offices are housed in similar premises across any sizeable town or city. They have had several guises over the years. The shop fitters come in, rip out the old fittings, slap on a fresh coat of paint and tart the place up to reflect what a modern shop or office should resemble. Another firm repeats the process eighteen months, ten years or several decades later, depending on the enterprise's success."

"What doesn't alter much is the original bricks and mortar," said Geoff, nodding his understanding.

"Exactly, until the building's fabric crumbles," said Gus, "and that got me thinking whether Tekin might have had access to the parlour upstairs. It was a record shop for years before Tekin opened his barbershop. Did the owner live over the shop? Was it a storage space for his business? Maggie Monk wanted two businesses in operation, providing her with a regular income. When Tekin took over, did he hold on to a key for that side door without her knowledge? Tekin got a key made, and as soon as Hickerton asked about access, he realised the game was up and lashed out."

"We'd better get in to see the ACC," said Geoff, "he was checking on Theo's progress. I want to hear how he is."

"I heard that," said the ACC as he took his seat at his desk, "if I might add my hearty congratulations on another successful case, Freeman. The Chief Constable will echo those sentiments when she has time. She's otherwise engaged today."

"I'll miss her smiling face, Sir," said Gus.

"Yes, well, moving on. You'll be happy to hear that DI Hickerton will leave the hospital early next week. When he returns to duty at Gablecross is undetermined."

"The good news is he didn't die," said Geoff Mercer, "the bad news is his handling of the original case wasn't textbook."

"It was a shambles; let's not dress it up any other way," said the ACC.

"What do you think will happen?" asked Geoff Mercer.

"When these things come to light, it's vital that the public keep their complete trust in the service. DI Hickerton's next appointment need not be well-publicised, for instance."

"That would only happen if he were moving further up the ladder," said Gus.

The ACC nodded.

"I imagine Theo will learn that he has reached as high as he will ever go. To demote him seven years after the event only attracts unwanted attention. Far simpler to shunt the officer sideways."

"Nothing to see here," said Gus, "move along, please."

"Exactly," said the ACC.

"Theo's got a way to go before retirement," said Geoff, "he might jump ship and move into private security. If he feels he needs a greater challenge; or a larger salary."

"You're not tempted, Sir?" Gus asked the ACC.

"Never in a million years, Freeman. The wife would kill me if I didn't end my time here and leave at the earliest opportunity. Money isn't a motivator for me."

"There are those keen to scale the greasy pole, despite the associated problems," said Geoff.

"Forget it," laughed Gus, "you've already blagged your way to dizzy heights."

"I wasn't thinking of myself," said Geoff, "I'm happy enough with my lot. Suzie Ferris is ambitious, and our new Chief Constable is keen on advancing the careers of young females. Ms Plunkett encouraged Suzie to attend a training course this week. That's why you haven't seen her here this morning. I know you two are as thick as thieves."

"Suzie's a sociable person," Gus agreed, trying to keep things as brief as possible in that regard, "we always find something to discuss."

"I can't think what's holding up our morning coffee," said the ACC, "I'm parched. I hope Mrs Jennings is fit and well."

Gus could confirm she was fit but declined to mention it.

Geoff Mercer went to find Vera and Kassie Trotter. As soon as he opened the door, Kassie wheeled in her trolley.

"Thanks, Mr Mercer. Sorry for the wait," she chirped, full of the joys of Spring as usual.

Vera followed her in, carrying a tray covered with a cloth.

"We waited until Her Ladyship left the building," said Vera as Kassie poured three cups of tea. "We couldn't risk her catching sight of Kassie's fancies."

"No, that would never do," smiled Kenneth Truelove.

"Kassie has excelled this weekend," Vera said, removing the cloth with a flourish worthy of a magician's assistant.

"Ooh," said Geoff Mercer, "I can't remember the last time I had a cream horn."

"Those are for a special occasion," said Kassie, "they're to celebrate the official end of Vera's marriage."

Vera and Gus exchanged a glance. The ACC didn't spot it.

He was deciding which cake on the tray was the least damaging to his waistline.

On the other hand, Geoff Mercer chose the largest on offer, grinning from ear to ear.

"We are here to celebrate the decree absolute of the marriage of Vera and Monty Jennings," he began and winked at Gus.

Kenneth Truelove tutted.

"Monty and I had several wonderful years," said Vera, "but it was over ages ago. The children will continue to see both of us whenever the opportunity allows. Divorce doesn't bother the younger generation too much. They've carried on as if nothing has happened ever since the initial split. My first task is finding somewhere closer to work to set up my new home."

There was an awkward silence.

"Well, if everyone's happy with their mid-morning refreshments, we'd better get on," said Kassie, "I'll pop back in fifteen minutes for the empties. I'll leave the tray, Mr Mercer, just in case."

With that, Vera and Kassie left the room.

Gus battled with his cream horn, praying he could avoid getting its contents on his clean shirt. He hoped the ACC didn't continue discussing Vera's altered circumstances.

"Young Kassie is one of your success stories, Sir," he said, hoping to steer him away from the topic. "She's a ray of sunshine, and we'll miss her baking skills if she were to get married or move on to new pastures."

"Marriage and Kassie Trotter's life have something in common," said the ACC, shifting his cup of tea around the saucer with the tips of his fingers.

Geoff Mercer thought there was a joke on its way, but he realised his boss was serious.

"In what way, Sir?" he asked.

"They both have occasions when everything balances on a knife-edge, and one false move can lead to disaster. Kassie was experiencing a life-changing moment when I spotted her. Without the right help, she might have fallen into a life of drugs and prostitution. I'm sure we know colleagues who have been happily married, and an extended undercover operation or a social occasion offers the opportunity to stray. It's tough to resist in such circumstances."

Geoff looked at Gus. Was the ACC admitting to an indiscretion from his past? If he was, it had been a well-kept secret.

"I can't speak for Gus," said Geoff, "but a colleague of either sex has never propositioned me during my time in the police."

"What about members of the public?" asked Gus.

The ACC sat up in his chair; he ignored his cup and saucer. He was all ears.

"Don't panic, boss. I wasn't accusing DS Mercer of any impropriety. It happened to me last Saturday afternoon, and not for the first time. Donna, the madam that Terry Davis put me onto, suggested I stay longer than our interview session concerning potential suspects in our case. So I made my excuses and left in a time-honoured fashion. Several girls in Salisbury asked if I was interested while working as a beat constable or a young Detective Sergeant. I always declined, whether single, engaged, or married at the time."

"Glad to hear it, Freeman," said the ACC, "I was talking in general, you understand, not implying there had been any wrongdoing on anyone's behalf. Especially my own. However, our old friend Culverhouse has skeletons in his closet, as we know. Do we have any more information to aid our cause of getting our retaliation in first?"

"I appreciate the turn of phrase, Sir," said Gus, "but no, we've not found any further indiscretions to add to the ones we identified earlier. There was just one thing, though."

Gus had remembered something.

"There's an unfamiliar face in the village. A man in his fifties who drinks gin and tonic and reads one of the broadsheets. He's been in the pub frequently when I've been there. Nobody knows who he is. I might be barking up the wrong tree, but he could be in league with our new Chief Constable. Terry Davis told me his informant reckons she's actively seeking an excuse to close the CRT."

"How many more times will Davis do that?" said the ACC, exasperated. "His intelligence-gathering is superior to that of GCHQ. If I ever discover who he's receiving these tip-offs from, they'll be for the high jump."

"We need to discover who Culverhouse and Plunkett have in common," said Geoff.

"Exactly," said Gus, "somewhere in their past, these three have worked together."

"I'll let you two dig deeper into those matters," said the ACC, "I'll try to keep Ms Plunkett out of your hair. So that brings me to your next assignment."

"Ah, you have another cold case for us to tackle," said Gus, rubbing his hands.

"I do, and I'll give you the details in a moment. However, you and your team need to take the time to recharge your batteries. I suggest you start work on this case on Monday; I insist on it. Once we've finished here, I want you to get off home. The weather forecast is fine. It would be best if you spent time on your allotment and caught up with your reading by that Kierkegaard fellow you enjoy. I don't know your team's leisure interests, but I encourage them to pursue them for the next few days. They may not get a break for ages. This next case will be a challenge."

Gus imagined Neil would hate being home with Melody while she fretted over the early months of her pregnancy. As for Alex Hardy and Lydia, well, that might be a problem. Despite his warning, if Lydia wanted to move their relationship along, Gus imagined Alex couldn't stop her, even if he tried.

"I can always catch up with the tasks on my allotment in the evenings and at weekends, Sir," said Gus, "I need to keep busy."

"Never ignore your social life, Freeman," said the ACC.

Geoff Mercer almost choked on his second cream horn. Gus gave him the stare.

"What is it you have for us to look into, Sir?" he asked as Geoff Mercer brushed tears from his eyes.

The ACC handed both officers a copy of the murder file.

LATE ON A QUIET afternoon on Saturday, 10th January 2004, Dr Ian McGuire, a Southampton football fanatic, was working at his home in Amesbury. He had one eye on the kitchen door he was repainting and the other on the TV screen for the football scores.

McGuire had just boiled the kettle for a well-earned cup of tea. He paused his painting, laid the brush on the open can, and picked up his red-and-white mug.

Outside in the darkness, a killer crept silently through the small back garden.

McGuire blew on the hot tea and offered a prayer as the

newsreader gave the Premiership results for the afternoon's matches.

'Birmingham City 2, Southampton 1.'

He gave a deep sigh. Both teams expected to finish mid-table, but he had high hopes for a draw today. Prutton getting sent off just after the hour mark was a disaster. One advantage of the fixture list was that the Saints were home to Leeds on Monday night. That was a chance for three points.

Fingers crossed; work wouldn't prevent him from travelling to St Mary's stadium to watch the game. McGuire took several sips of his tea and placed the mug on the worktop beside him.

As he picked up his brush to resume painting, he caught another result. Bristol City had won away at Notts County. Typical. The Robins were having a successful season in the Second Division. His colleagues wouldn't miss the opportunity to rib him over the Saint's reversal of fortunes at St Andrew's.

Those colleagues never had that opportunity.

The person outside in the back garden fired two shots through the kitchen window from a pump-action shotgun.

The first shot whistled past Ian's ear and crashed into the door jamb. He turned as he heard the spent cartridge hit the concrete patio. The second shot hit him square in the chest. He fell to the floor, mortally wounded.

His attacker collected the spent cartridges and scaled the wooden fence at the bottom of the garden. He soon disappeared into the maze of properties on the estate.

Ian McGuire struggled to the doorway into the lounge. His mobile phone was on the couch. If he could reach it, there might be time. The Scottish League results faded into the background as he dialled 999. When the call connected,

Ian McGuire found it impossible to speak. He was too weak.

The emergency operator heard groans and shallow breathing and traced the call. An ambulance raced to the scene, but by the time they arrived, Dr Ian McGuire was dead.

"HOW ON EARTH did this Dr McGuire deserve to get murdered?" asked Geoff Mercer, "did he upset one of his patients?"

"He wasn't a GP," said the ACC. "When you read further than the first page, you'll learn he was a research scientist with a stellar list of awards and accomplishments. He was a highly regarded man in his field, as they say. That's what made this case so baffling. The detectives investigated several motives. None of them emerged as the definitive reason for the attack. One idea proposed was that it was a case of mistaken identity. As far-fetched as that may seem, the investigating team clutched at straws after several fruitless weeks."

"No wonder you want us to take a few days off," said Gus, flicking through the weighty murder file.

Chapter Two

GUS FOUND it hard to relax. It was all very well for the ACC to send him home on Wednesday lunchtime and insist he didn't think about work until Monday. Ever since he'd handed him a copy of the Dr Ian McGuire murder file, he'd been itching to get stuck into the detail.

His first job when he reached the bungalow in Urchfont had been to phone his team members. They were in the office clearing the decks of paperwork from the Laura Mallinder case and refreshing the digital version in the Freeman Files. He'd spoken to each of them. Gus passed on the ACC's congratulations on a well-done job and instructed them to follow his wishes.

Neil, Alex, and Lydia weren't aware of the contents of the murder file, so they wouldn't get burdened with thoughts of the case until Monday morning when they started the week at the Old Police Station office. Nevertheless, certain aspects were already scratching away at the dark corners of his brain. For Gus Freeman, it was ever thus.

Neil Davis hadn't been as glum as Gus expected to learn he had a free weekend ahead. Neil had news of his own. His father, Terry, was flying in from Marbella. It was his first trip home since he retired to the Costa del Crime in 2013.

Neil told Gus that Terry thought they needed to wet the baby's head, even though it was seven months before the new Davis family member was due.

Terry Davis hadn't struck Gus as a full-on family man based on the few conversations they'd had over the telephone. Perhaps he was mellowing.

Gus wondered if he could tear Terry away from the bosom of his family for an hour to question him further on his local contacts. He could threaten him with Donna's idea of flying out to catch up with him again after she retired from the game for good.

It might be a way to get something useful out of the enforced layoff, and it could help reduce the ACC's blood pressure.

Alex Hardy was planning to spend his free time in the gym. His leg muscles were recovering from the extended period he'd spent in his wheelchair, but work was still needed now that he was more mobile on his crutches. In addition, his upper body strength required attention.

Gus wished Alex well. He hoped his gardening kept him as fit as a sixty-one-year-old had any right to expect. Unfortunately, there was no way anyone could persuade him to invest in a gym membership.

Lydia Logan Barre sounded less engaged than usual when he spoke with her. The prospect of time off didn't receive the enthusiasm Gus thought it warranted. When Tess was Lydia's age, she would have squealed with delight. Instead, Tess always had a lengthy list of things to do and places to go and greeted every hour of unexpected leisure time with unbounded enthusiasm.

Gus reckoned Lydia had other things on her mind. He wondered as Alex was seeing his physio later and planning frequent visits to the gym. It signalled he was aware things were getting too serious between them. Perhaps Alex was erecting a few barriers; that chat they'd had last week might have hit home.

"What are your plans?" Gus had asked Lydia. "Anything in particular in mind?"

"I might travel home to visit my mother," she'd replied. That was the end of the conversation.

GUS HELPED Bert Penman on the allotment throughout the daylight hours on Thursday and Friday. The older man was in his element. Bert manoeuvred Gus around the plot on a succession of tasks. Gus knew that he would benefit when the vegetables they worked on were ready to eat. The prospect of an infinite supply of fresh produce made the back-breaking effort worthwhile.

Bert disappeared to the pub on Thursday evening. Gus checked his watch. Ten minutes after six o'clock. The list of items Bert had suggested Gus could complete before finishing for the day would keep him here until eight o'clock. The weather was perfect. It was no hardship to potter around on such an evening.

"Good evening,"

The Reverend Clemency Bentham had arrived. Bert must have an early warning system, thought Gus.

"Mr Penman not around today?" she asked.

"We've toiled away together since half-past nine this

morning. Bert's taking refreshment after his labours," said Gus.

"You mean he's in the Lamb drinking cider and avoiding me," said Clemency.

"Don't take it personally," said Gus, "he avoids the local GP too. Bert knows the Doctor drops into the Lamb two evenings a week. Thursday isn't one of them. He fears he will scold him for having the occasional drink."

"Thank you," said Clemency, "I can see I need to do my homework. But, once I learn which nights the Doctor is in the pub, I can guarantee Bert will be here or at home."

"If you're that desperate to save his soul, you could always visit the Lamb yourself," suggested Gus.

Clemency giggled.

"The Church doesn't concentrate on that stuff these days," said Clemency, "I want to learn what I can from him. Mr Penman's a proper countryman. So much knowledge could disappear if we don't talk with our old folk before they're gone. He's bristly toward me, but I know that Irene North thinks the world of him. Those gifts of vegetables he leaves on her doorstep when she's out are very much appreciated. He never gives her a chance to thank him."

That's a guilty conscience, thought Gus. Frank North's hapless gardening skills had allowed Bert to pinch fruit and vegetables from his allotment for years.

"What about you, Mr Freeman?" asked Clemency, "should I be concerned for your soul?"

"What have you heard?" asked Gus.

"Irene North tells me you're a widower. As I am, you're a newcomer to the village and destined to be an outsider for at least twenty years. However, you've returned to work as a consultant attached to Wiltshire Police and enjoy female company."

"Ah, the curtain twitchers have been busy," laughed Gus.

"Very little escapes villagers in any corner of the country, Mr Freeman. It's the nature of the beast."

"If the parties involved are unattached, I hardly think it's anyone's business," said Gus.

"Oh, you'll get no argument from me. I thought you should be aware, that's all."

"Duly noted," said Gus.

"Irene North also told me you have someone monitoring your bungalow,"

"A tall, angular-looking gentleman, aged around fifty-five, who carries The Times under his arm as he strolls along the lane. Is that who you mean?"

"Oh, you knew already. Do you have an undercover policeman keeping you safe? I didn't realise you needed protecting."

He's undercover, okay, thought Gus, and not doing a good enough job of it here in the countryside.

"Had you moved into the village when the police raided the outbuildings behind Cambrai Terrace?" Gus asked.

"I read about it. I was still buying my place here, but Irene told me the men involved in that nasty business were responsible for Frank's death."

"That gang broke into my bungalow and tried to scare me. So, I had a protection officer on duty in the lane for several days. That protection has now ended. The gentleman you mentioned has been in the Lamb when I've had a drink with Bert Penman. Nobody knows who he is or what he's doing in the village. He's not attempted to speak with me. As a consultant, restrictions are placed on me, so I'd need to report any potential crime through the right channels. I can't act on the information myself. On the other hand, walking along the lane and admiring the view isn't a criminal act."

"I moved here looking for a quiet life," said Clemency, "as each day passes, it gets more like Midsomer Murders. I've taken up enough of your time, Mr Freeman. It's time to get my digging done and let you continue your work."

Gus relayed everything Clemency said on Friday morning to Bert; and persuaded Bert to meet Irene North face-to-face to thank him for the produce. He was less successful in getting Bert to accept that the Reverend only wanted advice on her brassicas. Gus decided to bide his time. He could try to mend those fences another day,

"Our mutual friend was in the Lamb last night, nursing a gin and tonic," said Bert.

"Irene North and others from the village have spotted him," said Gus, "Clemency tells me he's keeping an eye on my place."

"What will you do about him, Mr Freeman?" asked Bert.

"I've asked my colleagues at London Road to do a little digging. They'll find out who he is and what game he's playing. Remember my warning to Frank North. Keep well away from him, Bert. He could be dangerous. I can't afford to lose you, and nor can the Reverend. She needs to learn from you yet."

Bert didn't pass comment. He had several more chores to complete before the evening. The two friends passed the time, steadily working their way through the list. Gus decided against a drink in the Lamb as they left the allotment just after eight o'clock.

Gus said goodnight to Bert at the pub door and walked home. The lane was empty.

As he put his key in the door, he heard the phone ringing. He was too tired to rush.

The answerphone had clicked in, and Gus played the message once he got indoors.

"Are you free tomorrow? I'm looking at houses. I'd appreciate the company."

It was Vera Jennings. He called back and arranged for her to collect him at ten o'clock in the morning. Gus stood in the darkened room and watched for movement.

Gus saw nothing untoward, so he drew the curtains, switched on the lights and poured himself a cold beer. He realised how hungry he was and wished he didn't have to cook for himself. With a sigh, he placed the half-empty glass on a side table and headed for the kitchen.

"YOU PICKED A PLEASANT DAY FOR IT," said Gus as he slipped into the passenger seat of Vera's Alfa Romeo the following morning. Passing clouds now masked the sun that had been so prevalent in the preceding days. The forecast was for showery rain by noon, which threatened to last until nightfall.

"We'll be indoors most of the time," said Vera, "quit moaning."

"Ouch," said Gus, "did someone get out of bed on the wrong side?"

"Only Monty," she replied, "my solicitor says he's arguing over trivial items we thought we settled weeks ago."

"I thought the divorce was amicable. You've been apart for so long; surely Monty didn't still harbour hopes of a reconciliation?"

"No, it's nothing like that. Monty's strapped for cash, as usual. He's looking for any angle he can exploit to screw me for a few thousand pounds to keep him afloat until his next get-rich scheme arrives."

"What does your father think?" asked Gus.

"You've not met him," Vera replied, "if you had, you wouldn't ask. My father would have him horse-whipped and thrown into the arms of his creditors. This rigmarole our solicitors are going through is why he placed financial restraints on our marriage in the first place."

"As long as those restraints hold firm, Monty will have to accept that there's no big payday in the offing. I'm not qualified to give legal advice, but if it were me, I might cut short the process by offering a one-time payment to settle all outstanding and further queries. Monty can take it or leave it. For your sanity, you need to draw a line under the matter and know that he's not knocking on your door every few months with another issue to resolve."

"I'll discuss it with my parents tomorrow at lunch. I don't want to commit too much to pay him off; it will leave me with a tighter budget for my next home. Talking of which, this place on the right is a two-bedroomed town-house on my list."

As they made a tour of the property with a bright young thing from the estate agency, Gus made two mental notes from his conversation with Vera. She had referred to her father and the fact that he hadn't met him. There was no 'yet' in the comment. Their relationship had a way to run then before she needed to introduce him to her parents. Gus wondered if Vera had even mentioned she was seeing someone. It also appeared he wasn't in her plans for Sunday lunch.

"What do you think, Gus?"

"Very nice," he replied, unsure which aspect of the property was under scrutiny.

"Really? The galley kitchen's far too small, and I'm not too fond of the layout of the second bedroom. Time to drive to my next option."

Gus and Vera spent the rest of the morning and early afternoon moving from two townhouses to a bungalow and from the bungalow to a cottage. The showers had arrived with a vengeance.

"Well, that's five places visited," said Vera as they returned to her rented cottage for a well-earned cup of coffee. "Three are a total write-off, and two are still in the frame. I could be happy in the cottage; that's only a ten-minute walk from work."

"The fuel savings will be significant," said Gus, "and the Green people will applaud your contribution to the cause. It benefits me too because that's one more space in the car park at London Road for my old banger."

"I'll weigh up the pros and cons over the rest of the weekend and make my decision. Are you hungry?"

"I've been in five kitchens and not had a nibble," said Gus, "that's a first. So where do you want to eat? I'm free for the rest of the day if you're going home tomorrow."

"The night too, I hope?" said Vera, "actually, we're not lunching at home. My father has booked a table somewhere."

"I imagine the red carpet is getting an airing as we speak," said Gus, "let's find somewhere to eat before the next shower. We can be back before dark and spend a quiet night indoors."

"Sounds good to me," said Vera.

GUS STUDIED the dark clouds overhead as he drove home on Sunday morning. His Friday fling with Suzie hadn't reached Vera's ears yet. Nevertheless, everything that happened between driving into Devizes for an Indian meal, the quiet evening at the cottage, and overnight cemented his opinion he and Vera were compatible. It was as if they'd known one another for years, not months.

Why was there still a persistent black cloud looming over his Ford Focus this morning? It appeared to be tracking him mile by mile as he headed towards Urchfont. With Vera leaving in an hour to spend the day with her family, Gus was alone.

Gus found that his gardening activities were on hold due to the inclement weather. Maybe he could get a head start on the new case by digging further into the murder file.

As he passed the Lamb and the Community Shop, he remembered his unwanted stalker. There was no sign of strangers in the lane today. He pulled into the driveway of his bungalow and parked the car.

Gus checked his phone. He'd received no alarm from his camera security system to warn him of uninvited guests. All this technology was still new to him. He scolded himself for not realising he could check every few hours to see what his cameras captured. Old habits die hard. He didn't want to get anal about referring to his phone screen every five minutes like the youngsters did these days.

Once inside, he visited the kitchen to see what the system had to tell him. Very little, it transpired. He walked into the lounge and found the last message on his landline was Vera's call from Friday evening. Billy No Mates. What-ever happened to Dorothy? No bugger wanted to talk to him, it appeared.

The next place Gus checked was his fridge-freezer. There were dozens of meals in there that he'd stocked up, thinking they'd be backwards and forwards to Swindon on the Laura Mallinder case for weeks. He closed his eyes and picked one. That was lunch sorted.

As he sat at his kitchen table enjoying a glass of red wine after his beef bourguignon, he wondered what Terry Davis was up to later. Gus dialled Neil's number. Melody replied.

"Melody, it's Gus Freeman here. How are you keeping?"

"I'm better at this time of the day than I am first thing, thanks for asking. Neil wouldn't bother. You-know-who is here this weekend. He's just as objectionable in the flesh as he is on the end of a telephone line."

"I was hoping to have a word," said Gus, "can Terry tear himself away?"

"Terry's not here. He took Neil out for a lunchtime drink. Neil won't get home until after the football's finished."

"Is Terry staying with you?" asked Gus.

"What do you think? I put my foot down. We had to stay in a hotel when we visited him. He'll get no favours from me. Terry's in a B&B in town."

"Where will they go to watch football? I'll take a spin into Devizes and see if I can catch them. Terry might put a name to a face for me."

"Neil likes the Cavalier out on Eastleigh Road," said Melody, "if you see him, tell him his dinner will be on the table at six."

"In the bin by five past six. OK, Melody, I'll pass on the message. You take care of yourself."

Gus rang off before she could sling more barbed comments Terry's way. He studied what remained in his glass and poured it back into the bottle. Waste not, want not; the ACC would blow a fuse if one of his consultants got nicked for drink-driving.

It was no hardship finding the pub. The Cavalier was one he passed as he drove into Devizes, depending on which route he took. The car park was busy, and empty spaces were relatively small.

Still, another dent in the Ford Focus wouldn't notice. Gus didn't bother looking for Neil's car. He would take a taxi home. Melody may have wanted him to cut out the drinking while she was pregnant, but Terry's visit warranted a free pass.

Gus pushed his way past a noisy crowd in the bar. Nobody faced the barman as every head turned towards the giant screen.

There were twenty minutes left in the televised game. Gus couldn't stand around waiting without a drink. So he ordered a slimline tonic with ice.

"Do you want a straw with that?" sneered the barman.

"A smile's out of the question, I see?" Gus replied.

Neil must have spotted him. He tapped his boss on the shoulder.

"I'll get that, guv," he shouted above the roar. Someone had scored. Gus didn't know who and didn't care either way. "Two more of the same for me and my Dad, Skip."

The barman replenished the empty pint glasses that Neil plonked on the bar. Gus's soft drink arrived without a straw. Neil nodded towards the far corner of the crowded room.

"We're over there, guv. What brings you here?"

"Melody said to be home by six," said Gus, "I wanted a chat with Terry. I need to tap into his vast knowledge of creeps that knew Dominic Culverhouse."

"Melody won't leave it alone, guv. Sit with us and enjoy your drink. The game's nearly over, and this place will be empty within five minutes. You can talk without shouting, and there won't be anyone earwigging at the next table."

Neil was right. The final whistle was equivalent to the barman calling time. Only a handful of die-hard drinkers remained. They weren't close enough to hear any conversation between the three men seated in the far corner of the bar. Even the barman ignored them as he collected glasses from abandoned tables.

"Afternoon, Freeman. You're roughing it today, then?" said Terry Davis.

"I wanted a word. You remember what happens when a copper needs to rub shoulders with the great unwashed to get information."

"I remember, but you're not a copper any longer. You're a consultant who keeps sticking his nose where it's not wanted. I've warned you about that. Why don't you listen?"

"I listen, Terry, but sometimes you can't turn a blind eye."

"They never charged me with any wrongdoing, Freeman. I travelled here without incident. Nobody was waiting for me at Bristol International on Friday afternoon. Come on, spit it out. You wouldn't have come here unless you wanted something."

"Ten days to a fortnight ago, a guy in his mid-fifties, smart dresser, cultured accent, turned up in the village. I've seen him in the Lamb. Other villagers tell me he's watching my bungalow. I wondered if he might have links to Culverhouse or our new Chief Constable."

Terry Davis shook his head from side to side.

"I told you to stop this consulting lark and stick to growing vegetables. This guy stands six-foot-one or two, yeah? He reminds you of a grey-haired Christopher Lee.

You've stirred up a hornet's nest this time, Freeman. That has to be Ricky Gardiner. He's an enforcer."

"I thought he was an ex-copper," said Gus.

"Gardiner's worked both sides for so long I don't expect even he knows which way is up," snorted Terry.

"How does he link to Culverhouse, and why is he called Ricky? It makes him sound like a teenager."

"That rich voice is part of his persona. He's from a council estate in South London. He switches accents as often as Mike Yarwood used to when he was on the telly. Ricky started as a beat copper in the Metropolitan Police in the mid-Eighties. They had a succession of corruption problems and rumours of dirty cops wherever you looked. Gardiner went undercover inside a drug syndicate. He gathered evidence on the corrupt officers every bit as much as he helped to bring down the gang. His back story got tested more than once. I heard they took him to a deserted warehouse, and one of the gang members stuck the barrel of his gun into Gardiner's mouth. He swore blind Gardiner was a copper. Your man laughed in his face. Whoever trained him did their job well. Ricky blagged his way out of that tight corner, and an hour later, he was buying a pint for the gunman in a pub in the East End."

"Did they get enough evidence to arrest the gang?" asked Neil. "What about the officers mixed up in the business?"

"Check it out, son," said Terry, "it went the same way as every other operation with a code name ascribed to it. You win some; you lose some. Gang members at the bottom of the tree got sacrificed. Two or three low-ranking detectives got charged. The ladder got pulled up on both sides of the law, so those at the top escaped punishment."

"You haven't explained the Culverhouse connection," said Gus.

"To get chapter and verse on that, you must dig into the time my ex-guvnor and Sandra Plunkett spent together."

"That's not a likely scenario," said Gus.

"I don't mean he was giving her one," said Terry, "your new Chief Constable bats for the other team. I know that. They were at Bramshill together. The staff college in Hampshire. Neither of us received invitations to attend that place during our careers. You might be lucky to go somewhere like that, Neil. If you keep your nose clean."

"OK," said Gus, "they were on the same senior management training course. When was that exactly? Did something happen during that course that led them to become allies? Why should Gardiner target me on their behalf? What on earth is it they're so desperate to hide?"

"Culverhouse was at Bramshill between 2001 and 2002. I can't be sure of the exact dates. His superiors signed him up for every accelerated promotion course going. He was a rising star."

"I read the file on Sandra Plunkett. She was a Chief Inspector in those days. After the Bramshill sessions, she moved to West Mercia as a Superintendent. They didn't bump into Gardiner then, surely?"

"Never in a million years," said Terry, "that place was well above his pay grade. I'd bet that Ricky was undercover somewhere at that time. Get Neil to chase those bright young things in the Hub to ferret the details of his whereabouts."

"I'll need to carry out any searches myself, Terry. The fewer traces of someone digging into their past, the better. If the shit hits the fan, I don't want Neil or any of my Crime Review Team in the firing line."

"You know you can rely on the three of us to be discreet, guv," said Neil.

"Thanks, Neil," said Gus, "but things could get very nasty. Let me get my head around this. Jump in and correct me if I go astray, Terry. So, it's plausible Culverhouse and Plunkett met for the first time at Bramshill in 2002. Sandra moved to West Mercia in 2003. Culverhouse had recently joined you at the Old Police Station."

"That's right, Phil Hounsell moved to the Serious Crime Agency in London. Dominic Culverhouse took over the reins."

"Since I returned to work, I've learned that you two worked on the Trudi Villiers case in 2003 and the botched investigation into Daphne Tolliver's murder in 2008. Culverhouse left for Portishead in 2013, just before you made a run for sunnier climes."

"That's your interpretation of events, Freeman. I prefer to say I had done enough years in the job to deserve a comfortable and lengthy retirement."

"We must find a joint operation covered by the forces they served with in the months, or years, following their first meeting. Gardiner must have an involvement, too, some-how. Nothing jumps out as being a likely candidate. Can you offer a suggestion, Terry?"

"West Mercia covers Hereford and Worcester," said Neil, "and Avon and Somerset Police are on the other side of the Severn. The two forces are next door to one another. There had to be something they worked on together."

"The timing's wrong, Neil," said Gus.

"Yes, son," said his father, "Culverhouse and I were on the same team until several months before I quit. Sandra Plunkett wasn't with West Mercia in 2013; she moved onward and upward regularly. That's how the real high-flyers do it. They don't stay long enough to make a difference. They only stay long enough to give their superiors the impression they're after their positions, then they get moved on again to become someone else's problem."

"It's a game of pass the parcel, Dad. Is that what you're saying?"

"That's a cynical version of what's happening, Terry," said Gus, "several make a difference with ideas they bring to the top table. I agree that more of them get promoted into a position where they can't do any more harm than they've already inflicted on their colleagues and the public."

"I don't suppose you know where Ms Plunkett was, Freeman?" asked Terry.

"Sandra got promoted to Chief Superintendent within two years of joining West Mercia. The next item might interest you, Terry; you were fortunate to avoid coming into contact with her colleagues. Instead, Sandra went to Hindlip Park, near Worcester, and stayed there until 2011."

"The soft-shoe brigade," said Terry, "as I keep telling you, Freeman, Professional Standards never had a thing on me that stuck. It doesn't surprise me. It's one of the prize spots the high-flyers aim for, that and counter-terrorism. They score heavily with the public when a Chief Constable or Commander gets their name and achievements listed in the media after a major appointment."

Gus allowed himself a brief smile.

"Sandra negotiated her way through the Strategic Command Course in 2009 with flying colours, and when she became an Assistant Chief Constable, it was on her old stamping ground in Staffordshire. She became Head of Counter-Terrorism in June 2011."

"When did she get the top job?" asked Terry.

"Three years later," said Gus, "as Chief Constable for the West Midlands."

"The window is narrowing," said Neil, "if Culverhouse was at Portishead from early 2013, and Plunkett moved eighteen months later, there can't have been many operations where they could have worked together."

"My memory hasn't suffered much damage in the Marbella heat," Terry Davis said. "One thing I know for certain is that Sandra Plunkett and Dominic Culverhouse never came into contact when he and I worked in the same station. He never mentioned her name in my company, and he didn't disappear on an assignment for weeks at a time when I didn't know where he was unless they met up when he flew out to Majorca or the Greek Islands for his summer holidays. Those were the only weeks when we were apart."

"I'm still struggling to place Ricky Gardiner with those two," said Gus, "they seem such an odd group of people. They've got nothing in common."

"Until you find out they have," said Neil.

"If you stay here much longer, your dinner will be in the bin, Neil," said Gus, "I can run you home if you wish. What are your plans, Terry?"

"Don't worry about me, Freeman. I'm out for the duration. I know the decent drinking holes in town. They haven't seen me in five years. I'll enjoy catching up with a few old faces. I won't say which pubs or which faces. One or two of them might have useful information. If you get my drift."

"Kenneth Truelove will find out who your sources are one day," warned Gus, "and they'll not be so keen to lift the phone to contact you after they've had their knuckles rapped."

Terry smiled and finished his pint of lager.

"What time's your flight tomorrow, Dad," asked Neil, "will we see you before you leave?"

"I don't have to get to Bristol before the early evening, Neil. I can sleep off the drink and take a taxi when I feel human. There's no need to get Melody to paint on a pleased-to-see-me smile. I'm happy for you, son. I can't wait to meet my grandchild. Now I've come home once; I'll do it more often. I'll pop back before Christmas anyway, with luck, to wet the baby's head for real."

"OK, Dad, I'll call you tomorrow at lunchtime," said Neil. Then, turning to Gus, he said. "I'm ready when you are, guv. I can earn brownie points by getting home before six."

Gus and Neil headed for the exit. The barman didn't thank them for their business as they left.

Terry Davis was in the Gents toilet, getting ready to walk into the town centre to visit his old haunts.

Chapter Three

Monday, 14 May 2018

"AT LAST," thought Gus Freeman as he eased his car out of the driveway and into the lane. Finally, the day had arrived when he could get his Crime Review Team together to begin the investigation into another cold case.

After dropping Neil Davis at home last evening, he returned to the bungalow in Urchfont. Gus decided against another lucky dip in his freezer. He only required a snack after his excellent lunch.

While listening to Mike Oldfield's 'Ommadawn', Cheese on toast and coffee seemed to fit the bill. Gus slept the sleep of the just.

There were no dreams and no midnight callers. He was thankful for small mercies.

Some things never change. Roadworks on the A350 slowed everyone's progress through Devizes. His usual twenty-minute trip took the best part of forty. Were the gods mad at him? What else could they throw his way to prevent him from tackling this case?

When he parked his car beneath the Old Police Station office, he wasn't surprised to find he was the last to arrive. Neil must have set off early to miss the traffic. Maybe Melody was awake at the crack of dawn with her morning sickness. She wasn't having an easy time of it. As a result, neither was Neil.

Gus didn't have a clue how much longer Melody would suffer the symptoms. Vera suggested three months was a turning point when they stood in a child's nursery at one property they'd viewed on Saturday. If so, Neil's home might return to normalcy in the next fortnight.

Neil wasn't the only team member Gus relied on to engage in the tasks ahead. As he entered the lift, he hoped Alex and Lydia had used their free time to clear their heads.

"To the barricades, we have an intruder," said Neil as the lift purred upwards.

Lydia yawned.

"Enjoyable weekend?" asked Alex.

"I took the train to Edinburgh on Thursday to visit my mother, Eleanor. Did you spend every waking hour exercising?"

"Don't be daft. I rested in between sessions, as my physio told me. I missed you, by the way."

Lydia squeezed his arm as the lift doors opened, and Gus Freeman joined them.

"Another day, another collar, guv," said Neil.

"We can only hope, Neil. Good morning, you two," he added, nodding in Alex and Lydia's direction, "I spent an hour in Neil's company yesterday afternoon, nursing a soft drink. While I did that, Neil and his father guzzled copious amounts of lager. Other than that, the weekend was quiet. I hope you took advantage of the break and are fit and ready for a fresh challenge the ACC has thrown our way?"

"Yes, guv," came the reply.

Gus glanced around the room. The whiteboards were clear of photographs and data from their last case. It was time to load those boards with items from the murder file he held in his hands.

"This case dates back to Saturday, 10th January 2004, Dr Ian McGuire was working at his home in Amesbury. At around five o'clock in the evening, he was painting a door in his kitchen when someone crept into the rear garden and fired two shots through the kitchen window with a pump-action shotgun. The first shot whistled past the victim and crashed into the door jamb. The second shot hit him square in the chest. McGuire must have turned towards the sound of that first shot. The wound wasn't immediately fatal. McGuire's attacker removed the spent cartridges from the patio and fled. McGuire struggled into the lounge, reached for his mobile phone and attempted to contact the emergency services. He was already incoherent and fading fast. When they traced the call, paramedics attended the scene, but by the time they arrived, Dr Ian McGuire was dead."

"Did the initial investigation uncover a motive, guv?" asked Alex.

"There were several ideas mooted, but none proved to be definitive," said Gus.

"Where did this Doctor work, guv? A hospital or at a general practice surgery?"

"No, Neil, he was a research scientist. From what I've read of him in this murder file, he was one of those guys they coined the word boffin to describe."

"The post-mortem examination revealed that he died from severe chest injuries and loss of blood," Gus continued, "after that, the mystery deepened. Fourteen years on and the crime remains unsolved, and it still baffles our colleagues from Salisbury. They uncovered no motives, no suspects, and no leads. The murder team had little hard evidence. Neighbours heard the two shots. The brief gap between them made people assume they heard a car back-firing. On a chill January evening, it wasn't hard for the killer to flee the scene without being seen. The weapon never surfaced, and the killer had the presence of mind to remove the cartridges. Over the preceding days, frequent frosts hardened the ground in the rear garden of McGuire's house. The killer left no footprints. The wound in McGuire's chest indicated that his killer fired from a distance of six feet."

"What lay behind the Doctor's home, guv," asked Alex, "an adjoining garden, a pathway, or open ground?"

"There was a five-foot garden fence enclosing the rear garden. The killer scaled that to make his escape onto the pavement. The roadway it skirted gave access to garages belonging to the houses further into the estate. Those houses had long, narrow gardens, so they didn't hear the shots. Or at least, that's what they told the detectives who interviewed them. It's possible. Those people lived a fair distance away, and most people stay in the warm with doors and windows closed at that time of the year."

"Nobody was parking their cars or working in the garages then, guv?" asked Lydia.

"Timing can be everything in these matters, Lydia," said Gus, "the killer might have observed McGuire and the habits of both him and his neighbours."

"That's true," agreed Alex Hardy, "you can get a lull in the foot and vehicular traffic at traditional mealtimes even though things have changed over the years. I remember my parents telling me that their parents insisted they got home by half-past four on a weekday for afternoon tea. Other families ate dinner in the evenings, and the timing of that meal centred on the main breadwinner's arrival home from work. So, in their day, there was a distinct activity drop on their housing estate between half-past four and half-past six."

"So, the killer planned this murder with sophistication," said Neil, jumping in. "The killer knew his best chance of avoiding detection when climbing into and out of McGuire's garden meant the murder needed to occur between, say, ten to five and ten past five on Saturday evening."

"I should have told you Ian McGuire was a football fan," said Gus. "I don't disagree with any of your logic. But the victim was watching the results coming through on TV. When the paramedics arrived, it was still tuned to the Sky Sports News channel."

"It confirms what you said, guv," said Alex, "the killer kept McGuire under surveillance and struck when he knew he was home. The fact it came smack in the middle of a traditionally quiet period was a bonus for him."

"Where did McGuire come from?" asked Lydia.

"Ian McGuire was born in Glasgow, educated at the High School, and took his degree at Cambridge University. He was thirty-five years old when he died. His friends described him as amusing and popular. According to them, he didn't have an enemy in the world."

"Where did he do his research after he left Cambridge, guv," asked Neil, "what field did he study?"

"He was involved in research into specific areas of inorganic molecular chemistry at an establishment in Southampton. Please don't ask *me* to explain. It wasn't what he worked on at the time of his death. There's more in the murder file to mull over before we get to his last job. McGuire married a fellow student, Dierdre, the year after they left Cambridge. There's a daughter, Izzie, from that three-year relationship. She was eleven when her father died."

"What was the nature of their relationship when the murder occurred, guv?" asked Neil.

"Dierdre lived in Southampton with Izzie. There's no suggestion that McGuire and his ex-wife had any issues. He was up-to-date with his maintenance payments. He had access to the daughter during the school holidays. Izzie enjoyed living with her mother but loved spending time with her father. The detectives never linked Dierdre to the case at any stage."

"Who ran the show, guv," asked Alex.

"That was Detective Superintendent Tony Brown. We were both based in Salisbury. Brown was a senior officer during my time there, and I don't think he was ever lax in his approach. I've read this murder file in depth. He remarked at the time that his team committed a lot of resources to investigate various avenues. It's rare not to find something that leads to a successful conclusion in time."

"Statistics suggest that the police solve most murders," said Lydia.

"McGuire's murder proved an exception," said Gus, "Tony Brown admitted that they got nowhere. Fourteen years after the killing, they are still no nearer, knowing whether they are looking for a random killer or an obsessive with a grudge. It might even have been a professional hit where the killer blasted the wrong victim. We know how quickly these murders need solving before teams get disbanded and reassigned. Tony Brown's team grafted for twelve weeks. They interrogated the HOLMES computer with names they gathered, took one hundred and eighty statements and called on two hundred and thirty-five local addresses."

"All that work and the total number of positive leads stayed at zero," said Lydia "it's hard to believe. So how did they tackle the mistaken identity angle?"

"They would have checked computer records of local criminals," said Neil. "and identified those of a similar height and build. Then they try to match the faces they had to the properties close to McGuire's. Because we're looking into it again, it means that idea went nowhere."

"I'm not surprised," said Alex, "if it was a gangland execution, the gunman was an amateur. Despite sophisticated planning, he shot McGuire from a distance and through a window. The first shot went high, and the second was not guaranteed to kill. McGuire crawled into the lounge, and the gunman left the scene before he confirmed his target was beyond help. A contract killer would have rung the front doorbell and shot him point-blank with a handgun. Then added another for good luck to finish him and have done with it."

"I'm inclined to agree with you, Alex," said Gus, "as for the random killer suggestion, Tony Brown looked at the likelihood it was a robbery gone wrong. If McGuire had heard a noise from the kitchen, it might explain why he left the TV on and went to investigate. The problem with that was McGuire was already in the kitchen. He was painting a door and had an unfinished drink on the worktop beside him. So it's more likely that he was watching and listening to the football results as he carried on with decorating."

"We don't hear of that many criminals carrying pump-action shotguns when they're off to do a spot of breaking and entering, guv," said Neil.

"No, thank goodness," said Gus, "McGuire had never suffered a burglary, and break-ins on the estate were low; another dead-end."

"Where do we start, guv?" asked Neil.

"I'll distribute these copies of the murder file," said Gus, "Alex, you can set up the digital record and compile a list of people we need to interview. Lydia, can you load the crime scene photos onto the boards and dig out an Amesbury street map? Your job, Neil, will be to set the Hub people on a search to identify any known criminals living in the area and their current whereabouts. Tony Brown retired four or five years after this murder inquiry. He's in his early seventies now. See if you can locate him. I want to talk with him if possible."

"Will we be liaising with detectives from your old stomping ground, guv?" asked Neil.

"I think we'll play it by ear, Neil. The Swindon case required us to involve Theo Hickerton and Jake Latimer. A lot of water has passed under the bridge since this inquiry. Very few people involved in the case are still in the same job. My gut feeling is that this case got handled properly at the time. It was just one of those annoying cases that frustrate those involved when they move the jigsaw pieces around and nothing fits."

Gus handed the file copies to his team. Then, he headed towards the restroom.

"Two whites, one sugar, and a black, one sugar coming up,"

While Gus wrestled with the Gaggia, the others got on with their given tasks.

The room buzzed with activity when he returned. He

sipped his black, no-sugar coffee and was content. Gus did not understand where this case would lead them, but there were rumours about drugs, an alleged row with neighbours, and Dr Ian McGuire lived near a convicted paedophile. In 2004, none of those things produced a positive result.

Gus wondered whether the answer lay in thirty-five-year-old McGuire's tangled love life. The vast majority of victims were known to their killers.

McGuire lived with Alison Hill, a medical student, in a modern block of flats in Salisbury until February 2003. Towards the end, their relationship became stormy. One argument ended when police responded after Hill attacked McGuire with a steam iron.

The move from Salisbury to Amesbury had signalled the final split. He put distance between himself and Hill and settled into his new surroundings.

The Doctor then started seeing Debbie Dallimore, a married woman from Bristol. It appeared McGuire was selling his new house to live with his lover. He was meeting Debbie to go to the cinema the night he died. When her boyfriend didn't arrive, Debbie drove to his home. The police were at the scene and informed her he was dead.

Tony Brown's notes written at the time wondered whether Alison Hill wanted revenge. Or perhaps it was Debbie Dallimore's husband who targeted Ian McGuire. Debbie and Victor Dallimore lived separate lives. There were no children involved.

DS Brown interviewed Alison Hill and Victor Dallimore at length. They both had solid alibis. Brown decided a personal motive didn't lie behind Ian McGuire's killing.

Nothing suggested the pair capable of committing or arranging the murder. Nothing in the background and circumstances of anyone close to Ian McGuire suggested they had a motive.

One of Tony Brown's last attempts to uncover meaningful clues was to cordon off the estate four weeks after the shooting. Unfortunately, this event took place at the exact time of the murder. His officers spoke to everyone in the neighbourhood but got nothing useful from the exercise.

The clock ticked on, and after twelve weeks, they scaled back the hunt.

Gus could feel the confusion and frustration in every report and comment the detective team had included in the murder file. Where did they slip up? Who was it they interviewed that lied to them? Someone knew who was responsible for McGuire's shooting, and Gus felt the name was in that file.

Alex and Lydia were engrossed in their work. Neil had set the ball rolling at the London Road HQ. He had to wait for the computer wizards to work their magic. He carried his mug of coffee over to Gus's desk.

"I know you don't want us to get caught up in the Culverhouse matter, guv, but I'm interested in this undercover business. Nobody has asked me to go deep inside a gang. I've spent hours on stakeout operations, where it's hard to stay awake when it's so boring waiting for something to happen. If you go undercover like this guy Gardiner, you discussed with Dad, that has to be a different ball game altogether, surely?"

"Terry mentioned Gardiner's persona yesterday. Gardiner was born on a rough London housing estate. He left school at sixteen and joined the police. Over the years, he's cultivated various legends. Gardiner can wear a weather-beaten leather jacket and confidently slip into the underworld. If he dons a

Savile Row suit and a club tie, he's a businessman with the sales patter to match. Covert policing can be a game-changer when a case reaches court. The undercover cop can supply irrefutable eyewitnesses and secretly recorded evidence. As a result, the chance of a conviction is greatly enhanced."

"I sense there has to be a downside," said Neil.

"Undercover work can become corrupted and self-justifying. Over the years, a mystique grew up around the role. Officers must maintain absolute secrecy, but senior officers can lose focus. They can exploit the fact that one of their people is inside an important operation to further their careers."

"There have been cases where going undercover for extended periods has gone wrong. Is that true?"

"Well, these situations can spiral out of control. The officers play a role. The criminals don't know someone's watching them every step of the way. At least, you pray that they don't; otherwise, the undercover guy dies. However, in one famous instance, because the Met had officers inside a money-laundering operation for over six years, a judge termed the evidence they presented state-created crime and chucked the case out."

"That doesn't seem right, guv," said Neil.

"It wasn't, but he thought the undercover officers contributed to keeping the operation going longer than necessary by posing as money launderers. They added cash from Met funds to back up their expensive lifestyle. Undercover officers undergo a regular debrief with their cover man. I believe they refer to them as uncles in the Metropolitan Police. They receive intelligence from the undercover officers and can offer emotional support because they've done the job themselves. They should spot any sign of a breakdown or flaws in the persona the officer has adopted."

"Do they see a shrink if necessary?"

"Their handler would insist on a visit to the departmental psychologist if they sensed things were coming unglued. Look, Neil, if it's something you reckon you could handle, I can mention it to Geoff Mercer. With a baby on the way, it might not be the best time for a major change. I've met several undercover officers, and they say the same thing. You're never the same again. It's an immense burden. Adrenaline levels are through the roof while you're on the inside and your friends and family become part of the conspiracy. You must keep things from them every bit like the gang members. When you return to mainstream policing, it can be as dull as ditchwater by comparison. Is it any wonder many undercover officers have drink and drug problems and failed relationships?"

"This Ricky Gardiner has done loads of this undercover work then, guv?"

"So I believe, Neil. As I said, you, Alex and Lydia should keep your distance. Terry has told me more than once that I should steer clear of Culverhouse. He's a small step away from one of the most senior jobs in the country. His reputation is flawless as far as the top brass is concerned. The doubt and damaged reputation smear landed at your Dad's door. The authorities believed Terry manipulated evidence to incriminate Dennis Lewington, and Culverhouse knew nothing about it. He has also successfully hidden his relationship with Trudi Villiers. If it came out that he was screwing her for months, not long after she left school, he could kiss his lofty ambitions goodbye. With your Dad in Marbella, there was never any pressure to bring Terry back to face a Professional Standards inquiry or even a court. It was best to sweep the matter under the carpet and do everything to keep it hidden. Anyway, I haven't seen Gardiner for a week. My neighbours have seen him in the village, skulking around over the past fortnight, but he's never approached me to issue a warning. I'm not suggesting Terry is wrong in his assumption that Culverhouse sent him to keep tabs on me. I don't think anyone needs to panic. When I've discovered what binds Culverhouse and Plunkett in a conspiracy against the CRT, then Geoff Mercer and I can reassess the threat level."

Neil Davis finished his coffee and returned to his desk. His thoughts on undercover work had altered dramatically in the past fifteen minutes. It might sound exciting, but even if the prospect of a few nights away from Melody was attractive, a shallow grave was not.

Perhaps working with Gus Freeman for the foreseeable future was a better option. If only there were something he could do to ensure his Dad's old boss Culverhouse didn't elbow Gus into the long grass of retirement.

"Have you finished your coffee?" Lydia asked Alex.

"Yes, thanks," he replied. "Why? Are you on washing-up duty this morning?"

"No, but we could visit the restroom together for a quick catch-up,"

Neil was deep in thought. Gus was flicking through the murder file, no doubt checking for discrepancies they could exploit later.

Lydia carried their coffee mugs, and Alex swung behind her on his crutches.

"So, you visited your mother over the weekend?" asked Alex when they were behind the restroom door. "As you visited Edinburgh, I assume this was your birth mother?"

"Yes, I went to stay with Eleanor. She lives in Craigmillar. It's an area of the city with a population similar to a town like Devizes. She's lived there for ten years. They had riots thirty years ago, but regeneration projects are underway now. We spent the time sightseeing there and in the city. Edinburgh Castle is only a forty-minute bus ride away. We shopped until we dropped on Saturday in the city centre. I left Waverley station at half-past eleven yesterday morning and arrived at Bath Spa a few minutes after half-past seven."

"A tiring journey," said Alex.

"You're not kidding," said Lydia. "The train was an hour late—half a dozen minor delays on the way south due to engineering work. I was fortunate not to have to detrain and continue part of the journey by bus. Once I reached Bath, the lack of comprehensive bus service on Sundays meant taking a taxi to my place on this side of Chippenham was necessary. Tiredness set in when I got indoors. I had hot cocoa and was in bed by ten o'clock."

"I bet you enjoyed spending more time with Eleanor, though?"

"We both laughed at my change in choice of clothes. First, I wore the garish stuff from my pre-Crime Review Team wardrobe. Then, when we were in Edinburgh on Saturday afternoon, I was picking out conservative tops and skirts. She couldn't make me out. It was just as I had hoped. We got on fine as if two school chums were meeting after a long gap."

"I'm pleased it went well. Did you mention anything to Eleanor about your plan to search for your father?"

"No, I don't think I will either. Eleanor's not pining for a lost love. It might be kinder to do my research with your help and see what comes of that. He might not want to see me. If we meet, and he asks after her, I'll ask Eleanor if she wants to get in touch. I'll leave it to her to decide."

"We'd better get back before Gus wonders what we're doing."

"That exercise has given you excess energy, has it? So why don't you come back to my place tonight? I'm fully refreshed after a long sleep last night."

Alex couldn't think of an excuse.

Lydia kissed him before returning to the main office.

"Neil," she said as she passed his desk, "did you know that Devizes is the largest Wiltshire town without a railway station?"

"Was that fascinating fact on one of our fresh tea towels?" asked Neil.

Gus looked up from his screen.

"When you lot have finished. There's something here to interest you. Hazel McGuire, Ian's mother, is still alive. She's seventy-two now and still living in Glasgow. Her husband died in 1980 when Ian was only eleven years old. We might need to travel up to Scotland to interview her. If you need a reminder of why we should concentrate on this case one hundred per cent, listen to what she told a reporter four years ago:

"It's ten years since Ian, my only child, got shot. His death is always with me. Not a day passes by when I don't miss him. Why would someone be so callous as to take his life and rob the world of a lovely man, a good father, and a great scientist? Ten years is a long time to wait for answers. There must be people out there that know something. They could help ease the stress of not knowing why this happened to my son. I pray that the killer searches their conscience and contacts the police."

"Sorry, guv," said Alex.

"I didn't mean to snap at you. This murder file teems with items that proved to be a dead-end in the initial investigation. The whole thing keeps sliding in my hands like a bar of soap. Question: What caused the break-up with Alison Hill? Answers from McGuire's work colleagues: She was a jealous type. Ian became engrossed in academic work and often forgot to drive home. He was popular with the other members of the research team. Ian loved the fact his job didn't have regular hours. He was thrilled to go into the laboratory in the middle of the night if something required his attention. Alison always assumed the worst. He was having an affair if he didn't make it home or disappeared before dawn. The list of comments goes on and on. The inevitable happened, and the relationship turned sour. They broke up. There was an attempted reconciliation, but Ian moved out of Salisbury and bought the house in Amesbury."

"Alison Hill had a solid alibi, guv," shrugged Neil, "maybe we just leave her off the list that Alex is compiling?"

Gus wasn't listening. He'd found another quote that riled him.

"Clive Breakwell, a fellow scientist, said he was always making fun of himself, even though they didn't always understand his broad Scottish accent. Ian was great company, had a tremendous sense of humour and loved laughter. Clive said they got on great when he met Debbie Dallimore, and a softer side to McGuire came out. It was only a short while before they made plans to live together. He had set a date in March 2004 to move to Bristol. After that, Ian first wanted to travel to Glasgow to visit Hazel, his mother, with his new partner."

"That echoes his mother's feelings, guv," said Lydia. "If he was such a popular, stand-up guy, who loved his daughter, and was friends with everybody, why was he shot?"

"Someone wanted him dead," said Gus, "that has to be the first thing we tackle. Who did Ian McGuire piss off so much that they blasted him to death with a shotgun?"

"I reckon I need to take a trip to the murder scene," said Gus, "I want to inspect every inch of the streets surrounding that house. Someone was living there who was up to no good. That Hub search you sent in earlier, Neil. That should uncover them. Did McGuire enjoy a drink? He was a friendly guy. Where's the nearest pub, and who drinks there? What reputation does it have? Do you know, there might be a light at the end of this blessed dark tunnel after all."

"Unless it's a train coming, guv," said Neil.

That comment produced the first smiles in the office that morning.

The phone rang on Gus's desk.

"This might be London Road," Gus muttered. "I expect the ACC wants to hear we've solved this already. He's in for a disappointment."

Gus answered the call. He listened to the message, gave a curt response and put down the phone.

"Neil. We're needed elsewhere," he said.

"OK, guv. What's occurring?"

"They have discovered the body of a man at the foot of a fire escape just off the Market Place in Devizes."

Chapter Four

"I'LL DRIVE," said Gus Freeman when they reached the ground floor.

The weather was bright and sunny again today, and the few clouds that floated across the sky were white and fluffy. They represented everything Gus wasn't feeling right now.

As they drove towards Devizes, Neil Davis sat beside him in stony silence.

Gus knew it was pointless offering his commiserations. The scene that awaited them was a familiar one to both officers. They'd attended similar crime scenes a hundred times over, but this time it was personal.

He parked his car behind the Black Swan Hotel. They walked towards an alley that accessed the enclosed area behind the bed-and-breakfast premises where Terry Davis spent the weekend.

A blue and white police crime scene tape prevented them from approaching the rough patch of land at the foot of the fire escape. A uniformed sergeant confronted the pair, and Neil Davis showed him his badge. Gus presented his consultant's card and explained that DS Geoff Mercer asked him to attend.

The sergeant nodded and lifted the tape. Gus and Neil ducked underneath and approached the group of people gathered by the body on the ground. White-suited scene-of-crime officers were everywhere. Sterile stepping mats indicate where those directly involved, and visitors should walk.

"Peter Morgan's here today, guv," said Neil, "I saw that Porsche Boxster of his parked next to the alley."

Morgan spotted the newcomers and walked across to greet them.

"Could you don these natty blue shoe covers, gents? I'm sorry, DS Davis; if you could formally identify the deceased, I'll try to explain why we've found ourselves here this morning."

Neil nodded. He and Gus slipped the covers on their feet and followed the police surgeon to the fire escape. They passed officers taking photos from opposite ends of the enclosed space using digital cameras.

One man stood to the side, watching their approach. It was the detective leading the investigation. DI Gareth Francis nodded to Gus Freeman and led Neil Davis to view the body. Peter Morgan followed them.

As soon as he'd reached the outside cordon, Gus had known that the dead man was Terry Davis. He still wore the same clothes as he had yesterday afternoon. Neil's identification was a necessary formality.

The young DS stared at the man on the ground. His father's skin was mottled grey. The way the body lay suggested he tumbled down the steps of the metal staircase from top to bottom, landing in a crumpled heap at the foot.

"It's my father, former DS Terence Davis," said Neil.

"Thank you," said Peter Morgan.

"I'm sorry for your loss," said DI Francis.

Gus closed his eyes. What a muppet.

"What happened?" asked Neil.

"We're still piecing together the events of the past few days," said Gareth Francis, "he arrived in Devizes on Friday. I believe it was to spend time with you and your wife?"

"I know what happened until five-thirty yesterday afternoon," said Neil, "that was the last time I saw him alive. He was leaving the Cavalier to walk into town for the evening. Dad planned to meet up with old friends. I was calling him at lunchtime today to make sure he was sober. His flight back to Spain from Bristol meant leaving Devizes by taxi later this afternoon. So how did he die?"

"My primary examination suggests he died from serious head injuries," said Peter Morgan. "You've both attended enough of these scenes to know that I won't commit myself to a definitive cause of death until I've completed the post-mortem."

"It looks like a tragic accident," said Gareth Francis, "if he'd been drinking all afternoon and evening, he would have arrived here in the early hours. He didn't sleep in his bed. Perhaps he got disoriented in his drunken state and believed he was heading for the toilet. Many of the rooms in this place aren't en suite. It's at the budget end of the market."

"My father didn't believe in throwing his money around," said Neil, "but two things spring to mind. First, even when drunk, it would be difficult to confuse a toilet door with an emergency exit; second, why weren't staff alerted to someone using the exit to the fire escape after midnight without reason?"

"I mentioned these premises weren't among the best. For example, the ceiling light in the corridor outside your father's room wasn't working. The manager swears blind it was functioning perfectly well earlier that evening, but when we arrived this morning, a uniformed officer found the lightbulb missing. When asked about the emergency exit, the manager admitted that the alarm got disconnected last summer. He said guests complained that the rooms at the top of the building were airless, and they kept opening the door to reduce the heat. He insists the door remained closed every night since last September, but if someone opened it last night, there would be no piercing alarm signal."

"Where did Terry Davis drink last night?" asked Gus Freeman, "and who was the last person to talk with him?"

"We haven't traced his movements yet," said Gareth Francis, "we'll visit the likely pubs and clubs in due course. Did your father smoke, Neil?"

"Dad stopped smoking cigarettes twenty years ago," said Neil, "since he moved to Spain, he's smoked an occasional panatela cigar. But, as far as I recall, he didn't have any on him yesterday. Why?"

"Maybe he wasn't trying to find the toilet. If he wanted a smoke last thing before going to bed, he could have come out here onto the fire escape. Instead, he might have lost his footing."

"Did you find any cigar butts?" asked Gus.

"We're still collecting items from inside and outside the property. It's too soon to say whether what we've collected is pertinent."

Gus wondered why they were ensuring they missed nothing and collected every scrap of evidence. Such a procedure was overkill if they viewed this as a tragic accident.

He knew how events played out last night.

"You have a comprehensive CCTV system here in the town centre, don't you?" Gus asked DI Francis.

"We do; it's run with the support of the Devizes Development Partnership on behalf of the community since the end of 2007. It's scheduled for an upgrade later this year. There are nine locations with sophisticated, high-definition cameras."

"Which areas do they cover that we think are relevant?" asked Gus.

"We may be better checking the lot," said Gareth.

"There was no reason to use the car park in Sheep Street," said Neil. "I never remember him drinking in the pubs near the Wadworth's Roundabout on the A361 either. Those cameras out by Rose's the Ironmongers and Morrison's supermarket are too far out of the centre to capture him moving between pubs."

"Well, in that case, the cameras to concentrate on are at The Brittox, at Sainsbury's, then the Old Post Office, the Castle Hotel, and the Market Place itself," said Gareth Francis.

"Neil, you know this system better than I do. So how does it work?" asked Gus.

"Video signals from each camera get beamed back to the control centre. The images get recorded twenty-four-seven on a massive hard disk array. The scheme's run by a part-time CCTV Manager and manned by volunteers from the community."

"It's part of the community safety initiative operated in conjunction with the Police and the local town centre stores that subscribe to the system," said DI Francis. "They can communicate with the Police Control Room and officers on the ground. As a result, we can react quickly to a live incident. The system provides recorded evidence to assist in the prosecution of suspected offenders. Since 2007 it has contributed to several arrests and successful prosecutions. It also monitored suspicious individuals and dealt with several other incidents. Those cameras have significantly reduced criminal damage and anti-social behaviour in the town centre."

"All excellent news, Gareth," said Gus, "it means that we have every chance of tracing Terry Davis's movements around the town centre last night. Together with the statements your people take from the landlords and any customers you can trace, we should find the people Terry spoke to and work out who saw him last."

"If he fell over and broke his neck, we could draw a line under things," said Neil. "Although, our conversation in the Cavalier yesterday afternoon puts a different complexion on what followed, guv."

"I'm not following, DS Davis," said Gareth Francis.

"We'll talk more slowly if it helps," said Gus Freeman. "We have a missing lightbulb—and a lack of security on these premises. An intoxicated guest was returning to his room. That person rarely smoked and, as an ex-copper, was astute enough to know which room was which on a hotel corridor. I find it unlikely Terry Davis used that door to the fire escape willingly. Instead, someone followed him around town. They entered the guest house, removed the lightbulb outside Terry's room and waited in the dark at the top of the stairs for him to return. As he fumbled for his key, they bundled him through the fire door and pushed him down the stairs. I'll bet you a fiver. Peter Morgan will find that Terry Davis suffered a sharp blow to the back of the head. Easy to dismiss that as having occurred on any of the metal stairs, but this was no accident."

"What possible motive could there be?" asked DI Francis, shaking his head, "What conversation in the Cavalier do you mean? You two must sit with one of our detectives and provide a statement."

"Happy to do so," said Gus, "but can you let Neil get off home for now? He has places to go and people to see. It's a difficult time for him."

"I'm fine, guv," said Neil, "I want to find out who did this, and I've got experience with the CCTV system. So I can be an asset to the investigation."

"You need time with your family," said Gus. "I'm not driving out to inform Melody. Your Mum needs to learn about Terry's death too. Even if they were divorced, I don't think she would appreciate reading it in the newspaper."

"How will I get home? My car is outside our office."

"I can ask someone to drive you to collect your car, DS Davis," offered Gareth Francis.

"OK," said Neil, "it's probably for the best."

Gus spotted a new arrival ducking under the blue-and-white tape and heading towards them. It was his friend and superior officer, DS Geoff Mercer.

"Good morning, gentlemen," said Geoff, "I wish we were meeting under better circumstances. Neil, may I offer my condolences. Take the time you need. We'll cover your position in the CRT if necessary."

"DS Davis was just leaving us, Sir," said Gareth Francis, "I'll assign a uniformed officer to get him back to his car. We're making progress here, collecting evidence. DS Davis offered to assist with the CCTV analysis. That could prove vital in locating Mr Davis senior's movements last night."

"Neil needs to spend time with his family, DI Francis," said Geoff Mercer, "we'll find a body to hunt through hours of CCTV images. Never fear."

Geoff turned to Gus Freeman,

"You must remember, Gus, that you can't be directly involved in a live case. You were re-employed specifically to handle cold cases. The ACC will have my guts for garters if I let you do more than I already have. I was happy for you to accompany Neil to identify the body, but that should be the limit of your involvement."

"I appreciate what you're saying, Geoff," Gus sighed. He knew he was right. "However, there are extenuating circumstances in this case. I'm heading for London Road to get the ACC to move the goalposts. I need to be in on this investigation."

"Until the situation changes, those are my instructions, Gus."

Neil made his way back to the alley and a waiting car.

For now, Gus accepted that his role in the investigation into Terry Davis's death was at an end.

"What will you do if the ACC says no, Gus," said Geoff as they left the crime scene.

"I'll threaten to walk away from the Crime Review Team," muttered Gus.

"Don't do anything rash," said Geoff. "Make your way to London Road, and we'll meet there. If we can see the ACC, perhaps he'll consider a temporary change in your status."

As Gus settled into the driving seat of his car, he had a thought. He smacked the steering wheel with the palm of his hand.

I'm an idiot, Gus thought. That could be what the Chief Constable wants.

Plunkett and Culverhouse would succeed in closing our unit. We've missed something.

I know the reason for them wanting us gone lies in their shared past. But, although we uncovered Culverhouse's fling with Trudi Villiers and his guiding hand in how Terry Davis dealt with evidence in her murder, there has to be something more damning to find.

They wouldn't entertain using a fixer like Gardiner for a matter that resulted in a slap on the wrist for either of them. However, one of the cold cases the ACC selected could contain an explanation. Culverhouse and Plunkett came together for a reason. Maybe a murder case. If they screwed up big time, his Crime Review Team was too bloody good at their job not to find out what it was.

It's an obvious answer, Gus thought, and anyway, what else could it be?

Gus left the Black Swan car park and headed for London Road. On arrival, he parked next to Geoff Mercer's car. His boss was inside the building. A glance at the upstairs window confirmed that the ACC was in his office.

The reception desk was a formality these days. Gus signed in with a nod to the officer on duty and climbed the stairs two at a time. When he reached the top, two faces looked up from their work. Vera Jennings and Kassie Trotter looked glum. Bad news travels fast.

"I'm so sorry, Gus," said Vera, getting up from her chair and coming towards him. "How's Neil?"

Gus took both her hands in his; there was little point hiding a change in their relationship. Vera was no longer married, and the fact she'd slept at Gus's bungalow in Urchfont was common knowledge among the village community. His car was undoubtedly spotted outside Vera's rented cottage at the weekend.

"Neil's gone home to break the news to Melody and the rest of the family. He'll be back here for an hour tomorrow.

We need to provide statements for Gareth Francis, as we met with Terry Davis yesterday afternoon."

"Really?" asked Vera, "I didn't think you and Terry had much in common."

"Terry Davis was a useful resource on cases he'd worked on in the past, and he knew plenty of local people. He was brusque in his manner with me and didn't appreciate me coming out of retirement. Terry warned me about sticking my nose in where it wasn't wanted. I didn't expect him to be the one to pay the price. It's my fault he's dead."

"The chat here in the building suggested Terry was drunk, and it was an accidental death. How can you be responsible?"

"Freeman, in here, please."

ACC Kenneth Truelove had moved from his office window and stood in the doorway.

Geoff Mercer was sitting in front of the ACC's desk already.

Gus took a chair beside him.

"What did you discuss with Terry Davis yesterday afternoon?" asked the ACC.

"My reason for barging into Neil and Terry's quality time in the Cavalier was to ascertain what Terry knew about a man stalking me. He recognised Ricky Gardiner's description and warned me he was dangerous. Terry also intimated that there was a connection between Gardiner and our mutual friend."

"Why didn't you mention this to us earlier?"

"Gardiner's never bothered me. I noticed a stranger in the bar of the Lamb public house one evening after I'd been gardening at the allotment. I was having a quiet drink with Bert Penman, who has the adjacent plot. The stranger looked like a copper or an ex-copper. My first thought was he was connected to Brendan Curran. Ricky was in there again last week when we closed the Mallinder case."

"You say he's never bothered you nor attempted to talk to you?"

"No contact whatsoever. I started asking questions after Clemency Bentham told me he was watching my bungalow."

"Who on earth is Clemency... what did you say the name was?"

"Bentham, Sir. She's the new vicar at the village church. Ms Bentham took over Frank North's allotment. Frank's widow, Irene, told her this chap was skulking in the lane, watching my place."

"Frank North, the chap who died. Yes, I can see why you thought Curran might be the link. He'd wangled a significant payout for the widow, but I'm not entirely happy with how he handled things on that Rexha affair. It would be best if you kept your wits about you, Freeman. Brendan told me that his fellow compatriots have long memories. I might need to resurrect that protection duty I suspended after the raid on Cambrai Terrace."

"Let's not panic, Sir," said Gus, "it's Gardiner who needs to be the focus of our attention."

"How did Davis know this Gardiner character was dangerous? Who is he, anyway?"

"Gardiner's an undercover officer who served with the Metropolitan Police for years, guv," said Geoff Mercer. "He left under a cloud around ten years ago, and rumours spread that he was closer to the criminals than his handlers. But, again, that was only a rumour because he's got the reputation of being another Chuck Norris. You won't find him; he finds you."

"This sounds rather theatrical, Mercer. Let's accept that

he's no longer a serving officer. What is he doing in Urch-font keeping watch on Freeman's bungalow?"

"We believe he's working for Dominic Culverhouse and Sandra Plunkett, Sir," said Gus.

The ACC leapt from his chair and ran to the window. Gus wondered whether he considered that spot his 'safe' place.

"Her car's not at the front of the building. Thank goodness. I can't afford for Her Ladyship to overhear any of this."

"Have you swept your room for bugs, Sir?" asked Gus, tongue firmly in cheek.

Kenneth Truelove looked at Geoff Mercer.

"How do we do that, Geoff? Do you know someone?"

"Relax, guv, on the list of likely scenarios, her bugging your office is too tiny to register."

"I always knew digging the dirt on Culverhouse was risky. So why did she have to get promoted to Chief Constable here in Wiltshire? All I asked for was another twelve months of calm."

"I can't promise you that, Sir," said Gus, "when I chatted with Terry Davis, he assured me that Culverhouse didn't liaise with Ms Plunkett until the middle of 2013. Terry had retired to Spain, and Culverhouse was yet to transfer to Portishead. We believe the pair likely met at Bramshill a decade earlier. How they came together a decade later and what subsequently went pear-shaped, we don't yet understand. Gardiner's skill set suggests he's offering his services to both sides of the law these days."

"A gun for hire, do you mean?"

"If necessary, Sir. Last night, I believe he attempted to make Terry Davis's death look accidental. If you allow me to liaise with DI Francis to scrutinise the CCTV images captured on the five cameras focused on the town centre, I reckon we can prove it."

The ACC returned from the window. He stood with his hands resting on the back of his chair. Gus thought he could see him ageing before his eyes.

"The Chief Constable wouldn't stand for it, Freeman. She's looking for any excuse to get the CRT closed. Remember her comments when you met her here in this office."

"I'm with Gus on this, Sir," said Geoff Mercer, "if we're going after Dominic Culverhouse, then we need to be as sneaky as him. So I propose we sanction Freeman's involvement in the case, but we keep it under wraps. Gareth Francis will continue as SIO, and I'll brief him on Gus's involvement. His handling of the Eron Dushka business didn't impress Gus, but Gareth's a decent copper. With luck, they'll trace the relevant data in the CCTV system, and we'll be on our way."

"If you're sure we can keep his involvement from reaching Ms Plunkett's ears, then okay," said the ACC, "you have my blessing to go ahead."

"Thank you, Sir," said Gus. "I don't want to urinate on anyone's French fries, but even if we can prove this Gardiner fellow murdered Terry Davis, we're no closer to establishing the connection between him, Culverhouse and Plunkett. As soon as we arrest Gardiner, those two will destroy any paperwork or digital record that might show they've ever met or been in contact."

"We can't let them get away with it," said Geoff Mercer.

"Terry's assessment of the man's character indicated that he wouldn't trade information for a softer sentence, and if he's still running with both the hares and the hounds, he can't afford to show weakness. The criminal element he works for would see him dead in a week."

"What do we do, then?" asked the ACC.

"Leave that to me, Sir," said Gus, "the less you know, the better."

"Are you sure there's nobody you can get to check this room on the QT, Mercer? To be on the safe side?"

"I can have a look myself, guv. I'll work late tonight and sweep the whole of this floor. People in the Hub can locate the right piece of kit. I'll tell them it's for a training exercise elsewhere."

"I'd better get back to the CRT office, Sir," said Gus, "my two remaining team members will wonder what's happening."

"Any progress yet on the McGuire case?" asked the ACC.

Gus gave a rueful smile.

"When Geoff rang this morning, I thought you would ask me that very question, Sir. I'm afraid we've not got far so far. There appeared to be no motive, no likely suspects and very little evidence based on the murder file. I'll visit the murder scene to get a feel for the locality. A lot could have changed in the intervening period. I might need to chat with officers who served in Amesbury back then. They can fill in the blanks on who was up to no good in the area. Maybe the good doctor upset someone. He was a gregarious chap and fond of the ladies. That suggests a jealous husband or partner might have wanted to sort him out."

"I can see a criminal gang taking offence if someone disrupts their business. Gangs can be violent in the extreme on those occasions," said Kenneth Truelove. "As for a jealous husband. I can accept sorting McGuire out with a few punches or kicks, but blasting him with a pump-action shotgun is way beyond what one would expect."

"We'll follow the clues when we uncover them, Sir," said Gus, "it might take longer to solve than the other cases due to the existing situation."

Geoff Mercer interjected.

"How would you feel if I assigned DS Luke Sherman to CRT as cover until DS Davis returns to duty?"

"I'm always happy to welcome someone who saved my life, Geoff. If he's free tomorrow, he can assist DS Hardy in setting up interviews and chasing items Neil Davis forwarded to the Hub. Thanks. Much appreciated. You can have him back in a day or two."

Gus sensed a collective sigh of acceptance on the other side of the desk.

The ACC clutched the back of his chair, but his eyes no longer darted side-to-side, hunting a hidden camera or microphone.

"We keep going," said Geoff Mercer.

"All for one," said Gus.

He left the ACC's office with Geoff Mercer. Geoff grabbed Gus by the sleeve when they were outside the closed door.

"The ACC's going to pieces, isn't he?"

"If we can keep calm and carry on, we'll help him through it. We have no alternative."

"You're right, of course," said Geoff, "what happened to Terry Davis makes it personal. But, on the other hand, he might have been a rogue...."

"But he was our rogue," said Gus.

Vera was hovering, trying to catch their attention.

"Any news?" she asked.

"We're continuing with our enquiries," Geoff replied,

"Gus will return in the morning for an interview with DI Francis. Can you reserve a room for the purpose, Vera?"

"Certainly," Vera replied, "call me later, Gus, if you get five minutes. I want to make sure you're OK."

Gus nodded and made for the top of the stairs.

The Chief Constable was in the building and heading his way.

"Good morning, ma'am," said Gus as he breezed past Sandra Plunkett.

Her Ladyship scowled at him and kept climbing.

The news that Terry Davis's accident was suspicious had reached her ears. Gus made a mental note to check with Geoff Mercer about DI Francis's loyalty card. Was it up to date? Or was someone else passing information to the new Chief Constable? Unfortunately, only a few candidates were from this morning's crime scene.

Gus drove out of the car park and joined a queue of traffic inching its way through the town centre. Nothing changed. The seven-mile trip took him thirty-five minutes. Neil's car had disappeared from the Old Police Station car park long before he arrived.

The cars of his other two colleagues were still in situ. He could only hope they were upstairs working and not making out. The lift made almost no noise as it ascended, so there would be little warning of his arrival if they were distracted.

Gus stared at the floor and took the extra precaution of a cough.

"Are you okay, guv?" asked Lydia Logan Barre.

"Is Neil not with you, guv?" asked Alex.

"You heard what I said to Neil as we left the office," said Gus. "someone found a dead body on the rough ground near the town centre in Devizes. It was Neil's father, Terry."

"Oh no, poor Neil," said Lydia.

"Poor Terry too," said Gus, "at first, the Police Surgeon guessed it was an unintentional fall from the top of the metal fire escape. But, after Neil and I arrived and took a closer look, we uncovered facts that suggested foul play."

"It was murder?" said Alex. "Who was after him, guv? Did he have enemies from his time serving here in this station?"

"Neil sounded so happy when he told us his Dad was coming home," said Lydia.

"Yes, when Terry heard about the baby, it seemed it might bring him and Neil closer together," Alex added.

"It's water under the bridge now," said Gus. "I chatted with Neil and Terry in a Devizes pub for over an hour yesterday afternoon. Tomorrow morning, I'm required to attend an interview at London Road. Neil will be there too, and he's not returning here to work for the time being."

"That's understandable. If you need us to keep things ticking over while you're away, guv, that's no problem," said Alex. "I've completed a list of people to interview, by the way."

"Thanks, Alex. We'll have another pair of hands here tomorrow morning. DS Luke Sherman is joining us on a temporary assignment."

"Is he dishy, guv," said Lydia.

"I could have hugged him in a heartbeat when he shot the bugger, trying to add two more holes to my head. Why do you ask? I didn't think you'd be interested."

"No fear. I was asking for a friend," she replied.

Alex kept his head bowed. He didn't want Gus to see his blushes.

"I'd better check this list, Alex," said Gus.

In the Old Police Station office, three-quarters of the

team passed the remainder of the working day, going through the motions. Unfortunately, a dark cloud hung over the office despite the bright sunshine.

On the other side of Devizes, Melody was coming to terms with the shocking news of her father-in-law's sudden death.

"Terry will never hold his grandchild now, Neil. That's such a shame. I know I didn't like him much, but he didn't deserve that. Who could do such a thing?"

"Gus Freeman has his suspicions, Melody, but I can't be thinking about that. I need to drive over to tell Mum. It's something I need to do face-to-face. Thank goodness I've had plenty of practice performing this thankless task as a copper."

Neil left Melody to drive to his mother's house.

His wife sat in the kitchen, nursing a cold cup of tea. She had never liked Terry Davis, but he was the only father-in-law she would ever have.

When the tears came, Melody swept them away with her hand.

"This pregnancy has a lot to answer for; look at me. I'm never emotional."

EARLIER THAT MORNING, the train carrying Ricky Gardiner slowed to a crawl as it entered Paddington station. He joined the queue of people moving towards the front carriages.

As he stepped onto the platform, he made a call.

"There's no chance of your past returning to bite you now," he said.

"You're sure it will get cleared as an accident?"

"I've done this before, you know. Call me when you need another problem sorted."

Ricky Gardiner ended the call and melted into the crowds heading for the Underground.

Chapter Five

Tuesday, 15 May 2018

ANOTHER DAY DAWNED. Despite the trials and tribulations the world threw his way, Gus acknowledged that day followed night, regardless.

He stared at the ceiling and pondered what lay ahead. He was due at London Road HQ at nine o'clock.

Gus had an interview with DI Gareth Francis. It wasn't to be under caution. That was a blessing. At least the little muppet didn't have Gus in the frame for Terry Davis's demise. Gus thought Gareth Francis believed it to be nothing more than an accident. Fat chance of that. Gus prayed that the post-mortem confirmed his thoughts.

No point staring at this ceiling, he thought. Instead, the condemned man should eat a hearty breakfast.

As he stood in the kitchen and cracked an egg into the frying pan to join two rashers of bacon and one sausage, he had two questions on his mind.

When could he give his undivided attention to the thorny issue of the Dr Ian McGuire murder?

What did they feed chickens on these days that made their eggshells so hard to break?

Gus hated a broken yolk, but he had had to strike the shell with such force that the knife sliced straight through the egg. Waste not, want not, but it spoiled the aesthetic effect when he served his breakfast. The only consolation was that it still tasted fantastic. After that, he was ready for whatever questions Gareth Francis threw at him.

Gus rang Neil Davis before leaving the bungalow.

"I'm heading into Devizes, Neil. I'll see you later. How did things go yesterday?"

"There were a lot of tears, guv. It affected Mum more than I thought, considering the ill feeling after she and Dad divorced. Mum's spreading the news to the more distant corners of the Davis clan. It might be a fortnight before we can arrange the funeral. Melody has been quieter than usual since I came home. No love was lost between her and Dad, but sudden death is, well, it changes things, doesn't it?"

"I agree," said Gus, "on every case I've handled where there's been a sudden or suspicious death, close family members rally around. The past gets forgotten for a few days. Then, of course, I've attended the odd wake two weeks later where old differences resurface after a few beers, and we've separated the warring factions."

"I'll bear that in mind, guv," said Neil, "but a liquid celebration is something Dad insisted on. Mum reckoned he put money aside in his will for the special occasion. Dad had so many contacts in so many pubs; it will be difficult getting them together in one place."

"You may need to put money over the bar in every pub

you can think of and let them get on with it, Neil," said Gus. "If there's enough to go around."

"It's a bugger. I still can't believe he's gone. There's so much to get done."

"Remember what we said yesterday. Take as long as you need. Luke Sherman is standing in for you from today. I don't want you back until you're ready to give our latest case one hundred per cent. I hope it's sooner rather than later, but don't rush things."

"Thanks, guv. I'll see you at around ten o'clock."

Gus ended the call. He finished dressing, ensuring his shirt collar was down, and his tie was straight. It was too warm for a jacket, but this was an interview, so Gus relented and grabbed his old leather. A glance in the hallway mirror reminded him he was due a haircut. Never mind, he'd tried, and it wasn't a job interview.

London Road was always hectic in the minutes leading to nine o'clock in the morning. Gus was glad to escape the commuter traffic and start the hunt for a parking spot not too far from the main entrance. He was in luck; he glided into an empty slot, parked and ran up the steps.

As soon as he stepped through the front door, he bumped into Kassie Trotter.

"It's all happening here since you returned to work, Mr Freeman," she said, "did trouble follow you around when you were a proper copper?"

"Good morning, Kassie," said Gus, "thanks for reminding me I'm a mere consultant. But, no, I can honestly say that these past few weeks have surprised me. I don't know what I've done to deserve it."

"You've been busy in other areas, too," the young clerk said, jabbing him in the ribs.

"Steady on," said Gus, "you may have cracked a rib with that sharp elbow of yours. What do you mean?"

"You know what I mean, you rascal. Vera's had a smile on her face for the first time since she and Monty ended hostilities. I'm sure you had a hand in that."

"You have a way with words, Kassie," said Gus as they climbed the stairs to the administration area together. "Were you baking last night? Do I have something delicious to look forward to?"

Kassie laughed out loud. Her noisy but infectious breed of laughter woke everyone on the first floor.

"Her Ladyship's around this morning. Baked goods can only get served in secret. However, DI Francis isn't a lover of my cakes. Gareth says they add pounds to his waistline if he even looks at them, let alone eats them. He's waiting for you in Interview Room One. That's over there in the corner."

"Thanks, Kassie," said Gus and headed in the direction she pointed. Gus spotted a fresh bluebird tattoo on the underside of her arm.

Gareth Francis sat at the desk when Gus opened the door.

"Ah, Mr Freeman, you made it on time. Good. Let's get started."

Gus took a seat and waited for DI Francis to arrange the paper on the desk until it aligned with the edge. The detective then removed several pens and pencils from his jacket pocket and placed them in a row across the top of his papers.

"Could I have a glass of water," Gus asked.

He hoped Gareth needed to fetch a drink from outside so he could give in to the urge to disturb the symmetry. No such luck.

Gareth pushed back his chair and collected a bag resting against the table leg.

He produced bottled water from a large bag and a vacuum flask. He unscrewed the cup and showed the bottle to Gus.

"It's Evian. Is that okay?" grinned Gareth.

"Perfect," said Gus. This guy was good. Perhaps he'd misjudged him.

An hour later, the ordeal was over. Not a trial, more an hors d'oeuvres.

Gus repeated the conversation word-for-word that he'd had with Terry and Neil in the Cavalier pub on Sunday afternoon. He left out the meeting with the unfriendly barman. Gus confirmed when he'd left the bar to ferry Neil home in time for his evening meal. Gareth asked where he was between when he dropped Neil at home and when he arrived at work on Monday morning.

"It's routine, you know that, but I need to ask," said Gareth.

"I've asked criminals the same question a million times," said Gus, "and frequently, I've known they were going to lie because they were guilty."

"Should I cut to the chase then and ask if you killed Terry Davis?" asked DI Francis.

"No comment," said Gus, "I've always wanted to say that. Thanks."

Gus paused for effect.

"OK, you got me. So I drove home, made a coffee, ate cheese on toast and listened to 'Ommadawn' by Mike Oldfield. I never left home until I drove to the Old Police Station the following morning, arriving twenty minutes later than usual because of roadworks."

"Oldfield? Not someone I've come across. Dance music, is it?"

Gus shook his head. The skilful trick with the bottled water was a fluke; the little twerp remained a muppet.

"I think that's everything for now, Mr Freeman. When DS Davis arrives, I'll conduct a similar interview and attend the PM with Peter Morgan. I will get confirmation there whether Terry Davis fell or someone pushed him."

"A PM with PM," said Gus, "when do you intend to interrogate those CCTV cameras? Have you heard that the ACC clears me to work on the case after yesterday's meeting?"

Gareth Francis tried hard to hide that he didn't appreciate having a dinosaur added to his investigating team. He failed miserably.

"I heard, Mr Freeman, and I'm sure you appreciate that I'm the SIO. My next task is to interview your colleague. If DS Mercer wishes to alter my schedule, he'll let me know."

Gus left the diminutive DI in Interview Room One, rearranging paperwork and returning spare pens and pencils to his jacket pocket. The game was afoot, and Gus needed to get involved in it whether or not the SIO liked it.

Neil Davis was talking with Vera Jennings and Kassie Trotter.

"DI Francis will see you now, Neil," said Gus, "he's a muppet. So rise above it, and don't lose your temper."

"Did you avoid thumping him, Gus?" asked Vera.

"You do have a reputation, Mr Freeman," added Kassie, "that Curran chap was as white as a sheet when he left the ACC's office after you confronted him last month."

"I heard it was Suzie Ferris who held you back," said Vera. "She said the ACC would have needed a new carpet if you took one more step."

"Blimey, guv," said Neil, "a different side of you gets revealed every day. Thanks for the warning. I'll tell Gareth Francis the truth about everything Dad and I discussed from Friday when he turned up at our place until I left the Cavalier with you. I can't do any more than that."

"Carry on, Neil. It's a formality we both needed to endure. Remind me again where to find this CCTV control centre?"

"The Crown Centre," said Neil, "it's a charitable building for elderly and vulnerable adults to assemble in a safe environment and get help if needed. I think it's been running since the end of the Sixties. Sad to say, it's on its last legs. Fewer people have used it in the past few years, and it's closing. The control centre will continue to operate from there as I understand it."

Neil left the trio to continue their chat and walked to the interview room.

"The Crown Centre's opposite the entrance to High Street off of St John's Street," said Vera, "you can't miss it."

"I'm surprised the place wasn't getting more use," said Gus, "the media suggests more elderly people suffer from isolation and depression than ever. Add in the vulnerable element of all ages I read about, and the demand has got to grow, not fall."

"It's that austerity business again, Mr Freeman," said Kassie, "the Council places are closing because of cutbacks, and the charitable organisations that rely on the public putting their hands in their pockets are finding fewer Good Samaritans."

"We won't solve the world's worries here on the administration floor of the Wiltshire Police Headquarters, ladies," said Gus. "I'll find my way to this control centre in a while.

In the meantime, have you seen Geoff Mercer this morning?"

"Mr Mercer left his office around thirty minutes ago," said Kassie, "he told me he was returning something he'd borrowed to the Hub. I expect he'll be back in a minute or two. Can I make you a coffee?"

"That would be lovely, Kassie. I'll chat with Vera while I wait."

"You two lovebirds, what are you like?" giggled Kassie.

"Yes," said Vera, "what are we like? When will I see you again?"

"I fear it won't be before the weekend. The Terry Davis business and the new cold case are my priorities. I'm sorry."

"I understand, don't worry. I've agreed to go ahead with purchasing that cottage we viewed on Saturday, by the way. The location and the price swung the deal. But, after discussing it with my parents over lunch yesterday, there's one other thing I decided. Now the divorce is finalised, I'm reverting to my maiden name. My father doesn't want any lingering link between the Butler and Jennings families."

"I don't imagine you care very much whether Monty gets annoyed or upset?"

"Not one bit," said Vera, "the more distance I can put between us, the better. My father agreed with your suggestion of tempting Monty with a sweetener. It will end these minor queries through his solicitors. Dad offered to pay whatever is enough to stop it for good."

"It's a sensible approach. As for the name change, I'll soon get used to not calling you Mrs Jennings."

"If you call me Vera at all times, it will never become an issue," said Vera with a smile. "If anything relating to a divorce can ever be straightforward, I guess it's the name change part," said Vera. "If there were any complications, I would have to change it by Deed Poll, but I simply took Monty's surname when we wed, and our marriage took place in the UK. We finalised the divorce in the UK, and I have the decree absolute. You don't normally require a Deed Poll to change your records with the relevant bodies. There's enough evidence if you can show your decree absolute, your original Marriage Certificate, your original Birth Certificate, and a signed statement that you are reverting to using your maiden name for everything."

"You've gone into this in some detail, then?" said Gus, "I didn't know that was what was required. Not that it was ever relevant in my case."

"I can't claim the credit for the details," smiled Vera, "my father was the architect behind that. He did the spadework and then kept dropping gentle hints through lunch and into the afternoon that I got on with it. Finally, I gave in at around seven o'clock on Sunday. I wanted to drive home for a quiet evening."

"Gus, you've finished your interview."

It was Geoff Mercer returning from his trip to the Hub.

"You can take your coffee with you, Mr Freeman," said Kassie, "or I can bring it to Mr Mercer's office with another cup and a surprise?"

"A surprise, please. Kassie," said Geoff, "come on, Gus, we need to talk."

"I'll call you later in the week, Vera," Gus promised.

Gus followed Geoff Mercer into the dark corridor leading to his office.

He glanced across the administration area. It was just a hunch.

Gus sensed someone was watching him. There was nobody nearby, but on the far side, he spotted Sandra Plunkett staring in his direction as she peered over the shoulder of another of her senior officers. Gus resisted the temptation to wave and hurried after his friend.

"How did your interview go?" asked Geoff as he closed the door behind them.

"As you might expect."

"You annoyed him, then?"

"It's hard to avoid it, but I appreciate he has a job to do. He's not happy I got the green light from the ACC."

"Gareth's not the only one. The Chief Constable gave the ACC a verbal volley this morning. She left little doubt that if you made a nuisance of yourself or impeded the investigation, she would hold him responsible. So both of you would be out the door, pronto."

"They're suffering from an attack of the Roy Orbison's, aren't they?"

"Before my time," said Geoff, "anyway, I don't follow you."

"Liar," said Gus. "I mean, they're running scared."

There was a knock at the door.

Geoff Mercer looked worried.

"Don't panic; it will be Kassie Trotter," said Gus.

He stood and opened the door. Kassie wheeled in her trolley. She placed two coffee cups on Geoff's desk, and after checking, Gus had closed the door and produced a plate of chocolate digestive biscuits from beneath a tea towel.

"Say no more," she said, tapping her nose. Gus opened the door again, and Kassie disappeared.

"Kassie told me you were returning something to the Hub," said Gus. "Can I conclude that you completed the sweep of the offices?"

"I did, and we have a green light in that department too. So if there were ever any listening devices or hidden cameras in this part of the building, they're no longer there."

"I checked the manual for my home security system last night," said Gus, "A brief interrogation proved that nothing sinister has happened at the bungalow either. So, Ricky Gardiner restricted his observations to wandering along the lane and peeping through the branches of the trees."

"Good. What are your plans for the rest of the day?" asked Geoff.

"Gareth Francis is attending Terry Davis's post-mortem in an hour. It will be mid-afternoon before he's free to take me through the CCTV information available. I want to get cracking on that straight away."

"Look, Gareth is the Senior Investigating Officer. I don't doubt you're right in suspecting foul play. If it isn't, Her Ladyship will throw the book at you. She will accuse you of wasting valuable resources analysing data that merely supports the theory that Terry visited half-a-dozen pubs. As a result, he got paralytic and did a forward roll at speed down a metal fire escape."

"I want to search for signs of Gardiner," said Gus, "but there should be no comeback on using the system for supporting the initial findings Peter Morgan put forward. You could say that we confirmed the route that Terry took. We checked with the bar staff to learn how much he drank and got a precise time for him to return to the bed-and-breakfast hotel. If his death were an accident, there would be plenty of evidence to support it."

"Hold on, what's this 'you' could say, and 'we' confirmed?" said Geoff Mercer.

"Well, you're my superior officer. In name, at least. Surely, you aren't abandoning me in my time of need?"

"Do you even know where the CCTV control centre is?"

"I do, but I might get lost in a busy town like Devizes,"

Geoff Mercer shook his head.

"Come on, finish your coffee. I'll come with you. If Ms Plunkett asks, I'll say the ACC asked me to make sure you toed the line. It might save us. Remind me again why I thought it sensible to have you back?"

"I'm good at what I do," said Gus, grabbing a second biscuit, "and I spot inconsistencies that a less-experienced detective misses. Even if he is a Senior Investigation Officer."

There was no sign of Sandra Plunkett when Geoff and Gus headed out of the building.

"Will we take your car, Geoff?" asked Gus.

"It's a bugger to park along there. We can walk it in fifteen minutes."

"If memory serves, this route takes us past the job centre," said Gus.

"Pick me up a few leaflets on the way back if you don't like what you find," said Geoff.

Fifteen minutes later, they arrived at the Crown Centre. Geoff introduced the part-time supervisor and the volunteer in the office that morning. The two detectives sat and waited while the volunteer loaded the relevant camera data for them to review.

"You're familiar with this system then, Geoff?" asked Gus.

"It's a while since I used it, but we can always shout for help from the supervisor if I get stuck."

"Let's set our timeline to start from six o'clock," said Geoff, "that lines up with when you took Neil home and Terry began his pub crawl. First, he left the Cavalier on

Eastleigh Road and joined the main road. Then, he proceeded along Nursteed Road."

"Geoff, you're not giving evidence in court, mate. Apply the KISS principle."

"Keep it simple. I've got it. So, Terry came into town via Southbroom Road and onto Long Street. Unfortunately, there's no sign of him on any of the five cameras we've sourced yet."

"I agree with Neil's assessment of where his father drank when he was living here, Geoff. Terry wouldn't go off the reservation. Which pub has been around for centuries on that road?

"The Lamb Inn, on the High Street, just off Long Street and on the left. There's been a pub there since the fifteenth century. It's a traditional pub, right up Terry's street."

"Make a note of that one. We'll interview the manager. They might have cameras of their own. One of his bar staff could recall serving Terry Davis early Sunday evening. Let's move on further."

"If he was making for the town centre, he passed the Town Hall. Unfortunately, he's out of range of the Market Place camera at this point. The next pub on his route was the Silk Mercer."

"Any relation, Geoff?" asked Gus.

"No, and Terry would avoid it like the plague. It belongs to that pub chain where they buy up old buildings, in this case, a fabrics shop, and turn them into pubs. They sell cheap beer and don't allow TV screens or music. The chain owner wants to stimulate conversation."

"Terry liked to talk, but you're right; he preferred a traditional pub combined with a sports bar."

"Got him," cried Geoff, "there he is, still walking in a straight line at this stage."

"What time was that, and where are we?" asked Gus.

"Terry's strolling along The Brittox into Maryport Street. That's at twenty past seven."

"Can you go slower? That's better. Where is he going now?"

"The Three Crowns," said Geoff, "he's consistent. That's another place with decent craft beers and a lively atmosphere."

"I'm searching for Gardiner, but I can't see many people walking nearby. Ricky is too wily to go inside any of these bars. Terry would have spotted him a mile off. Let's keep an eye on that Brittox camera. Let it run. See if you pick up anyone."

Geoff continued to trawl through the images. Finally, a few minutes before nine, Terry Davis crossed over to the White Bear Inn. A taxi pulled up outside, and a man climbed out five minutes after Terry entered the bar.

"Well, I'm damned," said Geoff, "Monty Jennings."

"No way were Terry and Monty connected," said an incredulous Gus Freeman. How could they have missed that?

"It's a third pub on the list to visit," said Gus, "and I've never met Monty. I kept my distance while the marriage was still in limbo."

"Do you think it wise for *you* to interview him?" asked Geoff.

"It might be an interesting conversation," said Gus.

The clock on the screen ticked on as the two men watched.

"That clinches it. I *will* have a word," said Gus.

On-screen, Terry Davis and Monty Jennings were

leaving the White Bear together at a quarter to ten. They stood on the pavement, talking for several minutes. Finally, a taxi arrived to collect Monty, and the two men shook hands before Terry crossed the road behind the cab and headed towards Market Place. The cab disappeared from view.

"Still no sign of Ricky Gardiner on any of the cameras," said Gus.

"Terry is now walking through the Market Place," said Geoff, "he's not going into the Black Swan. But, woah, he almost slipped off the pavement when he passed that bloke. He's had a skinful now. I reckon he's on his way to the Dolphin. That's a place past the Cinema on the right-hand side."

"What did I see on the left-hand side?" shouted Gus. "Freeze it. Can you see a shadow there?"

"It's someone on the opposite side of the road. Let me think. That's the Chinese takeaway lit up on that person's left, and they're throwing a shadow into the road. I'll let the camera feed run forward."

"So, we know that Terry visited the Dolphin. I've made a note of that. It's getting late. Where else would he go?"

"Hold it. Our shadow was on the move. Did you spot that? They darted across the road and hurried towards the Black Swan."

"Black hoodie, black jeans or trousers. A baseball cap pulled over his eyes. He had his hands stuffed into his jacket pockets. No idea whether he wore gloves. Did you see how he turned his face back towards the Dolphin? Nobody would blame him for checking there wasn't a car coming from Northgate Street into Market Place. I reckon it was Ricky Gardiner. He might have checked if Terry Davis only had a swift half in the Dolphin and came out again, but my money is on him keeping his face from the camera. He's a pro."

"The time on screen was five past ten," said Geoff. "Now we wait for Terry to reappear."

At almost eleven, Terry Davis finally made his way along the pavement to the Black Swan.

"This was his last port of call," said Geoff, "we won't see him alive again."

"Why not?" asked Gus.

"He'll have walked out the back entrance into the car park and across to his B&B. Unfortunately, there's no coverage there."

"We can check with the bar staff to see when and where he left. Is there nowhere we can see Terry Davis or Ricky Gardiner again?"

"No, that's as far as the CCTV cover extends. We know someone crossed the road while Terry Davis was in the Dolphin and made their way past the Black Swan. We can't prove it was Gardiner yet. The forensic people might work out his height and build. Good luck with any facial recognition with what the camera captured. Who knows if we can trace Ricky Gardiner full-face, wearing those clothes elsewhere in Devizes during the daytime on Sunday?"

"We've got to," said Gus. "We've got five publicans to chat with, plus Monty Jennings. It's a start. I know that Neil will be keen to offer his services if you feel there's a slight chance Gardiner's in that system somewhere."

"He was keen to help, wasn't he? He might still be there if we head back to London Road. If not, you could call him, tell him what we've learned so far, and see if he's up to spending a few hours here tomorrow."

When they arrived back on the first floor at London

Road, there was no sign of Neil Davis. So Gus asked Vera if he'd gone home.

"Neil went home an hour ago, Gus. He didn't stop to chat after he and DI Francis had finished the interview. Gareth disappeared to attend Terry Davis's post-mortem shortly after Neil left. We expect Gareth back around two o'clock. Are you stopping here until he's available?"

"I don't want to loiter in case Her Ladyship spots me. Have you eaten yet?"

"I brought in a packed lunch today. We could share it in the park if you wish. It's a lovely day."

It certainly was, but Gus sensed the next hour would be less pleasant.

"I'll tell Geoff Mercer where I'm going," he said, "and then we can pop out for a bite to eat and a chat."

While Vera tidied her desk, Gus headed for Geoff's office. He knocked and stuck his head around the door.

"I'm lunching with Vera," he said, "I need to broach the subject of how well Monty knew Terry."

"Tread with care," said Geoff, "there has to be a genuine reason. Don't ruin something good that's only just started."

"It's a risk I have to take," said Gus. "I want to understand why Vera never even hinted that the two men knew one another."

"Terry was a devious sort," said Geoff, "who knows how many clandestine relationships he developed over the years when he was a DS?"

"I'll be back within the hour. Vera reckons Gareth Francis is expected back in the office at two o'clock. Can you collar him to run us through the findings of the post-mortem? That will define our strategy in the future. Then, as you suggested, I'll ring Neil to see if he's ready to rejoin the action. Do you have a DC to spare that can accompany Neil when he interviews the bar staff?"

"I can't think of many sitting on their hands at the minute," said Geoff, "you do remember the cutbacks we've endured for the past five years?"

"Yes, but be creative, Geoff. Persuade whoever they're reporting to so that Neil can train the youngster in CCTV techniques. Sell it as a trade-off against trawling around five pubs looking for witnesses."

Geoff gave a wry smile.

"You never give up, do you? No wonder you always had a great success rate on your cases. I reckon you sweet-talked most of the felons into a confession. You convinced the poor devils it was for their own good."

"Confession is good for the soul, Geoff," said Gus.

Gus left his friend to ponder and closed the door behind him.

Chapter Six

VERA WAS WAITING for Gus at the top of the stairs when he emerged from the corridor leading to Geoff Mercer's office.

"Where shall we go for lunch?" she asked, "the Large Green by The Crammer can get crowded, but it's the nearest spot. Only a few minutes from here."

"That's as good a place as any," said Gus, "let's walk and talk."

"You sound serious. Have you had a bad morning?"

"When Geoff and I reviewed the CCTV images from Sunday night in the town centre, Monty arrived in a taxi and went inside the White Bear."

"That's not unusual," said Vera, "it's one of several pubs he visits in town. Of course, he avoids the Bear Hotel since I frequented it, but what does Monty have to do with anything?"

"Geoff and I saw Terry Davis go inside before Monty arrived. Forty-five minutes after Monty entered the pub, he came out again with Terry. They continued their conversation outside the White Bear for several minutes until Monty's cab arrived to take him home or to another appointment."

"What are you implying?" asked Vera.

"Nothing, but it surprised me you never told me they were friends," said Gus.

"It's the first I've heard of it," said Vera, quite taken aback. "It makes no sense. I've made no secret of how Monty behaves. He describes himself as an entrepreneur. My father prefers to call him a chancer. Monty aims to mix with the right people and create and cultivate contacts that advance his various businesses. Terry Davis wasn't moving in the same circles."

"How do you explain what we saw, then?" said Gus as they reached an empty bench and took a seat. Around them were small groups of people doing what they were, enjoying the midday sunshine and the invigorating fresh air.

"I can't," said Vera, "I wasn't there."

"We weren't privy to what happened inside the White Bear," Gus agreed, "but the timing suggested it was a pre-arranged meeting. Terry told us in the afternoon that he planned to catch up with *old friends* after Neil and I left him in the Cavalier. There are four other drinking places to check to learn who Terry might have met and possibly what they discussed. Monty could have been one of several old acquaintances Terry drank with that evening. So far, your ex-husband is the only one we've identified."

"They might not have spoken to one another *inside* the White Bear," said Vera, "it's conjecture. You need to check with the landlord to confirm whether they even acknowledged one another. Monty is a well-known figure in Devizes. Terry was a familiar face on the streets, in bars, and in nightclubs. Who's to say what you saw wasn't a casual chat of no significance? So why would they *arrange* to meet? What could they have had to discuss?"

"I sense you genuinely don't know what brought them together, Vera," said Gus, relaxing a little. "Which pleases me. But you didn't see the interaction on the pavement while they waited for Monty's taxi to arrive. If I had to describe the body language and the warm handshake, I'd say it was conspiratorial."

Vera shook her head.

"What you're describing flies in the face of everything I've ever known about Monty," she said. "I wouldn't say this in front of Neil, but people like Terry Davis were riff-raff as far as my ex-husband was concerned. Monty schmoozed the landed gentry and captains of industry, not middle-ranking police officers. He was a social climber who trod on the backs of men such as Terry Davis in a mad scramble for the top."

"It beats me," said Gus, "before Sunday afternoon, the last time I rang Terry, he asked if we still saw one another. He referred to you as Monty's missus. I said we had seen each other several times. Terry wished me luck. He said that you were always too good for Bernard Jennings."

"So, what's your point?" asked Vera, slipping her arm through Gus's.

The packed lunch was untouched. Instead, today was the most in-depth conversation the pair had had to date.

"Everything I know concerning Monty comes from you, Geoff, and Kassie. I've never met the bloke to form my own opinion. The view Terry expressed over the phone last month matched what I heard from the three of you. Geoff was as shocked as I was when we saw Terry emerge onto the pavement in close conversation with Monty. Terry pulled the wool over our eyes. He and Monty connected somehow, and it suited both of them for people to believe they were strangers."

"My father did his due diligence into Monty's past when we got together twenty-odd years ago," said Vera. "If he found Monty mixed up in something illegal, he wouldn't have let me see him. Monty always sailed close to the wind with his money-making schemes, but apart from civil proceedings at County Court for money problems, he's never linked to anything criminal."

Gus thought for a few moments.

"Perhaps, we should saunter back to work?" he said, standing up and offering Vera his hand. "Let's think this out logically. Monty sailed close to the wind. When he was a policeman, Terry Davis dealt with people who did the same but crossed the line. Terry also fostered relationships with dozens of men and women who drifted for want of a better word. He gathered a network of confidential informants in pubs and on the streets, enabling him to make enough arrests to stop his superiors from sacking him for his other shortcomings."

"Do you honestly think Monty was a confidential informant?" asked Vera.

"Perhaps I should ask you that question, Vera? Is it possible Monty did something years ago to bring him to Terry's attention? For example, could Monty have avoided prison by feeding Terry inside information on any business contacts who drifted too far from the straight and narrow?"

"It does sound like something he might do, especially if he thought it improved his chances of making another million, only if he was to lose it again on his next hare-brained idea. However, it's the first time I've considered that option a real possibility. When the Cambrai Terrace affair broke, you avoided raising the matter with me. Instead, you wondered whether Monty was aiding and abetting the Rexha Brothers in their marijuana manufacture. Was he more than the rascal we believed him to be? Was he a rogue who got involved with a gang prepared to kill poor Frank North? I still considered Monty harmless back then, but now I'm unsure."

"Look, whatever brought Terry and Monty together is ancient history, and I doubt it was too serious. I want you to rack your brains for any occasions in the past five years when Monty might have learned things of use to Terry. Was Monty the contact Terry kept taunting me with on the phone from Spain? Did he pump you for information when you two were still living together?"

Vera laughed.

"I told you what our marriage had become, Gus," she replied. "Monty was being entertained by one of his business associates one weekend and hosting a catered function at home the next. During the week, we barely spoke. After I moved out, the only conversations we've had have been through our solicitors. I didn't start working at London Road until the children were teenagers, so there wasn't much he could have gleaned from me for a large proportion of our marriage."

"So, Monty's contact has worked at London Road for a time," Gus mused. "I doubt there was any financial reward for opening their mouth, so we're looking for someone who enjoys flapping their gums, regardless of whether the subject is confidential. Do you have anyone in mind?"

"They have to be older, Terry's age," said Vera, "which narrows the field somewhat. I'll give it thought and forward any likely candidates I come up with at the weekend. We're still on for the weekend, I hope?"

"All things being equal," said Gus, "I'll ask Geoff for

permission to interview Monty in the interim. We might get lucky. Now his handler is out of the picture, he won't need to pass on information. Perhaps he'll tell me who was feeding information to him?"

Vera and Gus climbed the stairs to the administration area. Kassie gave a welcoming wave, nodded towards the ACC's door and then grimaced. Her Ladyship must be in the building. Gus pitied the ACC; he was under enough stress.

"I'll call you on Friday, Vera," said Gus, "thanks for the heads-up, Kassie."

Gus found Geoff Mercer at his desk, just as he'd left him over an hour ago.

"It's not compulsory to wear yourself out by skipping authorised breaks, Geoff."

"I know. Did you ring Neil Davis yet?"

"I've been enjoying the sunshine and clearing the air with Vera. She didn't have a clue Terry and Monty knew one another. It's probably shrouded in the mists of time, but somewhere Monty must have bent the law sufficiently for Terry to get his claws into him. Since Terry's been in Marbella, Vera swears blind Monty hasn't asked her for information he shouldn't be privy to, so someone else here in this building is the leak. They told Monty, who then passed the details on to Terry Davis."

"It wasn't me," said Geoff, "in case you wondered. Did Vera have any suggestions?"

"Vera's giving it thought. I might get your answer if you allow me to interview Monty Jennings."

"Call Neil first and check if he's still keen to get back to work. I found a young WPC tipped for better things. She can tag along with Neil for two days, maximum. Use her or lose her, Gus. While you're chasing Neil, I'll find out where

Gareth Francis has gone. He should be back from the post-mortem in the next few minutes. I need to clear any interviews with him. I know you have a hidden agenda with Monty Jennings, but as the SIO, Gareth needs to control the big picture."

"Understood," said Gus, "as soon as I convince Neil to get back in the saddle, we'll badger DI Francis for a peek at the results of that PM."

Geoff left his office and went in search of Gareth Francis. Gus called Neil, and after a brief conversation, it was plain Neil was more than ready to start work at nine o'clock tomorrow morning.

Gus told him to go straight to the CCTV control centre and wait for a uniformed female officer who looked keen to impress. They should then hunt for a sighting of Ricky Gardiner that could match the running man he and Geoff captured after ten-fifteen on Sunday night.

Gus told Neil their subsequent interviews would be in the five pubs his father had visited that night. Neil knew the questions he needed to ask. Gus could rely on him to gather the intelligence they sought.

It would also benefit the WPC, regardless of the shortness of the assignment. It was an experience that books and seminars couldn't replicate.

Gus heard voices in the corridor. Geoff was returning, and he had company.

Gareth Francis was regaling his boss with the details of the post-mortem. Geoff wondered how many Gareth had attended. He'd lost count himself. These titbits were not news to him.

"Peter Morgan wrote the post-mortem report because he was the pathologist who performed it," said Gareth as they came through the office door. He nodded to Gus and carried on talking. "Terry Davis's next of kin will learn of the result, and Peter will send a copy to Davis's Doctor in Marbella."

"Neil and his family won't get a copy automatically?" asked Geoff.

"They only have to ask," said Gareth, "because it's now a criminal case, there might be restrictions on the information provided."

Gus's ears pricked at that gem. But common sense prevailed, and Morgan agreed it was a criminal case. Happy days.

"Are they easy for the family to follow if they request a copy?" asked Geoff. He was sitting now and winked at Gus while Gareth kept digging a bigger hole.

"Most reports start with general information concerning the deceased's medical history and the circumstances of their death. Peter then describes the outside of the body and the internal organs. That section includes details of the organs' size, weight and appearance. In this case, it wasn't a surprise to discover that Davis's liver took a hammering over the years. They tested his blood-alcohol level but ignored tests for drugs, poison, or prescribed medicines in this instance. The final summary listed the main points and the cause of death."

"Fascinating, Gareth," said Geoff, "but let's get to the point. What was the cause of death?"

"Maybe we should wait for Peter Morgan, Sir," said Gareth.

"He's on his way here, is he?" asked Geoff Mercer.

"I thought you wanted to hear what he has to say, Sir, given the slant Mr Freeman put on things at the crime scene yesterday."

Two minutes later, there was a tap at the door. Peter Morgan entered the room. He glanced at Gus Freeman.

"Good, you're here. Let me take you through my findings so far. Serious head injuries cause most fatal falls from stairs. The first impact occurs within a second of the loss of balance, no matter how that slip began. In a case such as this, with no witnesses, the cause can be determined from external injuries on the corpse and circumstantial evidence. My initial assessment was that Davis, impaired by alcohol, accidentally stumbled and lost balance at the top of the stairs. He then fell to the ground. Scenes of Crime Officers gathered evidence inside and around the top of the stairs, indicating a struggle. The external injuries included severe impact blow marks on the frontal bone of the head with skull fractures and severe impact blow marks with a fracture of the right upper shoulder. In addition, the body suffered fractured ribs and bruise marks on the lumbar area. I also recorded a severe impact blow mark on the occipital area of the skull."

"I was right," said Gus, "he got clouted around the back of the head and thrown down the stairs."

Peter Morgan nodded.

"The blood test results won't be available for a month," he continued. "How drunk Terry Davis was didn't play a significant role in how he died. A sober man might have reacted to an attack more quickly and saved himself. Who knows? I shall conduct further experiments to substantiate my findings to present in court."

"So the major fatal cause of death came from the skull fracture and intracranial injuries," said Geoff Mercer.

"What experiments can you carry out?" asked DI Francis, always keen to add to his knowledge.

"Peter will have a dummy prepared and return to the

crime scene to test his theory," said Gus. "I assume you're thinking of creating the scenario of an intentional fall from shoving at a standing-still posture?"

"You've read my mind," said Peter Morgan, "I'm impressed. An adult will vigorously push a forward-facing standing dummy, weighted to match the corpse, at the top of the staircase. I'll check the damage points with those I recorded on Davis's body. The force of the shove necessary can be determined by which of the lower steps receives the initial impact of the skull. It might not be possible to prove when the blow to the head occurred, however. The attack started in the corridor, as you suggested. Evidence collected by SOCO supports that theory. Probably, the stunning blow to the back of the head happened there. They then opened the fire door, bringing Davis forward in front of them and shoved him off the top step."

"Thank you, Peter, that's been very enlightening," said Geoff Mercer.

"Had you ever met Terry Davis?" asked Gus.

"I've been Police Surgeon here since '05, so yes, DS Davis and I bumped into one another at various crime scenes before he retired to the sun. He was a slovenly individual who reeked of alcohol and earned the unfortunate Blister nickname among his colleagues. Davis and I rarely spoke to one another."

"Blister?" asked Gareth Francis.

"They have an annoying habit of turning up after work's finished," said Peter Morgan.

"Oh, I get it now,"

"I should add that although I had no time for the man, I had no wish to perform an autopsy on a chap around the same age as myself. Life can be so fragile. There but for the Grace of God and all that."

"Exactly," said Gus. "Did evidence collected in the corridor and at the top of the staircase provide clues about his killer?"

"Nothing tangible. Scuff marks on the tiled floor surface, furniture and fittings damaged, and the missing lightbulb, of course. SOCO collected fibres from Davis's clothing, and if we had a suspect, it might be possible to find a match, but if the killer wore a mass-produced garment...."

"A good defence counsel could argue a million other people wear the same hoodie or pair of gloves," muttered Gus.

"True," said Peter Morgan, "if there's nothing more, I'll crack on. Places to go, Y-sections to perform."

"I'll go too, Sir, if that's okay," said Gareth Francis. "I wish to question Peter further. It's a fascinating subject, isn't it?"

"Off you go, Gareth," said Geoff.

"Peace at last," said Gus after the door closed behind the two men.

Peter Morgan stuck his head around the door again.

"I almost forgot. We found no mobile phone in Davis's possession. Nothing on his person, nor in his room. It will be several days before his other belongings can return to his family. I thought it odd that Davis didn't carry a phone in this day and age."

"I need to check with Neil," said Gus. "When I've spoken to him in Marbella, I used the number Melody Davis gave me, which was a private line."

"We've moved forward a little more," said Geoff, "if a phone is missing, it eliminates any confusion about the accident theory. Is Neil on board for tomorrow?"

"Everything is set to go at nine o'clock in the CCTV control centre."

"WPC Amelia Cranston will join him there. I'll pass the message along."

"Monty Jennings?"

"I haven't asked the ACC yet. Leave it with me? Don't you want to drive over to the office to liaise with your Crime Review Team people? Luke Sherman will appreciate you taking an interest."

"You're right. I'll head there next. Expect a call from me first thing tomorrow to learn when I can arrange an interview with Monty Jennings."

"I admire your confidence," said Geoff, "now go away. I've got work to do."

Gus tried to recall what the ACC had said to him when he persuaded him to take up this consultant's role. Something about Geoff not having a cushy number.

Gus had laughed at the suggestion. Now he appreciated how talented Geoff was at keeping those plates spinning. If they ever created a spare evening, he'd persuade Geoff and his wife to join him and Vera for a meal. His friend was getting run ragged by the Chief Constable, the ACC and the half-dozen DI's that reported to him.

As he trotted downstairs to his car, he wondered how Suzie Ferris was. Still no sign of her returning from whichever management course Sandra Plunkett sent her to endure. Maybe he should risk calling her this evening?

Twenty minutes later, he parked behind the Old Police Station. Neil's space held a pool car he recognised. DS Luke Sherman drove here in a vehicle Gus remembered from his surveillance days. Gus went upstairs in the lift to the CRT office.

"The wanderer returns," said Lydia.

"Irreverent as always," chided Gus, "do you have no respect for your elders and superiors?"

"Sorry, guv," she replied, "can I get you a coffee?"

"You're a lifesaver. Thanks. I never had time for lunch."

"What progress, guv?" asked Alex.

"The PM confirmed Terry Davis's death was no accident. DS Mercer and I believe we saw his killer on CCTV ninety minutes before he attacked and killed Neil's father. Neil is working on the case from tomorrow morning. I suspect we won't see him back here before Monday. What do you have for me on the McGuire case?"

"If you refer to the Freeman Files on your computer, you'll find I've updated them. We have a list of interviewees and suggested timings. Of course, who carries out which interview depends on your availability."

"I have one interview related to the Davis murder to undertake. I should know the timing of that tomorrow morning. So rather than me trawling through my copy of the files, why don't you bring me up to speed, Luke? Good to see you again, by the way."

"You too, guv. Your first visit to Amesbury will be to familiarise yourself with the murder scene and the surrounding area. Detective Superintendent Tony Brown was the SIO on the case back in January '04. He lives in Downton, a spot I believe you know well. But Tony Brown's not in the best of health. His wife insists that we minimise the talking he has to do. Tony was a heavy smoker, if you recall, and suffered from emphysema. A lung disease that primarily causes shortness of breath due to over-inflation of the air sacs in the lung. His wife told me he needs an oxygen cylinder by the side of his chair in the lounge. She said it's only a matter of time."

Gus nodded. Another of his former colleagues from Salisbury wouldn't enjoy his retirement pension long.

"Who else have you traced?" asked Gus.

"Alison Hill, now forty years old. She was a medical student at the time of McGuire's murder. She switched careers and is now a recruiter for senior personnel in the care home sector."

"Hill was the feisty ex-girlfriend, wasn't she?" asked Gus. It was hard getting his head around this cold case with everything else cluttering his brain.

"That's her," said Alex Hardy.

"Both of the Dallimore's are prepared to be interviewed," said Luke.

"They're prepared but not happy," added Alex, "Victor is still driving lorries, and his ex-wife Debbie hasn't been in a relationship with anyone since McGuire's murder."

"There was an ex-wife for McGuire, too, I remember," said Gus.

"That's Dierdre, guv," said Luke, "and McGuire's daughter is twenty-five now. Izzie takes after her father. She's a scientist working at Porton Down. Dierdre is pushing fifty and unemployed."

"So that covers the family and his lady friends apart from McGuire's mother," said Gus.

"Hazel McGuire lives in Glasgow, guv," said Lydia. "If we need to interview her, perhaps Luke and I could travel north?"

"I'm not sure what we stand to gain from an interview with the mother," said Gus. "She never came south to spend time with her son and his family, according to the murder file. Put her on a reserve list, Luke. Who do we have that worked with him or knew him as a neighbour?"

"Clive Breakwell is a fellow scientist. He could be useful.

Mrs Julie Summers was a close neighbour. Both knew him well and liked the bloke. There are a couple of names I've added to the list. Neil asked the Hub for data, and I uncovered two people of interest on the estate near McGuire's address."

"Ah, this sounds interesting," said Gus, "who do we have?"

"Norman Strugnell, a convicted rapist, lived two streets across from McGuire. The properties shared the same number, and the street names were similar. He lives in Warminster now. So there was a theory at the time that McGuire wasn't the target."

"We'll chat with Strugnell to gauge whether he was a lucky man. He can provide leads to victims and their partners who might have wanted to see him dead."

"Have you heard of the Belafonte family, guv?" asked Luke.

"Singers, are they? No, I didn't think so; from your introduction, they must be criminals. I've not come across the name."

"Ruby Belafonte was a neighbour of Ian McGuire's. She lived opposite him in a council estate. You take the rough with the smooth, they say. McGuire lived on the smooth side of the road. The Belafonte's and Strugnell lived in the rougher part of town."

"There was me thinking the quiet town of Amesbury was senior citizens playing bingo and bowls," sighed Gus, "and the rowdiest nights were at the WI Christmas raffle. Is nowhere safe anymore?"

Gus realised he knew the answer to that. Even a village such as Urchfont, with barely one thousand souls in its environs, had experienced a murder, a home invasion, and a drug gang working from one of its rural properties.

Those events had occurred since he returned to work. Kassie Trotter might have a point. It was his doing.

"Are you OK, guv," asked Lydia.

"Sorry, my mind drifts from time to time. It must be my age. Was that the total sum of interviewees you collected, Alex?"

"They're the ones from the murder file that make sense to investigate, guv," replied Alex.

"History suggests those people will offer additional lines of enquiry, guv," said Luke Sherman.

"Quite," said Gus, "we'll start on that list tomorrow morning. Alex, you and I will visit the murder site. After that, we'll get what we can from Tony Brown. We'll return here in the afternoon to liaise with Neil Davis. I want to keep in touch with his progress, or lack of it. I have another interview to arrange, and feedback from Neil will influence how quickly I set a time and date for that. Luke, you and Lydia can talk to Alison Hill. Where do we find the Dallimore's? Do they both still live in the Bristol area?"

"Yes, guv," said Luke, "Debbie will be easy to get hold of as she's on the dole, but we must interview Victor at the end of his driving shift. I can fix a time with him before we finish here today."

"Good," said Gus, "we've had a slow start on this one. Twenty-four hours can make a huge difference. Let's make inroads into identifying the devil who thought Dr Ian McGuire deserved to die."

The rest of Tuesday afternoon saw the team confirming the interview schedule while Gus reviewed the contents of the updated Freeman Files.

Gus allowed his mind to drift as he drove home to the bungalow. He hoped Bert Penman was keeping fit and healthy. The days ahead weren't likely to offer much free time for the allotment. Gus decided to drop by for a chat.

Bert was chatting with Clemency Bentham as Gus parked the Ford Focus in the lane. They both looked up as he strolled through the gate.

"You look to have the worries of the world on your shoulders again, Mr Freeman," said Bert.

"I've got broad shoulders, Bert," said Gus, "I'll cope with the pressures of my current caseload. Unfortunately, it's leaving you to pick up the extra work on my allotment that's giving me more grief."

"It's a pleasure, not a chore, Mr Freeman," said Bert.

"How are things going between you two?" asked Gus.

"We've called a truce," said Bert, "I'm calling on Irene for a cuppa in future when I take her fresh vegetables from the allotment holders here."

"And I agreed to stop pestering him to come to church whenever we're gardening together," said Clemency.

"Although, the Reverend followed me into the Lamb for a small sweet sherry last night," said Bert, "and asked the landlord if she could leave copies of the Parish magazine on the bar."

"It's a coincidence that the stool you sit on was where the landlord thought could be the ideal spot for my magazines," said Clemency.

"I came here to apologise for my absence over the coming days," said Gus, "I can see that I shall miss it more than I thought. The everyday life of country folk portrayed on that long-running radio show has nothing on the pantomime you two could offer. Enjoy your evening. I'm off home to rustle up a meal and get a good night's sleep. I have a busy week ahead."

"Irene tells me it's all quiet on the bungalow front," said Clemency.

"No sign of the stranger in the pub either, Mr Freeman," said Bert.

"He's gone for the time being," said Gus. "I can't say more than that, I'm afraid."

"You'll get your man, Mr Freeman," said Bert, "you always do."

"I'll pray for you tonight, Gus," said Clemency.

Gus shrugged his shoulders. He decided tonight wasn't the time for deep conversation.

He was tired and hungry. A quote from Kierkegaard entered his head as he trudged towards his car.

"The function of prayer is not to influence God, but rather to change the nature of the one who prays."

Chapter Seven

Wednesday, 16 May 2018

GUS AWOKE, feeling sluggish. He regretted his actions last night. Food wasn't the issue; a salad was the most he could face preparing on a warm May evening.

The half-empty single malt bottle he'd drained while feeling sorry for himself hurt him.

He'd called Suzie Ferris but had to leave a pathetic message, which made him sound like a lovelorn teenager. Gus was no wiser where she was, and because Suzie didn't reply, he lay awake half the night.

Gus dragged himself to the shower. Breakfast needed to be a slice of toast and black coffee this morning. He couldn't stomach a fry-up—what a shit start to the day. The prospect of driving around Amesbury looking for villains from yesteryear and then grilling an ex-Superintendent at death's door gave him little comfort.

On days such as this, another kick in the teeth always lay in wait around the next corner. The Focus started the first time, and the lane wasn't busy with traffic or children hurrying to school. That raised false hopes. No, those infernal roadworks slowed his progress yet again. Why would anyone send six workers to a site when only two work at once? No wonder the experts say productivity in the UK is pathetic.

As Gus sat at yet another set of traffic lights, he tried to remember what else he should have done last night. It would come to him in time. He knew the one call he needed to make. He took advantage of the hold-up and called Geoff Mercer.

"Has the ACC green-lit the Jennings interview?" Gus asked.

"Hello, and good morning to you, too," replied Geoff. "Yes, with the usual warning, keep it under your hat and don't let Her Ladyship know what you're doing."

"Happy days," said Gus. Geoff chuntered in the background as he ended the call.

WHILE GUS INCHED his way towards the Old Police Station, Neil Davis breezed through the traffic from the other side of Devizes and parked his car on Sheep Street. He had visited the Crown Centre frequently. It would help to do something after mooching around at home since Monday lunchtime.

Melody was tired and emotional, which was nothing new these days. Their home phone rang every few hours with people wanting to convey their condolences. The modern world had become such a small place, yet news of a death in the family took just as long to spread as it ever did.

Neil was sick of telling people the funeral date was yet to be confirmed. As for the wake, well, his mother was right.

His father had left explicit instructions about how much money was set aside for a proper knees-up. So Gus needn't fret that there wasn't enough to cope.

Neil spotted the young WPC on the opposite side of the road.

It wasn't hard. A copper in uniform is a rare sight on the streets of a UK town these days. Amelia Cranston was window-shopping.

"Hello there," said Neil, "good to see you're on time. I'm DS Neil Davis."

"Hi, Neil, call me Amelia. I'm sorry about the circumstances that brought us here."

"Don't be," said Neil. "How long since you joined us?"

"Nine months," she replied.

"Then you must have made great strides to deserve the chance of a spot of detective work. For someone like DS Mercer to be aware of you so soon is a credit to you."

"Oh, I don't know," Amelia sighed, "trouble seems to follow me. My sergeant says I have a knack for being in the right place at the right time."

"Or the wrong time for the villains," said Neil.

That brought a smile to the young girl's face.

"Come on, let's get into the control centre, and I'll show you the ropes. It's a simple task this morning. We're hunting for an image of my father's killer."

WPC Cranston had to trot beside Neil as he hurried to the Crown Centre.

Neil was on a mission.

IN THE CRIME Review Team office, Gus and Alex prepared to leave for Amesbury. Luke and Lydia had left for Salisbury to interview Alison Hill ten minutes earlier.

"We've got twenty-five miles of hard road between here and Tony Brown's place," said Gus.

"Was he your boss, guv?" asked Alex as they travelled down in the lift.

"No, he worked in Salisbury while I was there, but we were on different teams. That doesn't mean we didn't come into contact. He was a good copper. It will be tough to see him struggling today."

"I'll drive, guv," said Alex. Gus noticed he'd left his crutches in the office. Things were improving.

"You'll get no arguments from me, Alex. I might still be over the limit from last night. I shouldn't have driven in this morning. Although I was stationary most of the journey."

"We go into Amesbury via the A345, guv. Which part of the town is it we want?"

"McGuire lived on an estate off the Boscombe Road. New housing developments have sprung up in the years since McGuire lived here. Most are on the far side of the town, past the Rugby Club. We can get a sense of the place as we drive around. But I always liked to feel the ground under my feet, absorb the local smells and assess distances when running a live murder case. This thing is colder than cold. Fourteen years will have altered the murder site so much it could be unrecognisable."

"Has the Terry Davis murder produced this negativity, guv?" asked Alex, "you're usually much more positive than this."

"It's Terry's death a few hours after we discussed his killer in the pub, plus the hangover. Thanks for the admonishment. I shall try harder."

Alex found Boscombe Road and cruised its length. On the first pass, he avoided turning into the estate where

McGuire used to live. Gus studied the mix of housing and the scattering of shops.

"The houses tell a story in their fashion," said Gus, "I mentioned yesterday that your first impression of a town such as Amesbury is that the age profile is higher than the average. I doubt that ten per cent of the population qualify as immigrants in any shape or form. There will be a high percentage of retired professionals, senior managers and skilled engineers. I can see what attracted Ian McGuire. He fitted in, and it was convenient for work without it being on the doorstep."

"I did my homework yesterday before you returned to the office," said Alex. "You're spot on with the statistics, yet twenty per cent of the working-age inhabitants here are semi-skilled, unskilled manual workers or unemployed. McGuire moved to the house opposite the estate where most of those less fortunate people lived."

"I wonder if that influenced his choice?" said Gus.

"Time to take a walk, guv?" asked Alex.

"Yes, Alex. Let's start at the former McGuire residence. We'll reserve the walk on the wild side until later."

"This is it, guv, No 28, the detached property: integral garage, lounge-diner on the right-hand side of the front door. The hallway has doors off to the lounge and garage, and the kitchen has doors off to the diner, utility room and rear garden. The utility and kitchen lie at the rear of the garage. Three bedrooms upstairs, one en-suite, and a family bathroom."

"A well-maintained pavement splits the grassed areas in front of the property," said Gus, "and someone's recently planted ornamental bushes close to the wall under the lounge window. McGuire was painting in the kitchen and could see the TV through the door, wasn't he?"

"Yes, guv, the crime scene photos show the TV was wall-mounted on the external wall on our right. McGuire could see the screen from the kitchen doorway with ease. The settee stood on the left-hand side, against the hallway wall."

"That's where he'd left the mobile phone he tried to reach before he bled out. Let's walk around the back of the property. It's quiet here for mid-morning, don't you think?"

"On this side of the road, I suspect the professionals are at work. The retirees are on a cruise or watching us from behind the net curtains."

Alex and Gus walked to the end of the row of houses and turned right. A path should have taken them to the back of the properties, and they could then check the five-foot-high fence the killer scaled to enter Ian McGuire's rear garden.

"That's a bugger," said Gus.

"This was an open space back then, with garages on the left belonging to the houses we can see."

"This is upward mobility in action, Alex. Fourteen years ago, lots of families were lucky to have a car. The speed bumps mean they can't park on the main road now. The front gardens aren't large enough for a driveway, and every other home has two or more cars. They've built a row of garages stretching from one end to the other."

"If you wish to check the enclosed rear garden, we need to contact the homeowner. There can't be anyone in. They would have soon let us know if anyone spotted us when we stood outside the front door."

"We'll still have that little wander, Alex," said Gus, "a quick tramp around this estate and then over the road into bandit country. We know that Norman Strugnell lived at No 28 Whatever Street. Where did Ruby Belafonte live?"

"She lives on the same street Strugnell used to occupy, at

No 12, guv. The family has been there a long time. Do you want to chat with Ruby today?"

"I think we'll postpone that pleasure for another day, Alex. Someone on the team will travel this way again soon. Luke and Lydia can ask the questions we need answering if they draw the short straw."

As soon as the two men crossed the busy main road, they noticed a difference.

"It's noisier over here," said Alex, "and more people are out and about."

"No big surprise, Alex," said Gus, "younger families live on this side. Single mothers with small children. Unemployed blokes are wandering the street, some up to no good. Ignore any minor deals you might spot. We're not here for that. Look at the front gardens. They're longer than on the privately owned estate, more chance to fill them up with old washing machines and motorbikes. Fifty per cent of the gardens have grass growing eighteen inches high. The net curtains on this side are grey, not white. Most families here can still afford satellite TV, so the benefits system hasn't failed them."

"The pubs are open, guv," said Alex, with a grin, "perhaps you should pop in for one? You're like a bear with a sore backside today. I thought you were trying harder."

"This *is* me trying harder, Alex. Don't you find council or housing association properties depressing in their conformity? Everywhere in the country, they sink to the lowest common denominator. That one house over there looks to be the only one we've seen where the occupier cares."

"Believe it or not, that's No 12, where the Belafonte's live, guv," said Alex.

"I thought they were a family of criminals. Always in trouble with the law," said Gus.

"The husband left years ago. Two sons are in their late thirties and are both in prison. The eldest daughter was on the game. I'm not sure where the youngest son and daughter are these days. They were both at school when McGuire died. Ruby doesn't live alone for long. She's had several male friends at the property since before the murder. I think the children's father left when the youngest children were four. So it's easy to see why the children went off the rails."

"I've seen enough for now," said Gus, "are you sure it wise leaving your crutches behind? We've walked quite a distance."

"Things are getting less painful every day, guv. My physio tells me I should challenge myself, so I'm avoiding using them today. I'll collapse in a heap when I get home after work tonight. But an hour in the gym later this evening will continue improving my core muscle strength, and I'll be good to go again in the morning."

"Right, I'll call and warn Mrs Brown that we'll descend on her and Tony in thirty minutes. Then, I'll race you back to the car."

"You're feeling better?"

"Now that I've seen the Belafonte's place, it's the one rose among a crown of thorns on this side of the road."

The Browns lived in a detached bungalow near the leisure centre in Wick Lane.

How the other half lived. The Browns had at least half an acre of garden at the front of the property. It was impossible to see what lay beyond the mature pine trees skirting the sides of the house.

Gus knew from experience when buying his place in

Urchfont that the home they were visiting today would be worth three-quarters of a million pounds if it came on the market.

"Ironically, they live by a leisure centre, guv," said Alex. "The poor bloke can't even walk there to watch someone participate in an activity, let alone join in."

Before Alex could press the bell next to the glazed front door, an attractive older woman answered.

"Hello, I'm Carole, Tony's wife. Come on through. He's in the back room."

Tony Brown looked all of his seventy-something years. He did not try to get up but nodded at the two men his wife brought to see him.

"I remember you," he said, recognising Gus Freeman.

"Hello, Tony. Thank you for agreeing to speak with us. Yes, I foolishly allowed myself to get persuaded to return to work as a consultant with Wiltshire Police. DS Alex Hardy here is a member of my Crime Review Team. We've re-opened the Dr Ian McGuire murder case from January '04. I'm sure you remember it?"

"Not my finest hour, Gus," said Tony Brown, "no matter who we looked at in Amesbury or further afield, we never uncovered a viable suspect. We failed to identify a motive, as I recall. He enjoyed a busier love life than I ever managed, and that was the focus of our attention."

"No doubt, your superiors were in a rush to move you on to another urgent case, Sir?" asked Alex.

"It was always that way, Sergeant Hardy. I'm guessing that you're married with young children. Am I right?"

"No, Sir," said Alex, "single at present."

"The way you walked into the room favouring your left leg, I thought you had trodden on a Lego brick in the past twenty-four hours. They tell me the pain is excruciating."

"Nice try, Tony," said Gus, "but you can leave the detecting to us. You had better explain, Alex."

"I had a high-speed accident as a motorcycle pursuit rider, Sir. I suffered serious damage to both legs and recently confined my lightweight wheelchair to the scrap heap. Leaving my crutches in the office this morning was a mistake. Gus and I did too much walking in Amesbury earlier, and I'm paying the price. It's my fault for wanting to prove I'm back to full fitness."

"There's little chance you'll ever convince the powers-that-be you are fit enough to resume your old duties, Sergeant. But, if you stick with Gus Freeman for any length of time, you'll come out the other side as a bloody good detective. There's always a future for chaps like that."

Tony Brown sank back in his chair. It was clear the effort of holding a conversation was taking its toll.

"Look, we won't tire you any further, Tony," said Gus, "perhaps we should return another time?"

"Give me five minutes, Gus. What was it you wanted to hear?"

"McGuire had a complicated love life; we know that, and we can interview those involved over the coming days. I've visited the murder site and the surrounding estates. There was talk of mistaken identity and potential discord between McGuire and his neighbours. However, we don't know which crimes contributed the most to the statistics at the time. Who was active in that area? Could McGuire have been connected in any way?"

Tony Brown set aside his oxygen mask. Finally, he was breathing a little easier.

"Amesbury and the surrounding countryside had its share of petty villains," he said. "We dealt with the odd car theft, joyriding, shoplifting and minor altercations at the weekends. Then, two or three years before the murder, we saw a real shift in the crimes we handled. Drugs, Gus, it was about that time that things spiralled out of control."

"You experienced county lines behaviour here in Wiltshire?" asked Alex Hardy.

"Yes, Sergeant, city gangs sending young runners into the Shires to sell crack and heroin was increasing even when I was a serving officer. I recall talking with dealers and sex workers to appreciate how things worked in their infancy. The public is well aware people commute daily from the West Country into Paddington and Waterloo to reach their place of work. Unfortunately, kids working in those city gangs started travelling in the opposite direction."

"Instead of a business suit and a furled umbrella, they wore hoodies, jeans and trainers, I guess?" said Alex Hardy.

Tony Brown nodded.

"The buggers earn more in a day than most office workers going into London," he said.

"They don't have the overheads either," said Gus Freeman, "the only things they carry when going country is a burner phone, a bag of drugs and a weapon."

"How many gangs were involved in your day, Sir," asked Alex.

"Over one hundred, and that's doubled in the intervening period based on National Crime Agency reports. Moreover, London is only one of the key hubs to join the party. Birmingham, Liverpool, and Manchester have sent dealers to the smaller market towns and rolling countryside since the mobile phone boom in the Nineties."

Tony Brown stopped speaking and raised a hand.

The lengthy conversation was a struggle.

"Sorry, lads," he gasped, "can we take five minutes for a

cuppa? I'll ask Carole to make us a coffee and dig out the chocolate digestives she hides from me."

Alex Hardy glanced at Gus. Nothing was said, but both men knew they needed to keep going. They required the background and potential leads that Tony Brown could provide.

Gus Freeman was impatient to make progress. One look at how his former colleague looked today suggested any delay in completing this conversation could be fatal.

After Carole Brown served their coffee and biscuits, she checked the oxygen canister and adjusted the nose clip on her husband's face. The look of love that passed between them made Alex and Gus uncomfortable. They were intruding on what might be one of the last days this devoted couple spent together.

"I'll leave you to it," said Carole as she cleared the cups and plates. "Try not to overtax yourself, Tony; there's a love."

After his wife left them, Tony gave the detectives a weak smile.

"She fusses. We won't celebrate our Golden Wedding anniversary now, but we've lasted longer than many of my former colleagues."

"Take your time, Sir," said Alex, "carry on when you're ready."

"That initial trickle from the capital is now in full flood. They've taken over the drug trade right across the South of England. I bet you can't name a town in Wiltshire that they haven't got in their grubby hands. The dealers are getting younger too, only children, most of them, some still in junior school. Well, they would be if they ever bothered to attend."

"There's an increased rivalry between the gangs, too, isn't there?" asked Gus.

"They stuck to traditional areas within London, as did gangs in similar areas in the other major cities. There was the occasional turf war; that goes without saying. One drug lord wants a bigger slice of the cake and tries to take out his neighbour. Since they started going country, the level of hostility and violence has risen tenfold. If a gang from the Midlands travels into Bristol and decides it wants a piece of the action in the towns surrounding Bath, and the lads from East London are on the ground already, there will be ructions."

"How did this affect towns like Amesbury?" asked Alex.

"When I first encountered it, I didn't understand how the gangs operated. I asked around. I soon learned how these newcomers impacted the host towns such as Amesbury. I arrested a nineteen-year-old from an estate in Epping. His name was Vince. He started selling heroin in Essex when he was still at school. By the time he was seventeen, he'd moved to Salisbury with a mate. They set up a business selling crack and heroin in Wilton, Old Sarum, Downton and Amesbury. Vince bought the product from a contact in Chelmsford and delivered it to his mate in Salisbury. They used local runners to sell the drugs through a twenty-four-hour phone line."

"Why didn't the police realise what they were doing earlier?" asked Alex.

"Vince and his mate were forever on the move, and the runners they used weren't the same lads every time. We were chasing shadows. Don't run away with the idea that this was a simple game. When these kids go country, it's harder graft and less money than flipping burgers in McDonald's. Vince exploited the kids who worked for him, and he was exploited by the kingpins back in Essex, who supplied him with his product. Everyone in the Shires works long hours on little or no wages, and they get punished for losing money or drugs."

"I've heard gangs deliberately mug their runners," said Alex, "so they become indebted to the guys who hold the purse strings."

"It's just business," said Tony Brown, "cutthroat and ruthless. Only the strong survive. We became more aware of city gangs gravitating across the countryside and that local people and their homes got used for cover."

"The cuckoo effect," said Gus, "where the city gang members supply a local druggie with enough product to convince them to allow their homes to get taken over. As a result, those addresses become stash houses, crash pads and dealing dens."

"Locals dependent on drugs can get taken on as drivers or low-level runners," said Alex.

"That's how the sex workers I spoke with got involved," said Tony Brown, "their role was to spread the word. Romeo arrives from London with a winning smile and ready cash, and the girls fall for it. Before long, they forget the idea that the guy was their boyfriend. Their place of work is now another outlet to peddle drugs."

"Did Dr Ian McGuire fit into this somewhere?" asked Alex.

"If he did, there was no evidence of it at the time," Tony said.

"Was there ever a reward offered for information?" asked Gus.

"There was. We arranged a ten thousand pounds reward through Crimestoppers, but it produced little of any significance."

"You carried out a reconstruction too, didn't you?" asked Gus.

"Not really. My idea was to stop traffic on Boscombe Road at five on a Saturday afternoon. Then, we asked people whether they had seen or heard anything unusual four weeks ago. You can imagine how well that went. It was another dead end, and within a week, my boss moved officers off the case and onto crimes with a greater chance of a result."

"The murder file didn't itemise much in the way of forensic evidence," said Gus.

"By accident or design, the manner of the killing meant no forensic evidence was left at the scene. That case was like a bar of soap. It kept slipping through my fingers."

"What other aspects did you consider?" asked Alex.

"We looked into his private life to see whether he'd ever received threats because of his philandering. There was no suggestion that Ian McGuire was in fear for his life. The nature of the killing also encouraged us to examine the possibility of a drug motive. But, as I said earlier, despite it seeming a legitimate line of enquiry, it led nowhere."

"Even though you said drug gangs were moving into the area throughout the early years of the decade," said Gus.

"McGuire didn't use heroin or crack cocaine. Nobody in Amesbury needed a supplier. People like Vince appeared on the scene. They were part of a network stretching from the capital to Land's End. You asked which other aspects of the case we investigated. We always look at the family and partners to see who benefits from a victim's death. Dr McGuire died intestate. His ex-wife Dierdre inherited the house. Not that he planned it that way. Events overtook him, and McGuire hadn't got his personal affairs in order. Debbie Dallimore suffered as a result. It was obvious they were getting married sooner rather than later. She was in love with him and was devastated by his death. I remember Debbie was allowed to return to the house with one of my officers to collect a few personal possessions. It was all very unsatisfactory."

"She hasn't been in a relationship since," said Alex Hardy.

Gus didn't think there was much to gain by extending this meeting.

"We'll call it a day, Tony. It was just one of those cases. We'll interview the neighbours and dig deeper into his private life. How we'll come up with an answer from the scraps we've got, I don't know."

"Perhaps I missed something, Gus," said Tony Brown.

"Don't sit here worrying over it after we leave, Tony," said Gus, "concentrate on staying as well as you can."

They left Tony, and Gus looked for Carole Brown. She was sitting in the lounge reading a book.

"Finished?" she asked. "Was Tony able to help?"

"Tony was a great help, Carole," said Gus, "we won't trouble him again. Many thanks for putting up with us."

"We don't get many visitors. However, a couple of Tony's ex-colleagues drop in for half an hour after they've played indoor bowls. Tony thinks it's because they get a free cuppa here, with a biscuit, and it saves them the high prices the leisure centres charge these days."

"Take care, Carole," said Gus, "be seeing you."

When they were in the car, Alex turned to his boss.

"Why did you tell her Tony was a great help, guv? He gave us background on the drug gangs, but according to him, there was no link to the victim."

"We won't know whether something Tony told us will prove a vital piece of information until we learn something new about this case, Alex. No interview is ever wasted. Sometimes, it isn't what they say; I consider what's left unsaid when I sit outside my allotment shed. Remember that jigsaw I frequently reference; we have pieces from Tony Brown that don't match anything. The worst thing we could do is discard them. But, tomorrow, an odd-shaped piece could emerge, and it's that piece of information which locks Tony's pieces into a cohesive unit."

"It's good that you've rediscovered your more positive side, guv," said Alex, "although I wonder whether it's misplaced for the moment. Anyway, I didn't think we needed to bother Tony again. Why say to Carole that you'll be seeing her soon?"

"At Tony's funeral, Alex. It won't be long now, I fear."

Chapter Eight

ALEX DROVE BACK to the Old Police Station. Gus was quiet on the return trip.

"Luke Sherman and Lydia are back, guv," said Alex as he reversed into his parking space.

"I wonder what Ms Hill told them. By the way, I want you to use those crutches for the rest of the day, young man," said Gus. "While I remember it, that was an interesting reply to Tony Brown's question about your status. What did 'single at present' mean?"

"Just that, guv," said Alex, "I'm still seeing Lydia, and we're taking it one day at a time."

"I can't argue with the logic, Alex. I found Tess was the only person in our relationship who knew what stage it had reached. I lingered in a state of confusion, deciding when to ask if we should get engaged and then, after the engagement, when to broach the subject of setting a date for the wedding. Tess said we would never have married if she'd left it to me. I thought she had left it to me, but all the time, it appeared that she was orchestrating matters."

"I'll bear that in mind, guv. I told you I'd tell you when things altered enough for us to let London Road get involved. So we're still in the clear, I hope. But, of course, based on what you've just said, Lydia might have a different view."

"I wonder how she gets on with Luke?" said Gus, "you might have competition."

Alex pondered that as the lift rose silently to the first floor.

"Welcome back," cried Lydia. She was heading for the restroom with empty cups.

"How was your interview with Alison Hill, Luke?" asked Gus.

"Interesting," Luke replied, "I asked her about her relationship with Ian McGuire. He was almost ten years her senior. They began seeing one another when she was eighteen, back in '96."

"A seven-year relationship? I hadn't realised that. Was it always volatile?"

"Lydia can profile her better than me, guv. McGuire had married Dierdre when they were both young and just out of Cambridge University. They lived and worked in Southampton. Dierdre had enough after three years and took their daughter, Izzie, with her when she left him. Alison Hill suggested McGuire was unfaithful."

"Alison wasn't the reason the marriage ended?" asked Gus.

"Alison wasn't on the scene then. She lived in Salisbury and was underage for some of that period, anyway."

Gus raised an eyebrow.

Lydia returned to the main office and overheard Luke's last comment.

"I reckon Ian McGuire was a randy goat, guv. He

couldn't stop himself. He liked young brunettes, not too tall and with curves. Alison was his type when they first got together, that's for sure. As to why Alison Hill put up with him for so long? She loved him."

"I asked Luke whether the relationship was volatile right from the start. What impression did you get?"

"Alison is fragile, guv, the needy sort. McGuire could have carried on chasing younger women throughout their seven years together. He might have mellowed. Either way, Alison's an insecure soul who always suspected McGuire of seeing someone new. She questioned him when he came home late from work or dashed out for a meeting during the evening. Alison suspected everything and everyone. One thing I'm sure of is she instigated any physical violence that occurred."

"Alison belted McGuire with a steam iron, didn't she?" asked Gus.

"That was the culmination of a long period of scraps the pair had," said Lydia, "it sticks out in the murder file because it was the only time the police intervened. But, according to her, Alison threw plenty of breakable items over the years."

"Was McGuire ever violent towards her?"

"Never, guv," said Luke, "often it was McGuire's lack of reaction that infuriated Alison. Whenever she accused him of cheating, he just shrugged and told her she was crazy. Then, when she lost her temper and lashed out, he raised his arms to shield his head and body and waited for the attack to fizzle out. Alison Hill lost count of the times they kissed and made up during the seven years they lived together."

"After she whacked him around the head with the steam iron," said Lydia, "McGuire moved out. He stayed at a mate's house—a male friend. Alison begged him to return within days. That was in mid-January, but by February '03, the pair parted company again, this time for good."

"Alison's alibi was rock solid for the day of the murder," added Luke.

"She cut short her medical studies and switched career to the care home sector," said Gus, reading from the Freeman Files. "Has Alison Hill formed any new relationships since finishing with McGuire?"

"She's never married, guv," said Lydia, "we interviewed Ms Hill in her office. I didn't see a photo of a significant other, but she loves black Labradors. I believe she owns two."

"They're a faithful breed who love exercise," said Gus. "Does she use social media? Check her status there if you can. It might be worth a second visit if she is portrayed as a vindictive man-hater who doesn't trust a bloke further than she can throw him. If not, I reckon we accept that the alibi is proof that Ms Hill didn't do it."

"I agree, guv," said Luke, "she had ample opportunity to kill McGuire while they lived under the same roof."

"Remind me, where did Dierdre, the ex-wife, move to with her daughter, Izzie?"

"Dierdre still lives in Southampton, guv," said Luke, "in Weston. So Izzie returns home at weekends. During the week, she rents digs near her place of work. It's only an hour's commute, but Izzie takes after her late father and works to a different schedule to normal people."

"Izzie McGuire is a scientist and works at Porton Down Science Park," said Lydia.

"Izzie isn't involved in the Ministry of Defence's Defence and Science Technology Laboratory," said Luke, "her company works in Life Sciences and the Defence and

Security technology sector. Izzie's expertise is in the control of infectious disease, vaccinology and vaccine production."

"Dierdre is unemployed," said Gus, "isn't that unusual for Cambridge University graduates?"

"The poor woman is fifty, guv," said Lydia, "I might struggle to find anyone prepared to take me on in a meaningful job when I reach her age. You'd be surprised how many graduates are in catering or bar work rather than utilising the degree they studied."

"It depends on the subject too," added Luke, "those from a Science, Economics and Mathematics background fare better than those who opted for Media Studies and History of Art. The IT people are the ones that find it easier to stay at work. They're always in demand."

"What was Dierdre's degree?"

"Sociology," said Lydia.

"Any idea what her last post involved?"

"A guidance counsellor at Chamberlayne College for the Arts. Dierdre lives within a mile of her ex-employer in Weston."

"Any particular reason for her leaving that post?"

"No, guv, austerity cuts meant her post got phased out and incorporated into a reduced HR department."

"I see no reason why her current predicament should be permanent," said Gus. "Her age will count against her with certain establishments, but she showed a good work ethic throughout the twenty-three years after she and McGuire married. Dierdre raised Izzie on her own with regular financial input from McGuire. She produced an intelligent young lady with a bright future. I hate to say it, but what possible motive could this woman have for murdering her ex-husband?"

Deadly Formula

"I agree, guv," sighed Lydia, "we're in Alison Hill territory again. McGuire was unfaithful during their brief marriage. If Dierdre were angry enough to do something, she would have done it while they lived together. If Izzie said that Dad had already moved on to someone new when she stayed with him at the end of the next school term, that could have incited Dierdre to violence. Ten years had passed since they parted company, and everything suggests they had no unresolved issues."

"Where to next, Guv?" asked Luke.

"For you two, it's off to Bristol to interview the Dallimore's. McGuire might have been a randy goat as you described him, Lydia, but Debbie had something that stood out. She changed him in a matter of months. They were moving in together, planning to marry. McGuire was taking her to see his mother, Hazel, in Glasgow. Since '93, when he and Dierdre broke up, he'd shown no inclination to marry. If Alison Hill was correct, he showed no sign of being a fan of monogamy, either. How did Victor Dallimore react to the situation?"

"Both Debbie and Victor were interviewed at length by Tony Brown, guv," said Alex, "their alibis were solid."

"Time can change the answers people give to a series of questions, Alex," said Gus, "a gap of fourteen years will have altered relationships. Someone prepared to offer an alibi for Victor Dallimore early in '04 could well give a different reply today. Test the alibis. Debbie was head-over-heels in love with McGuire. I'll send my beloved Ford Focus to the scrapyard if it turns out she killed her lover. Victor, on the other hand, had a motive. Even though they were estranged, they were still married. Concentrate on the people who provided his alibi."

"Whatever you say, guv," said Luke, "I'll phone his firm

now to see when he finishes his shift. Then, perhaps Lydia and I can drive to Bristol this evening."

"What about Debbie Dallimore?" asked Gus.

"She's not been in a relationship since her lover's murder, which supports the view that she and McGuire had something special."

"How did Debbie earn a living back then? How did she and McGuire meet?" asked Gus.

"We'll ask Debbie those questions later, guv," said Luke, "and check whether, in hindsight, she believed Victor capable of murder. Her current lack of a job will see her at home at six. So we'll make her our first visit and give Victor time to stew. If he has a temper, keeping him hanging around when he's got an early start in the morning might pay dividends."

"That's the ticket, Luke," said Gus, "apply subtle pressure."

"Do I need to dress for the part, guv," asked Lydia, striking a pose.

"Not unless you're going as a good cop and a drama queen."

Lydia and Luke began arranging their Wednesday evening interviews.

Gus wondered who Alex should concentrate on tomorrow morning. He could send Alex to Warminster to interview Norman Strugnell. That wouldn't take long. A thirty-minute drive took him back to Amesbury, where the neighbour Julie Summers lived.

The first interview should kill off the mistaken identity theory, and the second might throw up a list of people who fell out with the gregarious Scotsman.

Was there something more productive for Alex to do for him?

"Alex, can you build a family tree for Ruby Belafonte and her various connections? The dead, the living, and the unrelated boyfriends have lived in the house. Also, find out what happened to Vince, the drug dealer Tony Brown mentioned. Is he in prison, back in Essex or dead? If it's the latter, then how did he die? Don't rely on DS Brown for that detail. Instead, call Amesbury Police Station on Salisbury Road. It's on the list to close within three or four years, but you should find someone available to answer the phone tomorrow."

"Am I on light duties, guv?" asked Alex.

"You're showing signs of strain, Alex," said Gus, "you overdid the exercise while we had those free days. Take it from me. You need to rest if you want to stay the distance."

"OK, guv, the local villains and the county lines dealers could offer more useful leads than other names on the list."

"My thoughts exactly. Alex," said Gus.

"I take it you'll be interviewing someone related to the Davis murder enquiry, guv?" asked Alex.

"I'll be back by lunchtime, Alex. Before that interview, I need to check how far Neil got today with his part of the investigation."

Gus spotted Luke Sherman; he was giving him the thumbs-up.

Their evening interviews were on, and Alex must cope without Lydia. Perhaps he'd seize the opportunity for an early night.

There was still the issue of Monty's interview to solve. Gus needed a body with him to avoid the Chief Constable's wrath. Gus remembered what it was he'd forgotten to ask. He called Neil Davis.

"Where are you, Neil?"

"I'm still in the Crown Centre. We had an unsuccessful

morning, guv," said Neil, "Amelia and I searched from eight in the morning on Sunday until eight at night. There was no sign of Ricky Gardiner in The Brittox or the Old Post Office. It's a mind-numbing task, isn't it?"

"Geoff Mercer and I studied five cameras from six until midnight. It's only boring if you don't find what you're looking for."

"If you say so, guv. Anyway, after we had a coffee, we checked Sainsbury's camera. I spotted Gardiner leaving the store at around one-thirty in the afternoon. He was the right height and build and wore the same clothes you described when he followed Dad later. The camera never got a good shot of his face, though."

"Gardiner's a clever operator, Neil. The supermarket has got in-store surveillance…."

"Amelia phoned to check it was still available, guv. She told them to hold on to it for viewing later. So she's on the ball, that one."

"Any luck with the other cameras?" asked Gus, impatient to get to the punchline.

"We found him in the Market Place at three minutes past five, guv. The image is good enough for a passport photograph. It's irrefutable evidence Ricky Gardiner was in Devizes on Sunday. When we've been to the supermarket, we should have more images to add."

"Good, Neil, now there's something I need to ask you,"

"I've got something else, guv," said Neil, "Amelia asked whether she should be looking for other faces. I asked why. She'd noticed a freeze-frame image of Dad chatting to Monty Jennings outside the White Bear I had in the file I collected from DI Francis. Amelia reckoned she'd seen Jennings when we trawled through the earlier camera at The Brittox. How Amelia picked a face out in the crowd, I don't know. We ran the data to check what she thought she saw. It was Monty Jennings, alright. He was in The Brittox at five past twelve on Sunday lunchtime. I watched him walking towards the camera, and then he stopped as he met another chap, and they started chatting. You'll never guess who, guv,"

"Peter Morgan," said Gus.

"I don't know why I bother," groaned Neil.

"Sorry, Neil. I challenged Vera yesterday lunchtime on how the drip-drip of information from London Road could reach Monty's ears. Vera wasn't talking to Monty, so it wasn't her. I believed it had to be someone who'd worked at London Road for a lengthy period and they were high enough in the organisation to learn valuable gossip. Peter blabbed to Monty. Monty passed things on to Terry."

"What was the other thing you wanted to ask, guv?"

"Did your Dad own a mobile phone? Peter Morgan suddenly remembered SOCO never found one at the scene."

"Dad always carried a crappy old pay-as-you-go Nokia, guv. It was embarrassing. He had a landline in Marbella and insisted he only needed something to text his contacts with a day and a time for a meeting. The fewer characters he needed to key in, the better. I only recall Dad using it twice while he visited my place. One must have been fixing to meet Monty in the White Bear. No idea who else he messaged. Do you think it was Gardiner that took the phone? If so. why?"

"When are you visiting the bars where Terry drank?" asked Gus.

"We'll start on our pub crawl as soon as we've popped over to Sainsbury's," Neil replied. "We can grab a bite from the deli counter and collect their camera images simultane-ously. We should reach the Lamb Inn by six at the latest."

"Terry told us he was meeting old friends. One of the landlords or their bar staff must have seen him chatting with someone. If we can identify that other friend, it might help explain why the phone was important to Gardiner. I'll grill Monty Jennings for information on his topics of conversation with your Dad when we meet."

"OK, guv. Leave it with us; we'll snoop around for Dad's contacts," said Neil.

"I suggest you stay on the soft drinks this evening, Neil. And remember that WPC Cranston is your responsibility. We may need her eagle eyes on future investigations."

"Don't worry, guv. I drove into Devizes this morning and parked on Sheep Street. I know I need to curb my enthusiasm. It's been a long, warm day in this CCTV centre and a cold pint of lager sounds just the ticket. A non-alco-holic beer will have to do, though. Let's hope they stock them in the chilled cabinet beside the Holsten Pils and the San Miguel."

"Stop it, Neil, you're making me thirsty. Call me first thing tomorrow. I'm interviewing Monty Jennings. Any extra ammunition you can provide will be priceless. I don't know how much you can contribute after today's stint. Please stay home with Melody. Tell WPC Cranston I'll collect her from Reception at London Road at nine o'clock in the morning. Geoff Mercer said we had her services for a couple of days. She can accompany me to sit in on the interview with Mr Bernard Jennings. She'll meet someone she recognised today."

"It will square the circle, or whatever they say. I'm keen to stay active, guv. What if I extend the search for the phone beyond the areas covered by the forensic guys? Maybe Dad lost his phone in one of the pubs we're visiting this evening? I'll let you know what we learn in the morning. You'll see both of us in Reception at nine. If I can be of use on my Dad's case, tell me what you want investigating, and I'll get cracking."

"You've made a fair point, Neil. However, we might be overthinking things. It wouldn't be the first time someone lost a phone while on a night out on the lash. See what you can dig up, and I'll see you two youngsters in the morning."

Gus checked his watch. Four o'clock. Luke and Lydia were soon leaving to drive to Bristol. Debbie Dallimore's house was in Filton, and traffic was manic all day between here and the M32 exit from the M4. The city of Bath was a nightmare to negotiate at any time, and once the tourist season got underway, it got worse. Nevertheless, he didn't envy the journey, whichever route they took.

Alex was compiling the Belafonte family tree. Gus knew he could leave him to get on with things without supervision.

"I'll head home," he told his team, "we've another busy day tomorrow. I don't plan to be here until late morning tomorrow. I want the Freeman Files updated with tonight's interviews for me to review. I'll also expect a progress report from you, Alex, on the tasks I set. If any of you has time to spare, follow up on the social media aspect concerning Alison Hill and re-examine Norman Strugnell's history to rule him in or out. Luke, contact Julie Summers for an interview; you and Lydia can cover that. Lydia, you're the best person to chat with Hazel McGuire. I don't think it's worth a trip north for any of us. Telephone her, and arrange a Skype call or a video link if practical. I want you to observe her reactions to your questions. She's no killer and may not know enough details of Ian's love life to give us

137

more than a gushing testimonial for her late son. It might sound harsh, but cut it short if necessary. You'll need to be alert for any names or events that might ring an alarm bell. You'll know it if you see or hear it."

Gus left the three team members and went down in the lift.

"Blimey," said Lydia, "that was different from how he's spoken to us during the weeks we've worked with him. So what's going on?"

"Gus was in a strange mood this morning," said Alex. "He brushed it off as a hangover, but he's a regular drinker who doesn't normally suffer mood swings. I can't see that being the true explanation. There are aspects of Neil's father's murder case that we don't fully understand. The ACC and DS Mercer shouldn't micro-manage that sort of case. They could leave an SIO like Gareth Francis or Suzie Ferris to run the investigation. Geoff Mercer even sat in with Gus on the CCTV analysis. That's odd behaviour for a superior officer."

"I'll leave you to mull it over, Alex," said Luke, "we need to drive to Filton. See you in the morning."

Luke walked to the lift. Lydia hung back for a word with Alex.

"Are you alright?" she asked.

"Tired, but I've felt worse. I hope you get something positive from your interviews this evening. Good luck."

"I'll be thinking of you. Sorry, we can't spend tonight together,"

Alex watched Lydia dash to the lift. Luke smiled at Alex as the doors closed.

Why did Gus think he needed to be worried, he wondered?

WHEN LUKE MERGED with the rush hour traffic at the Chippenham junction of the M4, Gus Freeman had reached his bungalow in Urchfont. He changed into his gardening clothes and strolled along the lane towards the church with a large notebook under his arm.

The weather was dry and warm, and he needed an hour to clear his head in the fresh country air. Gus opened his shed, brought out his chair and made himself comfortable. He took a biro from his shirt pocket and scribbled several random thoughts in his notebook.

There was no sign of Clemency Bentham this evening. Bert Penman was at the far end of his patch. Bert raised a hand to acknowledge Gus's arrival and carried on working. Bert knew when Gus wanted time alone to ponder.

If Gus remained seated and scribbling even until sunset, Bert would still keep his distance. The older man would wave once more as he left the allotments for the Lamb.

On the evenings that Gus walked over and started a conversation, Bert knew Mr Freeman's study of the human condition was at an end.

Gus looked at the list of things he'd scribbled.

Friends. Message. Phone. Chippenham.

Belafonte. Neighbours. Relatives.

Misdemeanour. Morgan.

Courses.

Gus considered each line carefully. Finally, a logical explanation surfaced for the first set of items. He thought they could draw a line under that matter by tomorrow's close of play. There was one big hurdle to climb, though before, it was more than a dotted line.

The second set was a long shot. Everything pointed to a mystery that couldn't be solved. But, if the answer was anywhere, history told Gus these three words were vital to finding it.

Two interviews over the next twenty-four to thirty-six hours would allow him to scrub the third set from his list.

The final line held a single word, but that word had the answer to a myriad of questions. There was only one person who could handle that problem. Gus knew it was his responsibility. In one instance, it was too dangerous for the ACC and Geoff Mercer to get involved. On the other, he wasn't sure what to do with the answer when he found it.

As he continued to wrestle with the issues raised by the various problems he mused over, Bert Penman cleaned his tools and locked them in his shed. Mr Freeman didn't acknowledge his farewell wave this evening. If the Reverend came into the pub later, they needed to discuss the matter. They couldn't let their friend wallow in a pit of despair. This return to work seemed a successful move a month ago, but issues had taken on a darker tone this past week that Bert didn't appreciate the look of one bit.

Thursday, 17 May 2018

GUS DROVE the short distance from Urchfont to London Road. He parked in front of the building and gazed at the ACC's window. There was no sign of Kenneth Truelove this morning.

A glance along the row of cars showed that Geoff Mercer was present and correct. Vera's Alfa Romeo brightened the car park, and its driver headed his way. The ACC hadn't arrived as yet.

"Hello, you," she said, "I wish you luck with your interview."

"Monty's a pussycat, isn't he?" said Gus.

"He wasn't easily tamed," said Vera, "and he's been off the leash for a considerable time. Remember never to take a backward step. Monty's all bluff and bluster."

"The ACC is missing today," said Gus. "Any idea why?"

"The Chief Constable gave him an ear-bashing late yesterday afternoon. Your interview with Monty may have sparked that. I'm not sure where the rumour started, but Peter Morgan seemed to believe Neil Davis had made a significant breakthrough in his father's murder yesterday. That got her riled up even more, although I can't understand why."

"Interesting," said Gus, "I know the ACC wants to survive until he can retire with dignity. He might consider it politic to take two days off to steady his nerves."

"Geoff will know if there's something more sinister."

Gus and Vera entered Reception together. Neil Davis spotted them and was grinning from ear to ear.

"Morning, guv," he said.

Gus knew what Neil was thinking. Unfortunately, on this occasion, he had it wrong.

Vera climbed the stairs to the administration area.

Amelia Cranston appeared beside Neil Davis. She had been chatting to the lad on duty at the reception desk.

"Have you talked with anyone about what happened yesterday, Neil?" asked Gus.

"No, guv," said Neil, "we didn't finish until eleven o'clock. So I ran Amelia to her place and then drove home."

"My Uncle Peter was in the Three Crowns when we

arrived last night," said Amelia. "He asked how things were going."

Gus closed his eyes. He wondered why Geoff Mercer hadn't mentioned that the star WPC was related to Peter Morgan, Police Surgeon and Blabbermouth General.

"Not to worry," said Gus, "right, a quick update, Neil."

"Not possible, guv," said Neil. He showed Gus the images they'd collected from the supermarket.

"Here we have two more than decent photos of Ricky Gardiner, time-stamped, as he's wandering in different aisles inside Sainsbury's. There's no doubt that it's him. I'll pass everything we gathered from the Crown Centre CCTV and the supermarket to DI Francis. We spoke to the landlord of the Lamb Inn. He wasn't working on Sunday evening. He told us that he and his wife have Sundays off. I spoke to Mitzi, the barmaid who was serving when Dad arrived. I sent her a photo, but although she remembered pouring him a pint of Stella, she wasn't old enough to drink the last time he drank there. So, she didn't know him from the old days. The bar was half-full of regulars, and several seemed on good terms with Dad. Mitzi said they chatted for an hour, and then he left. I took the names of the regulars she could remember, guv, but you know what it's like."

"First names and nicknames. No idea where they live. Come back on Friday when it's payday; they're more than likely to be in here. It's their local."

"You've got it. So, then we moved on to the Three Crowns," said Neil.

Amelia Cranston blushed.

"Is that your Uncle Peter's local?" asked Gus.

"I don't know," she replied, "we don't have much to do with him. My Dad thinks he's a pompous prat. I'm sorry if I spoke out of turn."

Gus remembered that Vera Jennings had the same opinion.

Odd that Monty and Peter were friendly.

"Don't blame yourself. Learn from the experience. Peter Morgan is a skilled inquisitor. In his professional capacity, he is constantly probing for answers. Unfortunately, it appears he can't resist the temptation when he's socialising. What could the landlord tell you, Neil?"

Neil smiled.

"This is why I thought a quick update was impossible, guv. Dad met with someone while he was drinking there. I know who the second old friend was now. Her name is Donna."

"OK, Neil, I know the lady in question. Donna helped us with information on our last case. Regardless of her chosen occupation, Donna and several other working girls from Swindon gave Terry valuable tips over the years that resulted in criminals having their collars felt. There's no suggestion things went beyond a chat over a drink in a pub, the same as Sunday evening. If money did change hands, it was for the information, nothing else."

"That's okay, guv," said Neil, "Dad never went into details about what he did. It seems irrelevant now."

"Terry spent longer in the Three Crowns than he did in the Lamb," said Gus. "He walked through The Brittox at twenty-past seven, then crossed to the White Bear to wait for Monty Jennings just before nine. Carry on, Neil."

"Dad ordered another pint of lager and chatted to the landlord. They knew one another from the old days. Donna arrived at eight o'clock. She's a regular. Dad was ready for a refill. He bought Donna a large gin and tonic, and they moved to a table in the corner for a private conversation."

"I'm guessing the landlord was occupied with customers

and didn't wander over to catch any of that conversation?" asked Gus.

"We should be so lucky," said Neil. "The only thing the landlord did say was that Dad gave Donna an envelope before he left. Donna stayed behind after Dad went to the White Bear. She didn't leave until closing time."

"I wonder what was in that envelope?" said Gus.

"I told Neil, sorry, DS Davis, that we should ask the landlord where Donna lived," said Amelia Cranston. "In case what was inside the envelope was relevant to the case."

"He told us the address," said Neil. "We went around to see her. That was an eye-opener, guv."

"I know. I've been there, Neil. What did Donna say?"

"Donna was quick to invite us in. She said Amelia's uniform was bad for business. Nobody rang the bell while we were there. Donna told me she planned to visit Dad in Marbella after she retired. She had tears in her eyes, guv. I think Donna had a soft spot for him. She wanted to help me find whoever killed him. I asked about the envelope. Donna told me it wasn't for her, but she could hand it over as I worked with you."

Neil took a slim, white envelope from his inside jacket pocket and handed it to Gus.

"Donna never opened it. Dad said she should hang onto it unless something happened to him. So I asked her why she had not come forward on Monday when the news broke of his death. She said a client had told her it was an accident. When the two of us appeared on her doorstep, she realised he'd misled her."

"I don't suppose she told you who this client was?" asked Gus.

"We asked," said WPC Cranston, "but Donna said her business relied on client confidentiality."

Gus examined the sealed envelope. Terry Davis had merely written 'Gus Freeman' on the front. It could only hold a single sheet of paper, if that. He opened the envelope and removed a scrap of paper that looked torn from a newspaper. There was newsprint on one side, possibly an advertisement. Gus turned the scrap paper over and read the single-word message Terry Davis had left him in the event of his death.

"Oakley," said Gus.

Chapter Nine

"DAD CAN'T HAVE MEANT Annie Oakley, surely, guv?" asked Neil Davis.

"I doubt it, Neil, but it has to be important. I need to put on my thinking cap."

"Can you tell what was on the other side, Sir?" asked Amelia Cranston.

"It's part of three lines of a newspaper advert," said Gus, taking a closer look. "A dozen words in total. Something related to car insurance, or one of those 'where there's blame, there's a claim' sites.

"Could that be relevant?" asked Amelia.

"It's more likely to be the first thing Dad grabbed hold of to leave Gus a note," said Neil.

"Terry wasn't stupid, Neil. He had shortcomings as a detective, but a second clue may be hidden here. When did he write this, I wonder? Think back to our conversation in the Cavalier. We discussed Ricky Gardiner and his background, did we not?"

Gus realised the next topic of conversation was delicate. He couldn't let the young WPC overhear this.

"WPC Cranston," Gus said, "can you ask Kassie Trotter if we can use Interview Room One earlier than planned? Monty Jennings and I aren't due to start sparring until half-past nine, but Neil and I can use the time more effectively there rather than stand here cluttering up the foyer."

"Certainly, Sir," the young WPC replied and trotted upstairs.

"We have to be careful that nobody hears any of this, Neil," Gus whispered. "I warned you how dangerous things could become. Unfortunately, certain people will go to great lengths to protect their careers."

"We can't let them get away with it, guv. Not just with my Dad's murder, but whatever they're so eager to keep hidden."

Gus and Neil climbed the stairs to the administration area. Amelia Cranston waited in the far corner with Kassie Trotter. Everything seemed ready for them to go ahead. Gus didn't imagine anyone else wanted the room before him, anyway. The ruse had got Amelia Cranston out of the way long enough for him to check that Neil was on the same page.

"Can you look after WPC Cranston for ten minutes, Kassie? DS Davis and I need a brief private conversation before my visitor arrives. Amelia can escort him to Interview Room One after he's signed in."

"No worries, Mr Freeman," said Kassie, "us girls can compare tattoos."

Gus looked at the uniformed officer. There were no visible signs of ink. He decided it best not to speculate where they were. Instead, he needed to concentrate on the matter at hand.

Once the door was closed, Gus continued with the list of things they'd discussed with Terry on Sunday afternoon.

"I asked your Dad to get an accurate date when Dominic Culverhouse and Sandra Plunkett met for the first time. He believed it to be in 2002 at the staff college in Bramshill. We discussed several events where they may have met again over the next decade. Either on additional senior management training courses, at conferences, or involved in working on a specific case."

"Dad couldn't think of anything, could he, guv? He was adamant they never worked on a case elsewhere in the country before he left the police and retired to Spain."

"So, where does that leave us?" asked Gus.

"Amelia might have stumbled onto something then, guv?" asked Neil. "When you examine that scrap of paper, he didn't rip it out of the newspaper, did he? If I want to note a phone number when I don't have my notebook to hand, I might write it on the bottom of a newspaper's front or back page. This scrap came from the advert section inside a Sunday edition."

"I asked earlier, Neil. When was this note written? We know your Dad handed it to Donna in the Three Crowns. If Terry wanted to give me a clue in the Cavalier, he had ample opportunity. Instead, he insisted I keep digging. Your Dad suggested I get you to set the young minds in the Hub to uncover the link. I'm convinced Terry knew or thought he had the answer. Perhaps by claiming he uncovered their deep, dark secret, it was his insurance policy if things got hairy. Terry didn't realise that Gardiner was in town to remove the potential threat he posed."

"That newspaper must have been on the counter in the

Lamb Inn," said Neil. "Something or someone spooked Dad between his leaving the Cavalier and reaching the town centre. You and Geoff Mercer never spotted Gardiner tailing Dad on the CCTV cameras before that late-night sighting near the Dolphin, but I bet Gardiner was there during the early evening. Dad was too good a copper not to notice a tail. He knew what was coming. It doesn't bear thinking about, guv."

"I know, Neil," said Gus. "Terry realised Gardiner's mission wasn't to track my movements in Urchfont and scare me off digging into Culverhouse's past. Gardiner was in Devizes to deal with him. So Terry did the only thing possible. He used the hour in the Lamb to devise a cryptic clue for Donna to deliver to me. If she opened the envelope, neither side of the piece of paper meant a thing to her. It would mean nothing to anyone except Culverhouse and Plunkett. We cannot be certain that Gardiner is anything other than a hired gun. Nothing is tying the three of them together. Gardiner worked with the Met in the capital. Plunkett spent most of her career in the Midlands, and Culverhouse worked here and at Portishead."

"Dad came up with something devious to help you," said Neil, "although I can't see what it means."

"Let me try to use my phone for something other than checking my security cameras," said Gus, "right, Oakley is a large village in Hampshire. It's a thirty-minute drive from the former Bramshill College. Now that's interesting."

"What is there at Oakley, guv?" asked Neil.

"Wrong question, Neil. What happened at Oakley, and when? That's what we need to discover. I've got it. Here's an unsolved hit-and-run from 2012. Jason Whitworth, a twenty-two-year-old hotel worker from Basingstoke, was cycling home in driving rain. He was struck by a vehicle that failed to stop. A passing motorist found Jason's bicycle and body in a ditch by the side of the B3400 Andover Road the following morning."

"What links that to our suspects, guv?"

"First, there's the cryptic reference in the advert for injury lawyers. Add in the location of Oakley and its proximity to Bramshill House. Terry reckoned I'd work out the connection. That scrap of paper, taken as a whole, indicates the persons to blame for that young man's death. Terry was telling us that Culverhouse and Plunkett were in Oakley in 2012."

"They were attending something like the tenth anniversary of that first meeting, d'you mean?" said Neil. "Culverhouse was driving, Sandra Plunkett was a passenger, and they fled the scene of an accident. Is that possible, guv?"

"It's a reasonable suggestion, Neil. People who spend extended periods on these high-pressure training programmes develop a close bond, or so I'm told. We need to check who else attended the same course. Follow up on their whereabouts at the time of this fatal accident, Neil, and ask pertinent questions. Someone might place those two in the same car that night."

"I'll get on it, guv. What about the hunt for Dad's mobile? Amelia and I asked around last night. Nobody found a phone in the pubs he visited when they cleared up, and no one handed a phone over the bar."

"I wouldn't look in dark corners for it in town, Neil. You can use your time more effectively. Check the taxi firms. See who ferried Ricky Gardiner out to Urchfont and back. Ask if they drove him anywhere else. Nobody ever mentioned a car when those villagers reported him lurking in the lane by my bungalow. He was always on foot. The same thing stands out in those Sunday supermarket images. Gardiner's walking between the supermarket and wherever he went, not heading towards the car park. So, where does he live? London. How would he get there once he'd finished his task?"

"Train to Paddington, guv, from Chippenham station."

"That's the place to start then, Neil. You never know. He might have chucked it in a waste bin that's still overflowing, begging for someone to empty it."

"Oh, cheers, guv. I'd better change clothes before I drive to Chippenham."

"I've had a thought. Remember the Trudi Villiers case? Culverhouse screwed Trudi from the age of sixteen or even younger. He was seeing her until Krystal Warner joined her at the Ring O'Bells."

"I remember you told us you phoned Dad in Marbella, and he filled in the gaps in our knowledge about Culverhouse. And how he encouraged Dad to mislay pieces of evidence."

"One thing Terry thought funny was that Culverhouse always drove large saloon cars. His boss enjoyed the extra room in the back for him and his lady friends. Terry said Culverhouse switched to a sports car because he wanted to drive something matching his status as a Detective Inspector accelerating through the ranks. I wonder what make of car he drove at the time of the fatal accident. He had to get rid of it. There's another angle to pursue."

"Why was Sandra Plunkett in the car with Culverhouse that night, guv?" asked Neil.

"Heaven knows. Perhaps our Lothario believed he was in with a chance, despite her professed sexual preference. Sandra and her partner Naomi got together as far back as 1998. Her car might have broken down, or she had too much to drink. There could be a handful of reasons. I believe they were driving towards Basingstoke late at night in driving rain and hit that poor young lad from behind. Check hotels in Basingstoke to see whether a group of senior officers stayed there over the weekend. Culverhouse might have ferried Sandra to and from the venue in Oakley, where they held this possible 2002 Class Reunion. I'm guessing there's a place big enough to host a function of that nature in Oakley village. That's a misnomer, anyway. It's linked with another village called Deane, and five times as many people live there than in Urchfont. It's bound to have a venue big enough for twenty coppers to have a knees-up."

"Thanks, guv. That will keep my mind occupied. I'll leave you to this interview with Monty Jennings. He should be here in a second."

"Good hunting, Neil," said Gus, "I'll catch up with you later today."

Neil left the room. He must have met Amelia Cranston and Monty Jennings at the top of the stairs because Gus heard a knock at the door within seconds.

"Come in," said Gus.

"Mr Jennings is here to see you, Sir," said WPC Cranston. Gus got his first sight of Vera's ex-husband.

"Thank you, Amelia. Sit beside me, and observe. Please take a seat, Mr Jennings."

Gus indicated the single chair on the opposite side of the desk.

Monty Jennings sat and folded his arms across his chest. He wore a dark-grey business suit, a white shirt with a cutaway collar and a tie that Gus couldn't quite place.

It belonged to a Lodge of the Royal Antediluvian Order of Buffalos, another fraternal organisation Gus had never wished to join.

Bernard Jennings was a little older than Vera. Gus pictured him in his mid-twenties when the couple first met. Then, he was a savvy, good-looking entrepreneur who swept people along with his confidence and enthusiasm. But Monty, as everyone called him, had aged gracefully over the past three decades.

He'd added a few extra pounds on the waistline. His full head of fair hair now carried a sheen of silver. Monty didn't wear glasses. Perhaps that was vanity, and contact lenses corrected failing eyesight. These days the man sitting opposite Gus could have paid for laser surgery; it wasn't easy to tell. However, the defensiveness portrayed by those crossed arms was evident. It was time for the inquisition to begin.

"My name is Freeman, and I'm a former Detective Inspector who came out of retirement to act as a consultant with Wiltshire Police. I head up a Crime Review Team investigating cold cases..."

"I know who you are," Jennings replied, "you've been sleeping with my ex-wife for weeks."

Amelia Cranston sat straighter in her chair. Gus realised this was news to the young woman. The gossip might have reached most people working in the main building at London Road, but the uniformed personnel elsewhere were still in the dark. That would change as soon as the WPC rejoined her colleagues unless he had a quiet word.

"I was enjoying my retirement when you and Vera began divorce proceedings. We met here for the first time at the end of March. We've not met before today. I find your opening comment interesting. If you allow me to continue the preliminaries to this conversation, I can explain."

Monty Jennings shrugged his shoulders.

"Whatever, I agreed to attend this pantomime this morning even though it's my last free day for a while. I'm a busy man. Your lot want me in Swindon from tomorrow, giving evidence at Crown Court against the Rexha brothers."

At last, that case was going ahead. Gus thought. The Crown Prosecution Service hadn't dropped the ball on this occasion. He hoped everything went as planned and the gang received prison sentences that merited the severity of the crime. The ACC and Geoff Mercer would keep him informed of progress.

"If I remember the motto of the Buffalos," said Gus, "it says 'no man is at all times wise', isn't that so? That was certainly the case when you leased the buildings above Cambrai Terrace to that gang of violent thugs. Perhaps due diligence was less important than a big payday?"

It was Monty Jennings's turn to sit up straighter in his chair. One arm dropped to his side, and the other touched his tie. The older man opposite was sharper than he thought.

"Let's park the court case for now," said Gus, "as I started to explain, my role involves taking a fresh look at old cases that baffled my predecessors. I don't make enquiries relating to current cases. However, circumstances have changed since last weekend. The father of one of the Sergeant's on my team got killed. The man suspected of the murder was tailing me for two weeks before Terry Davis flew home to visit his son. On Sunday night, after Neil and I spent part of the afternoon in the Cavalier pub with him, Terry set off for an evening in Devizes. We know he contacted two friends and arranged to meet them. We've chatted with one of those people. I'm sitting across the table from the other. Terry died only two hours after you ended your conversation on the pavement outside the White Bear. Yes, we've traced Terry's movements thanks to the CCTV system in the centre. You arrived by taxi soon after Terry left the Three Crowns and joined him inside the White Bear. When you both came outside later, you continued chatting until another cab collected you."

"What do you want to know?" asked Monty Jennings.

"What did you talk about?" asked Gus.

"This and that. We hadn't seen one another for five years. So I was surprised to see Terry when I walked into the bar."

"I didn't come down with the last shower, Jennings," snapped Gus. "We *know* he contacted you via that crappy old Nokia he carried."

Gus kept his fingers crossed that Neil found the phone to prove they were on the right track. Then, with Monty on the back foot, Gus continued to press him.

"Since early April, I've called Terry in Marbella for background information on cold cases we were investigating. What concerned me was how much fresh local knowledge Terry had at his fingertips. He knew far more than one might expect for someone who retired to the sun to get out of the rat race. Any idea of how that happened?"

"I'm sure I don't know," said Monty.

His arms were across his chest again, and he tried to appear disinterested.

"Well, let me tell you what I think happened," said Gus, "you've done business deals in this county for thirty years. Friends and colleagues tell me you've been both a prince and a pauper on several occasions. Terry Davis was a Detective Sergeant who rooted around in the dirt for clues. These days officers of a similar rank rely on computers, forensics, and probabilities. They aren't fans of getting their hands dirty. At some point, Terry found dirt that stuck to you. I don't know what it was. I don't much care what it was, and I won't even check whether the statute of limitations has run out or still applies. Whatever it was, he had you in his grubby hands. A word to his superiors, and you were in trouble. He chose to keep you as a resource. When did he start calling in the favours? Did it coincide with Vera starting work here or earlier?"

"Vera never provided me with any inside information," said Monty.

Monty relaxed a little, realisation dawning that the game was up.

"I've learned to roll with the punches over the years, Freeman. When I made my first million, I thought I'd cracked it. I couldn't wait to get my next big money-making idea off the ground to build on what I had. Unfortunately, a bloke I went into partnership with stitched me up. There was no official contract, just a handshake between two fellow entrepreneurs, and I lost a fortune. The guy was a crook, and I discovered that what I had invested in breached the Trades Descriptions Act. If it had been made public, it would have finished me. Terry kept my name out of it."

"Terry kept your connection to that crime a secret in return for regular tips on entrepreneurs operating at the shadier end of the business world," said Gus. "That's what we thought. So, when he left for Marbella, Terry no longer needed tips for pursuing a possible offence. You must have thought you were off the hook, and then he squeezed you for inside information from here at London Road."

"I'm friends with lots of local people, Freeman. I drop into the White Bear at least once a week. People talk; I listen. Some of it interested Terry, so I passed it to him."

WPC Cranston gave a polite cough. Gus thought of something.

"Do you drink in the Three Crowns or any other Devizes pub?"

"I haven't been inside the Three Crowns since I was a teenager," sneered Monty, "too downmarket for me. However, several people from this building drink in the White Bear and flit from place to place."

"Be a devil and name one," said Gus.

Monty Jennings glanced towards Amelia Cranston.

"The Police Surgeon, Peter Morgan. He moves around and is always eager to chat."

"Would you say you were friends?" asked Gus.

"Hardly. I let Morgan gabble on, trying to impress me with whom he knows what he's heard. It went in one ear and out to Terry Davis. Apart from an earache, it never cost me a penny."

"Let's get back to Sunday evening. What *did* you and Terry discuss?"

"You won't believe me, but everything and nothing. Terry was nervous; I know that. He kept glancing towards the door. He mentioned your name. Terry said you were a good copper, and if things went badly for him, you would deal with it."

"Did he mention being followed?"

"No, but something spooked him. He was drinking heavily. We never met up while he lived in Devizes. I called him and passed the details over the phone. When he moved abroad, we carried on in the same fashion. Sunday night was the first and only time we shared any time having a drink together. We just never moved in the same circles."

"Odd isn't it?" said Gus, "when Geoff Mercer and I saw you shaking hands before you went your separate ways, we imagined it reflected a lifelong friendship."

"It's a British trait. We've been that way for centuries.

Think back to those Kings or Lords they beheaded. The executioner would apologise for what he had to do, and the chap on the wrong end of the axe would say it was alright. He forgave him. I don't know why I thought of that. Maybe going through it with you again this morning reminds me of what I felt. We both knew when we shook hands and said cheerio, it was for the last time."

"Where did your taxi driver drop you?" asked Gus.

"After ten on a Sunday night? I went straight home, Freeman," said Monty.

"What do you know about a place called Oakley in Hampshire?"

"I've driven through it. I never stopped there, as far as I can recall. Why?"

"I wondered whether Terry mentioned it."

"No, but I remember someone else mentioning it recently."

"Who was that?"

"Bloody Morgan rabbiting on how his friend spent the weekend there with her partner. They stayed at an eighteenth-century Hall with a terrific chef. One of the two women was born in the village. Oakley has been a regular haunt of the couple for years."

"Naomi," said Gus as another link slipped into place.

"Morgan might have mentioned her name, but it was your new Chief Constable that Peter was keener to bring into the conversation. He kept bragging about how much she valued his opinion."

"Did you pass that piece of gossip on to Terry Davis?"

"A couple of days later, yes. I left a message. New appointments and a change of leadership always spiked Terry's interest. Terry rang back the following night. He wanted to check that this Sandra had been visiting Oakley ever since she and this Naomi got together. I couldn't add to what Morgan told me."

"Well, I reckon we've closed the loops on that one," said Gus.

"Terrific," said Monty. "Is that it? Can I get on with my day now?"

"One final thing," said Gus,

He turned to Amelia Cranston.

"Can you see if Kassie Trotter's coming round with her refreshments trolley? I could do with a cuppa before my next guest."

The WPC left the room.

"One thing bugs me, Jennings," said Gus. "Your marriage was over years before Vera and I met. You were separated for ages before divorce proceedings started. Yet, you still seem to know every detail of her private life. Am I right in thinking Peter Morgan is the source of that gossip? I've seen him trying to engage in conversation with Vera. She tells me he's always wanted more than a friendly chat, and she's rebuffed him on every occasion."

"Morgan is a worm. I told you. When I arrive, he creeps into the White Bear and makes sure other customers see him speaking with me. I can't help being a celebrity. He thinks it will rub off on him. It goes with the territory; I make and lose millions. There are days I can barely scrape together enough change to buy a drink, but people know I'll bounce back. I always do. Most people never experience the rush of being on top of the world. Morgan thinks his car and chosen profession impresses people, especially women. I couldn't say anything in front of your colleague. Easy to see where that one gets her looks. Her mother, Philippa, was a cracker and married well, but she's a different character to Peter, her older brother. He never married, and the only women he's had sex with are prostitutes."

"Things are falling into place, Jennings," said Gus, "thanks for coming to see me. If you stick to your story that you didn't realise what the Rexha brothers planned to do with the property you leased them, you should be OK."

"That was the truth, Freeman. I didn't have a clue they weren't legit. The money was too good to refuse, that's true, but some people don't know the true value of something, do they?"

Gus smiled. "My thoughts exactly," he said.

Amelia Cranston re-entered the room. Monty Jennings was out of his chair and rushed away.

"Did you find Kassie?" Gus asked.

"On her way," replied Amelia, "I saw Uncle Peter waiting outside. Is he being interviewed too?"

"That meeting will be more of a chat than an interview, WPC Cranston. So I won't require your services any further today. Can I remind you that anything you heard this morning is not for discussion outside this room?"

"I understand, Sir," she replied, "and thank you for letting me work with you and DS Davis."

"There could only be one reason for you not having another opportunity, Amelia," said Gus.

"I do understand that, Sir. You only need to tell me something once. My lips are sealed. Anyway, Vera's lovely. You're a lucky man."

"A good detective knows the true value of things, Amelia. That always helps, I find."

"I'll bear that in mind, Sir. Good morning."

As soon as Amelia Cranston left the room, Kassie bundled her trolley through the door.

"One coffee coming up, Mr Freeman. How was Monty

today? He looked happier when he came out than downstairs in the waiting room."

"I think we understand one another now, Kassie. Are there any surprises on your trolley today?"

"Do you fancy a slice of my lemon drizzle cake?"

"Always, Kassie, always," sighed Gus. What was the point of worrying over his waistline?

"Can you ask Peter Morgan to come in when you leave?" asked Gus.

"I'll call out when I get far enough away he can't stare down my top. Mr Freeman. He's pervy that way if you hadn't noticed."

"Why don't you complain? You shouldn't have to put up with that."

"A fat lot of good that would do these days. Peter Morgan and Her Ladyship are so tight you couldn't slide a sheet of toilet paper between them."

"What a lovely image to leave me with, Kassie," said Gus.

Gus heard Kassie shout to Peter Morgan that he was free, as did most people with offices on the first floor. The Police Surgeon came in without knocking and took a seat.

"Right, what is it you wanted to discuss? I've got an autopsy at eleven o'clock."

"This shouldn't take too long, Peter," said Gus, "I need the answers to two questions. First, how often do you hear the Tina Turner song, 'Simply The Best'?"

Gus watched the man's reaction.

It was like watching a balloon deflate in front of his eyes.

Vera wasn't the only one who had described Morgan as a pompous prat. All the bluff and bluster that surrounded the man who entered the room seconds ago was gone.

"I don't know what…."

"You don't remember Donna's doorbell? Oh, you know it, Peter. She's got a few gentleman callers left on her books. Men who would miss her if she retired from the game. Donna told me about them when I called on her a fortnight ago. Last night, she also told Neil Davis that a client told her his father's death was an accident and that she did not need to bother the police. Donna's too wily to have told you what she and Terry discussed in the Three Crowns, but you couldn't take any chances, could you?"

"You're making a big mistake...."

"I'm wondering how deep in this mess you are, Peter. Would you falsify an autopsy report for the Chief Constable, for instance? How well did you know Dominic Culverhouse?"

"Now, look, you've lost me, Freeman. I knew Culverhouse when he was here, but we weren't close. The new Chief Constable has confided in me since her appointment. I always got on well with her predecessor too. Sandra thought an accidental death was the obvious conclusion based on my initial examination of the body."

"Did she pressurise you into signing off on it quickly?" asked Gus.

"I didn't see it that way. Everyone is keen to move cases on as soon as possible."

"My second question concerns Oakley in Hampshire. What can you tell me?"

"The Hall serves exquisite food, and the hotel accommodation is to die for. She's been visiting the area for twenty years. It's where she met Naomi, her partner."

"So, I understand. Did you know that Bramshill Staff College was just up the road from that village? Sandra Plunkett was there between 2001 and 2002 for various training courses. Of course, it's closed now, but I've heard that certain class reunions occurred close to the old training centre. What jolly japes they must have had getting together to celebrate how far they've progressed up the greasy pole."

"Why, I believe your jealous, Mr Freeman," said Peter Morgan.

"For every jolly jape, there's a not-so-pleasant episode, Morgan," said Gus. "When people relay bits of gossip on matters that should stay within this building, it can end in something worse than an unpleasant episode. Do you follow?"

"I can't say that I do. I need to be at that autopsy."

"We're both too young to remember seeing the wartime slogan 'Loose Lips Cost Lives' posted everywhere, but it still holds today. So I strongly advise you to watch what you say in the future."

"I'll heed your warning, Freeman," said Peter Morgan, "you won't mention the other matter to anyone, will you?"

"That depends on you, but it also depends on the next steps taken by those who orchestrated Terry Davis's murder."

The look on Peter Morgan's face convinced Gus he was a hapless fool in no way complicit in the cover-up undertaken by Culverhouse and Plunkett.

Peter Morgan was another pawn that they moved around the board, creating havoc.

"Get lost, Peter," said Gus.

The Police Surgeon scuttled out of the room.

Chapter Ten

GUS WAITED in Interview Room One for ten minutes before leaving London Road and heading out of town. He needed those few moments of calm.

Peter Morgan was the leak that the ACC wanted to castigate at least, if not to castrate.

Morgan's casual remarks in the White Bear to Monty Jennings started the ball rolling. Monty called Terry Davis. Terry put two and two together and made Oakley the place that inextricably linked Culverhouse and Plunkett. The event was simple to find, as Gus had proved.

With both of them continuing to climb the ladder in their careers, the sudden revelation that they covered up a fatal hit-and-run would be devastating. Many would hang their heads in shame and crawl away from the ashes of their humiliation if it came out, but not those two. Instead, they conspired to keep their secret hidden by utilising Ricky Gardiner to eliminate the threat.

Once they realised Terry Davis had the pieces in his possession to complete the picture, he was a dead man.

Gus knew that he was next if Culverhouse and Plunkett learned that Terry passed the missing link to him via Donna.

When he arrived at the Old Police Station and rode the lift to the Crime Review Team office, he tried to wipe his mind of negative thoughts. The team needed his mind focused on Dr Ian McGuire and the characters that surrounded him fourteen years ago.

GUS SPOTTED a familiar face when he exited the lift.

Neil Davis held up an evidence bag.

"I thought you'd come here after your interview with Jennings, guv. Guess what? I asked if they had CCTV coverage first thing on Monday morning. I told them I was checking whether a suspect caught the earliest Paddington train. They took a while to sort out, and I wandered along the row of waste bins. A guy on the opposite platform called out and asked what I was doing. I shouted back that I'd lost a phone. He pointed towards Lost Property and said they had dozens in there."

"I'm guessing you soon noticed an ancient piece of technology among the smartphones?" said Gus.

"The bloke in charge took one look at Gardiner's picture and told me he handed it in. Gardiner said he'd found it outside in the car park. Then he showed his return ticket at the gate and crossed over to the London Paddington platform."

"What time was this?" asked Gus.

"Around a quarter to five, guv."

"The taxi firm should remember a trip that early," said Gus.

"You could walk it in less than four hours, guv," said Luke Sherman.

"That fits the time frame, guv," said Neil, "if Gardiner set off to Chippenham straight after he checked Dad was dead, taking the phone with him."

"Get that phone to the forensic people for checking, Neil. We need to see what it contains. Gardiner had ample time to wipe his fingerprints before handing it in, but you never know. When Chippenham has located the CCTV for the middle of the night on Monday, we should have enough to prove Gardiner handed the phone in, regardless."

"I'll head home after I drop this phone into London Road, guv, if that's okay? I want to spend time with Melody."

"Understood," said Gus, "you can work from home when the opportunity arises over the next couple of days. Keep chasing those management course attendees and dates when any of them you can identify stayed at Basingstoke hotels. Get in touch with the hotels and confirm if those dates coincided with reunions. Find out Naomi's surname and dig into her background."

"Did you get anything from the Monty Jennings interview you wanted to update me on, guv?"

"Not now, Neil. I'll discuss matters with the ACC and DS Mercer. They will guide us on how we proceed going forward."

Neil recognised bullshit when he heard it. Perhaps Gus thought the less he knew, the better for the present. Dangerous times lay ahead. Neil wanted justice for his father, but it wouldn't happen if they acted in haste.

"I'll be off then, guv," said Neil, "I'll see you guys on Monday, maybe."

"Right," said Gus, "I'm sure you have plenty to tell me.

Alex, I'll run through the Belafonte family tree as soon as I hear from Luke and Lydia.

"No problem, guv," said Alex.

"A quick update on Alison Hill, guv," said Lydia, "I looked at her social media footprint. Her Twitter account comprises holiday snaps, recipes, and comments on popular culture. I found nothing sinister in her posts. Alison's Facebook and Instagram accounts followed much the same pattern. She's not a frequent contributor to either. The content is bland. I can't see any evidence that shows Alison Hill as someone with unresolved issues with Ian McGuire."

"Agreed. Strike Alison Hill off the list," said Gus, "moving on?"

"We interviewed Debbie Dallimore in Filton," said Luke Sherman.

"Debbie's warm and cuddly, guv," said Lydia, "fifty now, but I can imagine how attractive McGuire found her when they met. It was in a bar after a football match. McGuire had been to the game, and Debbie was on a night out with girlfriends from work. She said their eyes met across a crowded bar. It was love at first sight."

"Any hint of her alibi not being genuine?" asked Gus, cutting to the chase.

"No, guv, everything gelled with what Tony Brown's investigation recorded," said Luke.

"Where did you find Victor Dallimore?"

"He lives in the south of the city at Withywood, if you can call it living," said Luke.

"Victor's rough," said Lydia, "the area has its problems, but I've seen worse. It's hard to imagine him and Debbie's marriage lasting for as long as it did."

"Victor smokes, drinks and eats junk food," said Luke. "He includes at least one swear word in every sentence. The money he earns as a driver allows him to survive, but if he has any money left over at the end of the week, it's gambled away."

"I can tell you liked him, Luke," said Gus, "but could he have killed Ian McGuire?"

"Not possible, guv," said Lydia, "we told him we were questioning his alibi to gauge his reaction. I think Luke hoped he'd get violent."

"Did he?" asked Gus.

"No, guv," said Luke, "he showed us a photograph taken in Bristol on the day of the murder. There were eighteen people dressed to impress, grinning at the camera. Victor attended a mate's wedding, just as he claimed."

"I don't remember that photograph from the murder file," said Gus.

"Victor didn't have it at the time, guv," said Lydia. "He explained that there was a mix-up and guests didn't receive their copies until three months after the wedding. Tony Brown's officers only had verbal testimony from mates Victor had suggested could alibi him."

"It wasn't a wasted trip," said Luke, "we're clearing the decks of possible suspects. Only a few left now. So that means we're nearly there."

"Or we haven't identified the right ones yet," said Gus. "are you off somewhere this afternoon, you two?"

"Yes, guv," said Luke, "I'm driving to Warminster to talk with Norman Strugnell."

"I'm staying here, guv. I'm speaking to Hazel McGuire at three o'clock."

"That leaves me to pick up Julie Summers, the neighbour. Alex, you can accompany me on that trip if you feel up to it."

"I'm fine, guv. A good night's sleep helped."

"Take me through the Belafonte clan and all its roots and branches, Alex, and then we'll get over to Amesbury."

Luke Sherman collected the things he needed for his visit to Warminster and left the office.

"If you're leaving before three, I'll have this place to myself when I speak with Ian McGuire's mother. It might help her to be more open, not hearing the hustle and bustle of a busy office in the background."

"The hustle and bustle?" said Gus, "Progress is what I want to see. We're making precious little of that. How did you get on with that Vince character, Alex? Where is he?"

"He's dead, guv. The local officers at Amesbury were a great help. Unfortunately, Vince Walsh died of an overdose in 2008."

"I don't recall Tony Brown mentioning that Vince used drugs, do you? Often the dealers keep well away from the product they supply. They're aware it seriously damages your health, and all they're interested in is finding more and more mug punters willing to shoot up and keep them in business."

"I learned there was a question mark over who administered the fatal dose, guv," said Alex, "Vince had a falling out with his mysterious mate. As a result, money destined for the suppliers back in Essex went missing. Unfortunately, the police never determined whether Vince or his mate was responsible for the shortfall."

"So, Vince might have been clean. The Essex gang leaders needed to tighten control of the supply chain, and someone disposed of Vince. It's standard practice when they wish to send a message from the top to the runners on the ladder's bottom rung. Did Amesbury ever look for his killer?"

"I think they treated Vince as one more casualty of the

war on drugs, guv. Whether it was an accidental overdose or someone topped him, it wasn't worth losing sleep. They were glad to see the back of him and moved on to another problem."

"That's another name out of the frame," said Lydia.

"There's been no suggestion that Ian McGuire met a low-life like Vince or his mate. So why has that mate never been identified? Tony Brown never named him, either. Is that significant, I wonder? I can't see the connection, though."

"I've had a thought, guv," said Alex.

"All contributions gratefully received, Alex," said Gus, "they're thin on the ground."

"Tony Brown might have turned him, guv. Maybe he was an informant and didn't want to give up his name."

"That's one possibility. Another is, did Tony have anyone working undercover?"

"Should I ring him, guv? Or is it better for you to call Salisbury? You could get to fill in the gaps if you know more people there. It's out of date now, anyway. The undercover officer will be retired."

"Based on Vince's experience, an informant isn't above ground either. So I'll ring Salisbury later and call in a favour."

"Right, guv, let me take you through the Belafonte story. Without the rare exception, the family are a bunch of reprobates. Eugene was the first to arrive on the Windrush in 1948. He married Eralia Brown in 1950. They had five children. Ruby was born in 1955. She had four brothers, two older and two younger."

"Where did Eugene settle when he arrived?" asked Gus.

"London, guv, Canning Town. The ideal breeding ground for the junior Belafonte's."

"What did Eugene do for a living?"

"He worked as a bus conductor by day and stripped lead from church roofs at night. He received several custodial sentences over the years. Eralia brought the kids up on her own during most of the Sixties. Ruby took over the household duties from her mother when she was fifteen. Unfortunately, Eralia had a weak heart and died the week before Eugene came out of Wandsworth after yet another three-year sentence."

"I can see where this is heading," said Gus.

"Eugene was a mess when he got out. He'd used drugs before he went to prison for what proved to be the last time and had no bother getting supplies while in Wandsworth. Eugene attended Eralia's funeral and then disappeared for two days. After that, he went on a drink and drug-fuelled bender. Ruby's four brothers were not at home when that ended. One was in prison. One was selling drugs on a nearby street corner while her younger brothers played football at the local youth club. So Ruby was alone when her father reached the block of flats that the Belafonte's called home. Eugene tried it on, and Ruby kicked him in the shins. He punched her several times in the head and said she was taking Eralia's place in every way. Eralia was raped by her father almost every day for the next three years."

"What hope did they have?" said Gus. "A large family living on the breadline in one of the most dangerous parts of London. The boys were guaranteed to gravitate towards the gangs and get in trouble. Did the youngest two boys escape through their football skills?"

"Not a chance," said Alex, "Eugene was violent towards the boys too. The eldest, Kelvin, moved out after he left prison. Kelvin didn't want to return to live under the same roof as his father. Kelvin's luck never changed, and he returned to prison within eighteen months. Someone stabbed him in the yard during a mini-riot. They never found his killer. The drug dealer, Devlin, tried to protect Ruby and was hospitalised after Eugene attacked him with a crowbar. Six months later, Devlin walked into the flat and shot his father three times in the chest as he lounged on a leather settee watching television."

"So, Ruby escaped at last," said Gus, "how did she end up in Amesbury?"

"A colleague of Devlin's got her pregnant. Nobody knows how she dodged a bullet with her father, but within weeks of Devlin bringing this Tyrone character to the flat, Ruby was expecting her first child. Devlin was arrested for his father's murder and received a life sentence, which back then was longer than today. He's still in HMP Belmarsh after killing another prisoner in the late Eighties. Rumour has it that he evened the score for his brother, Kelvin. When he got arrested, the crew Devlin ran with felt the heat because the Met had cracked down on the drug gangs. It was one of those frequent purges carried out back in the day designed to soothe the public's concerns."

"I remember," said Gus, "they lasted five minutes and did no good whatsoever."

"Well, this one got several of Devlin's pals banged up, and Tyrone fled from London to find a home for his family. Somehow they ended up in Amesbury, and Ruby's first child was born in 1979. Unfortunately, Tyrone lacked imagination, and the poor devil was named Tyrone Junior. The confusion at home didn't last long, however, as Tyrone missed the bright lights of London and crept back in 1982. Tyrone Junior had a lot of uncles as Ruby decided her only skills lay in the bedroom. A succession of men moved in to live with her. Their financial contribution varied depending on whether they were unemployed or earning big money through criminal activities. Ruby supplemented whatever they brought to the table through prostitution."

"Ruby's father has plenty to answer for," said Gus, "he robbed her of her innocence and self-worth. The poor woman never stood a chance."

"The white father of Michael, her second son, born in 1983, is not recorded. Tammy arrived two years later, and the birth marked the start of a stable period in Ruby's life. Ricardo Jackson became her lover towards the end of 1984. Jackson moved from St Paul's in Bristol to live with Ruby. He was on the fringes of the drug scene in Bristol and wanted to broaden his horizons."

"You mean he moved to an area with potential," sighed Gus. "An area where he could develop a drugs business of his own. How did that turn out for him?"

"Police stopped Jackson late at night as he drove through Salisbury and found significant quantities of heroin, cannabis and ecstasy in his car. He claimed it was for personal use. Ricardo Jackson served two years in prison. He returned to live with Ruby and his daughter Tammy. In early 1989 Ruby gave birth to twins. They named the boy Kai and the girl Kayleigh. Jackson found honest work for a while, and Tammy, Kai, and Kayleigh briefly saw normal life. However, old habits die hard, and Ricardo was a habitual cannabis user. When the twins were four years old, he disappeared. Ruby hasn't heard from him since. She hunted for him in St Paul's, but he wasn't there. It's possible he left the country and moved back to where his family's roots were in Barbados."

"So, Ruby Belafonte never married," said Gus, "one imagines that none of the children's fathers ever wanted to cement the relationship so she could claim maintenance.

Ruby was on a constant cycle of abuse in one shape or form. How did she get that house of hers looking so pristine?"

"Time changes things for everyone, doesn't it, guv," said Alex, "she had five kids under the age of ten living with her as the Nineties began. She had her regular clients to supplement the child benefits and anything else she could claim. But, until the new millennium, she resisted having anyone move in with her. You will recall what Tony Brown told us of the county lines scourge emerging. Things were changing in the county. Ruby's older children were at risk, with no father figure. She did her best, but Tyrone Junior was already thieving to feed a habit. He was twenty-one at the start of the new century and had left school with zero qualifications. The only things he was proud of on his CV were the number of CA's he could claim."

"Court appearances?" asked Gus. Alex nodded.

"They view them as a badge of honour, guv, and it raises their street cred with the other clowns in the gang. Every misstep they make is one move closer to getting imprisoned or killed by someone they cross. Michael, at nineteen, didn't fit in with the rest of the family. His lighter skin colour set him apart. He was a loner who rarely spoke to his mother. Michael spent most of his time at the bookies, where he proved himself a successful punter. Michael searched for companionship among his cousins. We know what happened to Kelvin and Devlin, but Ruby's younger brothers moved away from Canning Town. Michael looked them up in Southampton. The Thornhill estate is one of the most deprived areas in the country. Clyde and Donovan's footballing days were behind them. They blew their one hope of escape through women, drink and drugs."

"It's twenty years ago now, Alex," said Gus, "they were a

product of their times. In a more fragmented society, the family unit is not what it was. Marriage as an institution is now frowned upon in certain quarters. London and several major cities saw no-go areas developing where the immigrant population gathered. The organised crime gangs and the religious fundamentalists held sway. Violence increased, and Clyde and Donovan got caught between a rock and a hard place. They were always out of a job, never actively seeking work. They drew the dole, stole what they could to scrape a living, and lived in atrocious conditions. A move from Canning Town to a coastal port such as Southampton must have appeared a wise move. The trouble is, nowhere is any different when you're cast adrift by society. One slum landlord is much like another, whether in Salford, Saltley, or somewhere else up north beginning with S that I can't remember."

"Clyde and Donovan always attracted a female following," said Gus, "whether they were playing football, clubbing, or just wandering the streets to fill their day. Both men were in their early to mid-forties and married with teenage children. Michael preferred their company to his mother and any of her lovers."

"Dr Ian McGuire spent time in Southampton, didn't he?" asked Gus.

"He did while still with his first wife, Dierdre. It's doubtful he ever contacted any of the Belafonte clan, even though Ruby lived across the road from him in Amesbury. By the time he moved in, she was almost a local."

"What happened to Michael? Did he get into trouble with the law?"

"What do you think? Michael and his cousins were frequent visitors to Southampton police stations and the courts. There were seven of them altogether; five boys and two girls Michael associated with during the Nineties. He never had a permanent address; he moved from flat to house, from house to high-rise and slept on the sofas of his relatives. Who knows if he felt more kinship with them than he had with his brothers and sisters?"

"How old was Tammy when McGuire died?" asked Gus.

"Eighteen, going on nineteen, guv," said Alex, "and you've guessed it, she was already on the game. Tammy had a child while still at school. She put it up for adoption. Again, there's no evidence to suggest McGuire knew Tammy Belafonte. However, there was a big change in Ruby's circumstances before McGuire's murder."

Gus Freeman clapped his hands.

"I scribbled a few thoughts the other evening as I sat by my allotment shed. I wrote Belafonte, Neighbours, Relatives. Because I knew a lead had to be in there somewhere. I can't see it yet, but it's coming."

Alex Hardy couldn't imagine how the background he'd researched could offer a solution to a fourteen-year-old murder mystery. Instead, he saw it as a familiar story of disenfranchised folk who eke out an existence on the fringes of a society they believe abandoned them.

"Tell me, Alex, what happened to rock Ruby's world?"

"Michael and two of his cousins died. They overdosed on crystal meth."

"Where did they get it?" asked Gus, "was our old pal Vince supplying it?"

"No, guv, his patch didn't cover Southampton. The detective who investigated the deaths believed they were testing their self-made product. Instead, they found a laboratory in a garage on the Thornhill estate."

"So, Ruby saw Tyrone Junior going the same way as her

older brothers, Tammy started turning tricks as a teenager, and then Michael died from a drug overdose. Had she kept in contact with Clyde and Donovan?"

"Not as far as we can tell, guv," said Alex, "Tyrone didn't invite them to live at home in Amesbury when they moved west after Devlin's murder trial. Tyrone had enough problems with a wife and child. Social services in London got involved with her two younger brothers after Devlin killed Eugene. The boys lived in group homes until Clyde reached eighteen. They were lucky they stayed together; many siblings don't. Clyde and Donovan left their group home on Clyde's birthday, and after a far-from-glitzy life in London, they headed for Southampton. I don't think Ruby ever met any of her nephews and nieces until the funerals."

"Who can we talk to?" asked Gus. He glanced at his watch. If they wanted something positive out of this afternoon, they should drive to Amesbury.

"We can visit Ruby. She's over sixty now. Her earning days as a prostitute are over. Men still lived with her since McGuire's death, but there were no more children after the twins."

"Come on then, fill me in on the rest in the car. I'll drive. You can sit back and relax. I need to protect my asset."

Alex grinned. Gus wouldn't let it lie. He took his crutches on this trip to give Gus one less thing to moan about. They travelled to the ground floor in the lift and headed away from the Old Police station. Lydia set up her video conference in the CRT office with Hazel McGuire.

"Where's Tyrone Junior these days?" Gus asked as he fastened his seat belt.

"Somewhere you visited last month, guv. HMP Bristol, out at Horfield."

"What about Tammy?" asked Gus as he pulled out of the car park, "what's she up to?"

"She no longer lives with her mother, guv," said Alex. "Tammy lives in Salisbury now and is trying to get her act together. She was a prostitute for over a decade. When I talked to the local officers at Amesbury, they reckoned Ruby and Tammy operated separately, or as a double-act at the outset, if the money was right."

"Ye Gods," said Gus, "it gets worse. I dread to think what those twins are doing. But, let's visit McGuire's neighbour, Julie Summers, first and then fix a time to see Ruby and Tammy in the morning."

"Do you want me to arrange an interview in the afternoon with Clive Breakwell, guv?"

"He was a close colleague of McGuire's, wasn't he? So, yes, he might supply the answers we seek."

Gus stopped outside Ian McGuire's former house at a quarter to four. Julie Summers was in her garden, two doors away. Alex noticed she straightened her back carefully as he got up from tending her flower borders.

"You must be the police people I'm expecting," she said.

"Is it that obvious?" asked Gus.

"There are only a few professions that bother wearing a suit and tie these days," she replied, "and someone phoned to say two detectives were calling on me this afternoon."

"We could use bright people like yourself, Mrs Summers," said Gus.

"I don't think you're looking for people in their early eighties, Inspector, is it?" she said, "and call me Julie. It makes me sound younger."

"Well, Julie, I was a Detective Inspector before I retired," said Gus, "now I'm a consultant for Wiltshire Police. The name's Freeman, Gus Freeman. My colleague,

Detective Sergeant Hardy, and I are taking a fresh look into Dr McGuire's murder."

"Oh, that was a dreadful business. Come indoors. I'll make us a cold drink. Would a glass of lemonade be alright?"

"More than welcome on a warm afternoon, Julie. Lead on."

Gus and Alex followed Julie Summers as she hobbled to the ramp that led to her side door. Even as they stood in her kitchen, they could tell how house-proud she was. The inside of the house was as immaculate as the garden they had just walked through.

Julie nodded towards the door leading off the kitchen.

"Find somewhere to sit out there in the conservatory. The outer door is open to let what breeze there is blow through. I'll follow you in a minute."

Gus and Alex did as instructed. The room was more a sauna than a conservatory, but the rear garden matched its custodian's prim and proper appearance.

"It's lovely out here, Julie," said Gus, loosening his collar. He could feel the beads of sweat trickling off his forehead. Alex sat closer to the door, wishing they were in the shade of the apple tree he spotted in the far corner.

"There we are," said Julie, setting a tray on the glass-topped table in the centre of the room, "take your pick."

Gus had to admit the ice-cold drink was just the ticket.

"How can I be of assistance?" asked Julie.

"We know Ian McGuire wasn't your neighbour for very long, Julie," said Gus, "but what did you make of him?"

"I was a school teacher for forty years, Mr Freeman. Ian was someone I dreamed of having in my class. He was the cleverest person I'd ever met. So I popped along to introduce myself the day Ian moved here, and I like to think we became friends. He was always courteous, with a wicked sense of humour. I could talk to him on any subject under the sun."

"A meeting of like minds then," said Gus, "but not everyone shared the same opinion of him, I suspect? People can be jealous or even suspicious of those who display eye-watering levels of intelligence. Were there neighbours who didn't get on with Dr McGuire as well as you?"

"I suppose you're referring to the riff-raff from the other side of the main road. The council-owned properties and those places run by the housing association have been a problem for years. I wish I'd sold up and moved to Seaton in Devon to be closer to my sister before they built the last batch of houses. But, unfortunately, house prices on this side of the road haven't kept pace with rises around the county. It's too late now. I could never afford a bungalow by the coast."

"Does anyone spring to mind, Julie, who had words with Dr McGuire?"

Gus realised that the clock was ticking. The lemonade was helping, but he couldn't allow Julie Summers to wander too far along memory lane.

"Ian worked such odd hours." Julie replied, "he never liked to leave his lab if a task was unfinished. It wasn't unusual for him to disappear for forty-eight hours at a stretch. Then he'd come home and sleep during the day. I kept an eye out for him and popped around to see if he needed things from the shops. If he rowed with anyone, then I never witnessed it."

"Did he ever have dealings with any of the families from the other side of the main road?" asked Alex, "kids causing trouble, perhaps."

"I have to think; it's over ten years since he died. One

year is much the same as another when you get to my age. That dreadful Strugnell character lived on the estate in those days."

"Norman Strugnell?" asked Alex.

"The things he did to the young girls on that estate. He seemed such a quiet, reserved man. What a monster he was. The local lads threw bricks at his windows, slashed his car tyres and ripped off his wing mirrors after he came out of prison. I'm sorry to say this, but the police arrested and charged the lot of them. Dr McGuire offered to pay the fines for the younger ones caught up in the campaign."

"How about the Belafonte family?" asked Gus, "any of those involved in that caper?"

"I've lived here for years, as you know, Mr Freeman. So, I remember when Ruby Belafonte first arrived in the area. Her house is far enough into the estate that I couldn't witness the comings and goings, but it was common knowledge what went on—credit where it's due. Ruby got left with the twins to bring up after her older children left, for whatever reason. She threw out the last of her gentlemen friends and told Tammy to move out if she couldn't quit the drugs. Maybe losing Michael was the final straw. He was no good, just like the older brother, but things couldn't continue as they were. Ruby's a born-again Christian, Mr Freeman. If religion has saved the soul of someone as wretched as her, there must be something to it. But I didn't believe it could work before I saw what it did for Ruby Belafonte. As for the twins, Kai and Kayleigh, they're chalk and cheese compared to their siblings."

"We took a stroll around the estate the other day," said Gus, "and I remarked to my colleague DS Hardy that one house stood out from the shabby row of dwellings. He told me it belonged to Ruby Belafonte."

"Did Ruby or Tammy ever meet Dr McGuire?" asked Alex.

"I should sincerely hope not," said Julie. She looked indignant. "I understood from Ian that a long-term relationship ended before his move to Amesbury, but he wasn't a man who needed to resort to visiting prostitutes. Ian worked long hours, and when he wasn't working, he travelled to Southampton to watch football or visit the local pubs. He loved his music and his sport. He was amicable, not a loner who paid for female company."

"Did you ever meet Debbie Dallimore?" asked Gus.

"Oh, Ian introduced her to me," said Julie, "she was just what Ian needed. When I was their age, it was social suicide for a married woman to seek a new relationship before the marriage officially ended, but times have changed."

Gus swallowed hard.

"They were happy together, would you say?" asked Alex.

"I should say they were," said Julie, "Ian was smitten with Debbie, and I was so happy for them both. It was cruel beyond belief that someone killed him the way they did."

"You appear to have known Ian better than many others in the area, Julie," said Gus, "did you ever wonder who might have done it? Was there anyone you thought the police should have considered that Detective Superintendent Brown overlooked?"

"I sat at home in the evenings following that dreadful January evening, Mr Freeman, wondering who it could have been. Ian was such a nice chap, so well-liked. He never hurt anyone. It must have been one of those drug addicts desperate for cash to buy their next fix. When he made that offer to pay the fines for the young ones, I told Ian that it was misguided. He might have put the idea into their head that he kept lots of cash in the house. So many of them carry a weapon these days, don't they?"

"They do, Julie," said Gus, "knives mostly, even fourteen years later, but pump-action shotguns are still thin on the ground, thank goodness. Yes, I can see Dr McGuire's offer of help might have caused a scallywag to think of breaking in to hunt for cash; however, he was at home, in a brightly lit kitchen with the TV on in the lounge. The timing doesn't fit a break-in. The choice of weapon points to a criminal who meant to kill."

"Oh my," said Julie Summers. Her hand flew to her mouth.

"Don't worry, Julie," said Gus, "you're perfectly safe. Whoever it was is long gone. They targeted Dr McGuire for a specific reason. We don't know what it was yet, but when we do, we'll understand where we need to start our search for the culprit."

"You've finished your lemonade," said Julie, "is there anything more I can get you?"

"You've helped us a great deal, Julie," said Gus, getting up from his seat, "we must visit others involved in the case to see what they can add."

"Of course, I hope you find Ian's killer. Have you talked to Debbie at all?"

"We have," said Gus, "she's well and living in Filton, in Bristol."

"Did she remarry? What about the children she planned to have with Ian??"

"Debbie hasn't been in a relationship since Ian's death," said Alex, "no children."

"Oh, what a shame. She was looking forward to becoming a mother so much."

Alex glanced at Gus. His boss nodded.

"I've got her phone number here, Julie. If you wanted to get in touch."

"Bless you," said Julie, "I'd like that very much."

Julie Summers walked with them to the door and stood and waved until Gus drove out of sight into the estate opposite.

"You made her day, Alex," said Gus, "now let's see if we can catch Ruby Belafonte at home."

Chapter Eleven

RUBY BELAFONTE ANSWERED the doorbell and stood with her arms open wide.

"Welcome," she said, "what a wonderful day God has blessed us with today."

"Ms Belafonte," said Gus, "my name is Freeman. I'm a civilian consultant working with Wiltshire Police. We want to ask you what you remember of the events surrounding the death of Dr Ian McGuire fourteen years ago. May my colleague Detective Sergeant Hardy and I come in?"

"A shooting? Fourteen years ago? That was across the road, on the other estate. We had nothing to do with that."

"Nobody suggested you did, Ms Belafonte," said Gus. "Perhaps we can go indoors to stop your neighbours hurting their necks peeking around their curtains checking who's on your doorstep."

Ruby turned and waddled into the lounge. The bright colour scheme of the walls, carpet and leather furniture didn't surprise Gus. What surprised him was how spotless the room looked. It was immaculate.

Ruby plonked her large frame in a leather armchair and waved a podgy hand to encourage Gus and Alex to follow suit.

"What year are we talking about, sweetheart? I can't do the sums in my head."

"The murder took place in January '04. Dr McGuire lived at No 28, the house directly opposite the entrance to your estate. He died on a Saturday evening, just after five o'clock."

Ruby crossed herself.

"May he rest in peace. He was a doctor. I didn't know."

"Not a medical doctor," said Gus, "he was a scientist. Did you never meet him?"

"My life has changed since then. I'm a different person now."

"Is that so? Can you enlighten us?" said Gus.

"Ricardo Jackson, that sinner, left me with five young children ten years before that happened. Tyrone Junior gave me no respite. Like his father, he was born to be in trouble with the law. Michael was sullen and moody. His father made him that way. Not that he stayed long after Michael was born. I tried to keep them both from harm, but I was as guilty as them. I was a sinner too. Then I lost Tammy, my beautiful daughter. She was weak and gave in to the sins of the flesh—too many men. Too much hurt, and the only way to blot out the hurt for Tammy was with drugs. I had to ask her to leave so I could try to save myself. Without God's help, I couldn't hope to save Kai and Kayleigh from following the wrong path like their brothers and sister."

"The cross on the wall behind you," said Gus. "The statue of Jesus Christ on the table in the corner. Does this show that your religious beliefs helped you through the worst times?"

"I'm born-again, Mr Freeman. I have repented of my sins and turned to Christ for my salvation. I wish to become part of God's family forever. That can only happen when I allow God's Spirit to work in my life. By nature, we aren't members of God's family, and because of our sins, we have no right to inherit eternal life. I rebelled against God before Michael died, and in God's eyes, even one sin is enough to keep me from heaven. You have no idea how many sins I committed before I begged for salvation."

Gus knew he was the wrong person to listen to Ruby's confession. If, indeed, that was what it was. She clearly believed the doctrine fed to her by the church she followed. He had no faith. Everything Ruby preached to him was an anathema. He knew he must ignore the diatribe and concentrate on Ruby and her family alone.

"We've interviewed everyone who could offer an insight into Dr McGuire's background and how he might die in such a brutal fashion," said Gus. "Forgive me if I bring back unhappy memories. Where was Tyrone Junior at the time of the murder?"

"Tyrone was on remand. He got charged with breaking into a shop and stealing money collected for a cancer charity. I got no sympathy for that fool. His father was no good, and Junior was always his father's son."

"Your son, Michael, passed away before the murder, didn't he?" asked Gus.

"My son abandoned me, Mr Freeman. He mixed with other sinners like my younger brothers and their children. I lost touch with them after I left Canning Town. Tyrone brought me here to escape the madness; I was foolish and allowed the madness to follow me to this house. But Jesus Christ came to save me and make me part of His family forever. He did this by dying for our sins on the cross and by conquering death through His resurrection."

"Can you concentrate on the question, Ruby, please? When did Michael overdose on the crystal meth he and his cousins made?"

"How could I ever forget that day?" wailed Ruby Belafonte, "no matter what a sinner Michael might have become. It was Friday, the tenth of January 2003. The day of the twin's fourteenth birthday."

A light went on in Gus's head.

"So, Tyrone Junior was on remand one year later when Dr McGuire died? Where was Tammy?"

"In Salisbury, I told her to leave within months of Michael's death. I had to repent my sins and make this house proper for Kai and Kayleigh to live in. Tammy was still selling herself and using heroin when that thing happened."

"Where can we get hold of Kai and Kayleigh to speak with them?" asked Gus.

"Kai is in Thailand at present," said Ruby, with evident pride, "he's worked abroad since he left school with different charitable organisations. I pray God keeps him safe and brings him home for Christmas this year."

"And Kayleigh?"

"Kayleigh is living in London now, working as a MacMillan nurse. She volunteered with Raleigh International when she left school. Kayleigh's three trips are available to read on her blog. Let me show you where to find it."

Gus looked at Alex for the second time. This conversation wasn't going in the direction they thought. It just goes to show you should never assume. After Tyrone, Michael and Tammy expected a teenage pregnancy, a rebellious single mother with no future. What a difference fourteen years can make.

Ruby returned with the link and scribbled Kayleigh's phone number on the sheet of paper.

"Tell Kayleigh that Mummy loves her if you call. She'll visit and bring my three grandchildren to see me when she can."

"Kayleigh seems to have got the wanderlust out of her system and settled into steady work and family life," said Gus. "They're both twenty-nine now, is Kai married?"

"Not him," said Ruby, "he's thrown himself into good works, and there's so much hurt to heal in the world. Kai says he never has time for a relationship. God needs him to help people worse off than him. One day, perhaps, he'll take a breath and look for someone with whom he can share his life."

"Thank you for your time, Ms Belafonte," said Gus, "it's been enlightening. Unfortunately, DS Hardy and I need to return to the office."

"Don't rush away, Mr Freeman," said Ruby, "I feel you're searching for answers in other parts of your life, not just concerning the murder you're investigating. I have leaflets that might help."

Gus was already halfway out of the door. Alex paused before he followed his boss.

"You've turned things around and produced two children you can be proud of, Ms Belafonte," he said.

"My prayer is that you, too, may be born again and become part of God's family. Say a prayer with me, Mr Hardy, and read from this card. Dear God, I know I'm a sinner, and I ask for your forgiveness. I believe Jesus Christ is Your Son. I believe that He died for my sin and that you raised Him to life. I want to trust Him as my Saviour and follow Him as Lord from this day forward. Guide my life and help me do your will. I pray this in the name of Jesus. Amen."

Alex let Ruby finish and shook the podgy hand she extended.

"You can't save everyone, Ms Belafonte," he said. "Take credit for saving your twins."

Alex joined Gus in the car, and they headed away from Amesbury.

"You looked glad to get out of there, guv," said Alex. "Religion isn't your thing. You didn't fire any of Soren Kierkegaard's thoughts back at her, though?"

"I wanted to get home before dark, Alex. I learned long ago that arguing over politics or religion is pointless. Each of you believes what you believe, and no amount of argument will alter that. I thought she would hand out hymn sheets," grunted Gus, "and get us singing along with her."

"Ruby's heart's in the right place, guv," said Alex, "what do we do about the twins now?"

"Don't take their mother's word for anything, Alex. First thing in the morning, we'll set Luke and Lydia on checking their careers since McGuire's murder. Then, you and I will interview Tammy Belafonte. Please don't mention that we've spoken with her mother. I want to hear the unexpurgated version of the lives of Ruby, Kai and Kayleigh over the past fourteen years."

Gus drove into the office car park, dropped Alex by his car, and with a short beep on his horn, went home to Urchfont.

Tomorrow was another day, and Gus knew he had a decision to make.

Friday, 18 May 2018

ONLY one more day to suffer, thought Gus, as he raised his head from the pillow.

It had been a long week with so many dead ends. Finally, after days of attempting to make sense of Ian McGuire's killing, yesterday saw a breakthrough.

Gus didn't know what to do with it.

He showered, and dressed, then drove to the Old Police Station. Alex, Luke and Lydia were waiting for him when he reached the CRT office.

"Good to see you're in early," he said. "I hope that means you've updated the Freeman Files?"

Three voices sang out, "Yes, guv."

"A rapid recap then, Luke. How was Norman Strugnell?"

"He's still a sick individual. Nothing in his statement suggested he was the target that evening. Strugnell never met McGuire. I think we can cross him off our list."

"If you had been with me yesterday afternoon, Luke, we wouldn't have bothered driving to Warminster. Try to forget him. What did Hazel McGuire offer us, Lydia?"

"The sun shone from somewhere south of her son Ian's waist, guv. She's a lonely woman. I'm afraid I let her witter on for far too long. I couldn't see the point."

"We might have to write this one off to experience, Lydia. It happens."

His three team members shared a glance. Was this the first loss recorded on the Freeman Files?

"There are a couple of things you two can check while Alex and I are in Salisbury," said Gus, retrieving the scrap of paper Ruby Belafonte handed him yesterday afternoon.

"Follow up on these two. I want to know what they did and where they've been from the tenth of January '03 to today."

"Why '03, guv," asked Luke.

"It was their fourteenth birthday," said Gus, "funny that, don't you think? I don't like coincidences."

"What's on your mind, guv?" asked Alex as they left the office ten minutes later.

"Something's not adding up, Alex. Michael was a loner, a misfit. Although his mother might have treated all her children as equals, his white father made him feel like an outsider."

"He left home and went to live in Southampton with his cousins. Ruby's younger brothers, Clyde and Donovan, were of African Caribbean heritage. What if one of Ruby's brothers was in a mixed marriage? We haven't pursued that angle. Maybe he felt more at home mixing with that crowd."

"It's possible. I don't profess to understand how that works. Take Lydia, for example, with an African father and a Scottish mother. She's a feisty, intelligent singleton who gets on with anyone. I can't imagine her feeling like an outsider or a misfit, can you?"

"Lydia attributes that to her foster family, guv," said Alex, "they raised her that way. Now she's in contact with her birth mother; that solid grounding has been invaluable in bridging the gap that inevitably existed."

Alex bit his tongue. Did Gus realise Lydia and her mother were in touch?

Gus carried on driving. He stored that knowledge away to mull it over one evening at the allotment.

As they headed across the Plain to Salisbury, Gus immediately turned his attention to Michael.

"We know that heroin and cocaine were readily available in the area in the early Noughties, thanks to Vince and his crew. So does it seem odd to you that Michael and his cousins overdosed on this crystal meth stuff?"

"A little, guv, if I'm honest," said Alex. "It was becoming a popular pastime in the States, but production and usage in the UK were small compared to the other drugs."

"That production and usage soared several years after they died when the credit crunch bit. Michael Belafonte and his cousins were ahead of the curve for the first time."

"With tragic results," said Gus.

"There were twelve million illegal drug takers in the UK at the start of the Noughties," said Alex. "I've got no sympathy for them, but during an earlier economic down-turn, the much cheaper drug they called speed was an alternative high."

"Less ready cash threatened the drug dealer's income," said Gus, "and they looked for alternatives the same as any legitimate business."

"Cocaine use increased significantly in the Nineties and into the new millennium. My forte wasn't getting involved with drugs or vice when I worked in Salisbury, but I thought I read that the trade was worth two billion pounds a year."

"It was, despite us seizing record amounts, guv, you're right. The growth in cocaine abuse reflected the economic boom of the Nineties. There's always a bust to follow a boom. Michael and his pals anticipated the big dip on the horizon and planned to swamp the South and West with crystal meth."

"Our canny shoppers want value for money, and drug consumers are no different," said Gus.

"Others have followed in the footsteps of the Belafonte pioneers," said Alex, "it's got more than a toehold in the UK these days."

"I'm damned if I can see the attraction, Alex," said Gus, "the user gets a brief false sense of well-being and energy followed by a severe crash after the effects wear off. That's bad enough if it's a one-time thing, but regular use leads to a physical and mental breakdown."

"Michael Belafonte and his pals didn't experience disturbed sleep, nausea, hallucinations and bizarre behaviour that typifies short-term to medium-term use, guv. However, the Medical Examiner's report indicated they suffered convulsions and seizures that resulted in death due to the purity of the high dose they took."

"A little knowledge is a dangerous thing," said Gus, "I wonder how three kids who rarely attended school concocted a recipe for this stuff in the first place."

"From people who know people, I guess. That's how the drugs world operates," said Alex, "nobody is born knowing how to inject drugs. It's an acquired skill. But, if you mix with the right people, they'll teach you. I never did, thank goodness."

"Nor me," said Gus, "anyway, in my teenage years, the acquired skill was how to make the perfect roll-up cigarette."

As they negotiated the heavy traffic in Salisbury, Gus realised that the block of flats where Tammy Belafonte lived was a distinct contrast to the pristine appearance of her former family home.

"It's grim around here, guv, isn't it?" said Alex. "On which floor is Tammy's flat? The lift's out of order."

"Take it steady climbing the stairs, Alex," said Gus, "and be thankful it's only the second floor. Even so, the stench from this stairwell will linger in the memory for days. How anyone can live this way is beyond me."

Tammy Belafonte lived behind the door marked No23 in white paint but seemed in no rush to open her door until Alex leant on the bell and refused to budge. He struggled to believe the woman who answered was only thirty-three. Tammy looked ten years older. Gus thought Tammy and Ruby could pass for sisters. Perhaps that's how they played it years ago when they offered double the pleasure to the punters.

"Oh, it's your lot," Tammy grumbled, "I forgot you were coming,"

"We'll try to make it quick, Ms Belafonte," said Gus, "and let you get back to bed."

Tammy pulled the lightweight dressing-gown tighter around her and flopped into the nearest chair.

"What did you want to talk to me about again?" she asked.

"DS Hardy, my colleague, told you on the phone. My name is Freeman, and we work with a Crime Review Team for Wiltshire Police."

"I remember now. You want to dig into the death of that McGuire bloke. I can't help you. I never met him. He could have lived on the moon for all I knew. When I saw a paper that said where he lived, I realised the murder happened just up the road from our house."

"The house where you and Ruby, your mother, lived off immoral earnings," said Gus.

"What else is a girl supposed to do? I was not too fond of school and couldn't wait to leave. I wasn't sitting at a supermarket checkout for eight hours daily."

"You left before the end of the school year, Tammy," said Gus, "you were expecting a child while you were only fifteen."

"Mum told me to get rid of it, but I had to carry it full

195

term. So I left it too late to tell her I'd missed several periods."

"Was it your mother who persuaded you to have the baby adopted?"

Tammy nodded and stared at the wall behind Gus and Alex.

"When did you leave Amesbury?" asked Gus.

"I was a mess back then," said Tammy. She got up and walked to the coffee table, where she collected her cigarettes and lighter. When she had taken several drags of her cigarette, she continued: -

"The only way I could be with those men that came to our house was to blot out what they were doing to me," she said. "The money was better, depending on how much you wished to suffer. Mum was more used to it. Do we have to talk about that? What's my drug-taking got to do with the murder?"

Alex was wondering the same thing. Something encouraged Gus to continue.

"We won't know until you tell us something that tallies with what we already know."

Tammy shrugged in resignation.

"After Michael died, things changed. We argued more about drugs than before. Not that I ever tried that meth crap. I've got good teeth, and I want to keep them, thank you very much. I've always had a fuller figure, the same as my Mum. A lot of men prefer that in a woman. If I took that meth stuff, I'd look as thin as a rake and older than Mum. I can't remember the exact date that year, but Mum chucked me out. I came to Salisbury, found a place on the other side of the city, and worked from home."

Tammy looked at Alex.

"A pity you didn't visit me, DS Hardy. We could have had fun."

"That's enough of that, young lady," said Gus, "let's stay on track, shall we? You were still using and working as a prostitute. What was the name of your supplier?"

"Jax saw me right. We got along at first. I didn't like his mate much, though."

"That would be Vince?" asked Gus.

"Yeah, the Essex kid," Tammy laughed. "He thought he was the big man, but he was just a cog in the wheel. I couldn't see it then because I was using it so much everything was a blur. Day, night, summer, winter, it didn't matter. Vince was under the cosh from the real big men back in Essex, and he started getting mean."

"Did he harm you?" asked Gus. Tammy shook her head.

"Not him; he wasn't around much after that. Vince died five years after Michael."

"That was an overdose, wasn't it?" asked Alex.

"You *can* talk then," said Tammy, giving him a thousand-watt smile. He caught a glimpse of the attractive girl that she'd been around the time she left school.

"It might have looked like an OD," she said, "but someone wanted his turf."

"The county lines gangs were moving into the county in numbers," said Gus, "a flat such as yours was a typical target."

"How was it when they descended on your place and were living all around you?" asked Alex.

"Most of them were five years younger than me, if not more. They were just kids to look at, but they never had a proper childhood. Those kids were quiet and withdrawn. They spent the day lounging around my living room, watching TV, listening to music, and playing video games. Their mobile phone was never more than a foot away from their hand, day or night. That's no life. I was earning what I could to feed my habit, and food isn't a priority when you're hooked. As for the kids who squatted in my place, they had never had a home-cooked meal in two years. They would have starved to death if the fast-food joints had closed."

"Who took over from Vince Walsh? Was this Jax the main man now?" asked Gus.

Tammy shook her head.

"More than my life's worth to tell you that. They've still got a stranglehold here in the city."

"Then what happened?" asked Gus.

"Two years later, I had a total breakdown," said Tammy, "I was vulnerable and desperate for a fix. Jax kept tormenting me and withholding the drugs. That breakdown saved my life. It took me several attempts to get clean. This past year is the first since I was fifteen that I've spent clean. Finally, I'm mentally strong enough to keep the dealers from my door."

"I'm glad to hear it," said Gus, "does your mother know how much better you're doing?"

"There's no talking to her since she got religion," said Tammy, stubbing out her cigarette.

"What about the twins? Do you keep in touch with them?"

"I haven't been near either of them since I got chucked out."

"That's not what I asked," said Gus.

"OK, I talk to Kayleigh on the phone from time to time," snapped Tammy, "there's no law against it. We've got the same mother and father."

"Ricardo Jackson is your father, isn't he?" said Gus.

"If he's still alive," said Tammy, "he was a proper father for a while."

"Did this Jax come from Essex, the same as Vince?"

"No idea, he sounded as if he came from London way, but he never said. I wanted his drugs, not his life story."

"You said the two of you got on?"

"Did you ever use your body to pay for your drugs?" asked Gus.

"I told you, everything was a blur. I'd do anything for a fix."

"What about Vince?" asked Gus.

"I must have held on to some standards," said Tammy, "I never gave myself to that weasel."

"What's Kayleigh been doing since you left home?" asked Gus.

"She sat two A levels in 2006. They were one-year courses in Sociology and Biology. She wasn't sure if she wanted to go to University, so she took a year out to experience other things. Kayleigh volunteered with Raleigh International and undertook three trips. In Tanzania, she worked with a team on environmental projects. Her next trip was to India, where they built a tree nursery. Replanting trees is important in reducing climate change, or so she said. Finally, Kayleigh returned to Africa and helped build a toilet block at a junior school in Namibia. She said what she learned about the world was great, but what she learned about herself was invaluable. When she returned to the UK, she had a stronger sense of direction for her future career. Kayleigh went into nursing, caring for cancer patients."

"Kayleigh's married and has three children, I believe?" asked Gus.

"Two boys and a girl. She met Jamie, her husband, in

Tanzania. So, maybe, one day, I'll get to meet them. Not while Mum's alive, though, I bet."

"One last thing, Tammy, and we can leave you to get on with your day," said Gus, "Your brother, Kai."

"Saint Kai, you mean?" laughed Tammy.

"How did he get on at school?" asked Gus.

"Kai left at sixteen. As soon as one of those charities he works with took him on, he flew out of the country. Kai comes home to see his mother once, maybe twice a year. The main one he worked for was Christians Abroad. Kai travels around the world doing good work. He says he doesn't covet material things. As long as he has clothes on his back, shoes on his feet and a toothbrush, he's content. He makes me want to spit."

"Where did he get this missionary zeal?" asked Gus.

"From our mother, she brainwashed him. Kayleigh followed her own path. Kai went where his mother ordered him to go. He's never come home for more than a few days a year."

"I'm sorry to have taken up so much of your time, Tammy," said Gus, "we have another appointment straight after lunch. So we'll be on our way."

Tammy saw them to the door.

"Have a nice day, DS Hardy," she whispered as Alex walked past her.

Gus didn't say a word. Instead, he drove them to the edge of the city centre.

"Sergei Skripal got released from the hospital the other day," said Alex, "things are starting to look more normal now."

"I thought we could boost the economy by eating lunch here," Gus said.

"What did you make of Tammy's responses?"

"Tammy confirmed what Ruby told us of Kayleigh's story. Our colleagues won't have dug up any dirt there. Tammy was vague on detail with Kai, didn't you think? Luke and Lydia might uncover something. Other replies she gave were disturbing."

Alex shifted his position. His leg ached more today. He wondered what Gus was driving at by saying things were disturbing.

The only thing he noticed was Tammy Belafonte hitting on him. On more than one occasion, that dressing gown was unsuccessful in covering her assets.

Chapter Twelve

AFTER LUNCH, Gus drove to the research establishment to meet with Clive Breakwell. The complex included the department where Dr Ian McGuire worked at the time of his death. Security was tight.

Gus wondered what they were researching here. It wasn't overtly military, not like Porton Down. It purported to be research relating to the chemical industry. There didn't appear to be much chance of them letting anyone in on the secret.

Alex and Gus waited in a sterile-looking ante-room for Clive Breakwell to collect them. Finally, a tall, thin man in a white lab coat entered the room one minute before the appointed hour of two o'clock. He looked around fifty years old, a contemporary of Dr McGuire.

"You must be Freeman and Hardy," he said, with a grin, "Ian would have loved you. Did you leave Willis in the car?"

"Not on this occasion, Sir," said Gus, "as you know who we are and why we've come, we can get cracking."

"Follow me," said Clive Breakwell, "I'll show you where

we worked when Ian was here. There are new bits of kit, but the basic layout is unchanged."

Although the department they entered might not have changed, there was little or no activity. Alex spotted just two white-coated employees on the far side of the large laboratory.

"Quiet today," said Gus.

"There are currently no projects available for this section," said Clive.

"We wouldn't understand them even if you were at liberty to explain what they entailed," said Gus.

Clive Breakwell smiled.

"How can I help, Mr Freeman?"

"Before we get into what you recall of the details surrounding Ian's death, can you throw light on a subject that has often cropped up since we reopened the investigation?"

"If I can, of course."

"The original detective, DS Brown, discounted drugs from playing any part in the murder. He found no evidence Dr McGuire used them. He didn't believe Ian came in contact with anyone associated with the gangs creeping into the area. What do you have to say about that?"

"Ian never got into that scene, Mr Freeman. He liked a drink and visited pubs where they had live music, but drugs never tempted him. But, sadly, almost every pub has a level of drug activity on its premises these days. Deals get made in plain sight in the worst-offending premises; lines of coke get snorted off the lid of the low-level cisterns in the toilet cubicles. Most places have removed the doors now."

"What do you know about crystal meth?" asked Gus.

"Crystal meth has become a relatively common drug of abuse because it works quickly, produces an extreme high, and is easy to make. Those on meth will smoke, snort, inject or swallow it. The problem is that the effects dissipate as rapidly as they arise, which means the abuser is constantly bingeing on the drug. In addition, crystal meth is something users can make at home, and the substances required to produce it are readily obtainable."

"Where do they get these ingredients," asked Gus, "online or from backstreet dealers?"

"Most ingredients are in your local chemists, although access is more restricted than at the turn of the century. So cold medications, nail polish removers, lithium, ammonia aren't suspicious buys if you're careful not to pile them in the same basket when you go to the checkout."

"How do these drug dealers, or users, understand how to mix the ingredients in the right proportions?" asked Gus. "Don't you need a proper recipe? I hope I can't Google it when I get home tonight or watch a YouTube 'How To' video."

Clive Breakwell laughed.

"If you know where to look on the Dark Web, there's chapter and verse on anything you wish. Drug abusers are resourceful. They've developed a shake-and-bake method of producing meth, mixing the chemicals in a plastic bottle and shaking it vigorously. Even though the ingredients are highly combustible, they do it, and the bottle could explode when they open it. So I suppose if you're desperate to experience that extreme high again and again, you'll take the quickest and easiest option."

"I'm not suggesting that you would do something illegal," said Gus, "but would you and Ian McGuire understand how to prepare a high-quality product of this nature?"

Clive Breakwell didn't appear fazed by the question.

Instead, he stood up and stretched his legs. It was an acknowledgement that this meeting was more than a brief refresher of the statement given to Tony Brown fourteen years ago.

"This was bound to raise its ugly head at some point," he said, "the police were convinced drugs didn't play a part in his death. But, unfortunately, I couldn't see the connection until later."

"You need to explain," said Gus. Alex took his pen from his pocket and opened his notebook. He needed to take notes. Gus wasn't switched on this afternoon.

"When it comes to making meth," said Clive, "you need to acknowledge there's a difference between cooking and synthesis. Anyone can cook meth whether or not they have a chemistry education. It's just riskier than cooking a Sunday roast. A lack of chemical knowledge puts the cook and anyone near them at serious risk of injury. A skilled chemist like Ian McGuire understood chemistry, allowing him to adapt the synthesis as necessary. Ian had easy access to the chemicals. He extracted the pseudoephedrine from over-the-counter cold medicine and combined it with iodine and red phosphorous in a boiling flask and water. Ian had to be wary of the phosphine gas that heating his concoction produced. This lab needed to be well-ventilated. After he'd completed the cooking stage, he extracted a basic solution with an organic solvent. Ian was a genius. He refined his synthesis to produce a purity value above ninety-eight point four per cent. He viewed it as an exercise in demonstrating what was possible if you had a brain the size of a planet. It was a challenge for him, nothing more."

"What did he do with the batch he produced?" asked Gus.

"He destroyed it," said Clive, "he had no intention of

ever using it or selling it for profit. It was science, pure and simple."

"Was he aware how potent that mixture could be if it ever hit the streets?" asked Alex.

"Oh, he was well aware the test formula was deadly," said Clive, "but every dealer reduces the strength of their street-level drugs to maximise profits, don't they? Laypeople know that fact every bit as much as we scientists."

"If he destroyed the only batch he ever made, how did three people die from meth using this deadly formula?" asked Gus.

Clive Breakwell sat back in his chair.

"We had a break-in. Security back in '03 was lax compared to today. We arrived one Monday morning to find someone had gained access through a broken window and trashed the office and storeroom. They must have thought we had drugs on the premises they could sell. They emptied the petty cash box, but they were lucky if they stole a fiver."

"Is that all they took?" asked Gus.

"Most of our computer kit wasn't user-friendly for the local yobbo, but a laptop was missing."

"Dr McGuire's, I presume?"

Clive Breakwell nodded.

"Ian always mislaid his laptop. You've heard what a workaholic he was. Ian could be here for dozens of hours, then take work home. He thought he'd left it in his house. The uniformed officers that came here took notes and asked him to let them know if it turned up at home, but we never heard from them again."

"They didn't ask, so Ian McGuire didn't bother telling anyone it was stolen and the laptop contained something that could be lethal."

"The break-in was between Christmas and New Year, and we returned to work on the sixth of January. I read a report of the deaths in the newspaper a week later. They died on Friday night; let's see, that would have been on the tenth. Whoever broke in was involved. Ian's laptop was password-protected, but with his Southampton mug and his workstation plastered with team photos, I expect they tried 'saints' before anything else. I don't know what happened to the laptop and its deadly formula. The police thought the three lads miscalculated the dosage, and the coroner's report recorded it as an accidental death. Within a week, it was no longer news. Ian got himself another laptop and carried on as usual. His mind was soon occupied with other things because he'd met Debbie in a pub in Bristol. He never stopped talking about her. Ian was head over heels in love. The decorating he did the day he died was part of a final tidy-up of his place before putting it on the market. They were moving in together in Filton, getting married, planning children, the complete package."

"A year later, to the day that those three youngsters died, someone shot him. Does that not strike you as odd?" asked Gus.

"In hindsight, yes," said Clive.

"The police didn't know about the laptop," said Gus, "if Dr McGuire reported it stolen and stressed the dangers of it falling into the wrong hands, it could have prevented those deaths. DS Tony Brown couldn't hope to find a link between Dr McGuire and drugs unless someone told him about the stolen laptop."

"Ian didn't think it worth bothering. He thought kids broke in here, and they would only use the laptop for playing video games. It was naïve."

"How did McGuire react when you told him people died?" asked Alex.

"He shrugged his shoulders and said – serve the buggers right."

"This opens the door on a series of new leads," said Alex, "we need to establish whether the three victims were in an organised gang. The other gang members would seek retribution. Parents of the victims are now firmly in the frame, as are friends and relatives. Each of them has a motive."

"Many gangs have weapons at their disposal," said Gus, "so some of those you've listed also had means and opportunity."

"Do you think you'll find the killer now?" asked Clive Breakwell.

"I've no idea," said Gus, "but at least we have somewhere to look that might be productive. Between you and Dr McGuire, you ensured that's been impossible. It cost him his life. How it will affect you when this is over isn't for me to say. I'll leave it with my superiors and the CPS. Good day, Mr Breakwell."

Alex needed to hurry behind Gus to keep pace.

"Where are we off to, guv?" he asked.

"Salisbury Police Station," he said, "I need to ask questions of anyone who worked there in the winter of '02 through to McGuire's murder."

The drive to the Police Station took a mere fifteen minutes. It felt longer to Alex. Gus was quiet.

Gus explained to the desk sergeant who they were.

"I'll ask someone to come to see you, Mr Freeman," he said, "your name is the stuff of legend around here."

"Time marches on, sergeant," said Gus, "high time someone else made a name for themselves."

Five minutes later, a man not much younger than Gus appeared.

"Bob, I thought they put you out to grass not long after me," said Gus, shaking his hand.

"They kept me on out of spite, I reckon," replied DS Bob Martin, "but I'm out of here at the end of next month. So what was it you wanted to know?"

"Tony Brown mentioned a lad called Vince, who came here fifteen years ago. He was from Chelmsford and in the drugs game. His mate, Jax, helped this Vince find the runners."

"Vince died ages ago, with help from his friends. It wasn't an accident. Jax Jackson is still around. He's inside at present, but it won't be long before he's back on the streets, and we'll be trying to catch him all over again. Some people never learn."

"Jax Jackson? That makes sense," said Gus, "does anything come to mind after those lads died of a crystal meth overdose in '03?"

"Now you're asking," said Bob, taking a moment to reflect. "They were nothing to do with Vince and Jax, Gus. Those three were from the Belafonte clan and always in trouble with the law, but they weren't dealing, not here in the county."

"Did they find a laptop at the scene when they discovered those three bodies?"

"I'd have to check, but it doesn't ring a bell. Forensics should have a record. I'll give them a shout."

Gus handed Bob Martin a card.

"Ring me when you find out, Bob," said Gus, "did Jax and Vince ever get raided around that time? I wondered whether they might have found a stash of weapons."

"Again, I'm drawing a blank, Gus. It's so far back that I didn't have grey hair. I'll check it out and get back to you."

"Thanks, Bob," said Gus, "and just in case I'm out of the office, enjoy your retirement."

"I intend to, Gus," said Bob, "and you won't catch me slipping back in the side door looking for a cold case to solve."

"Sometimes I wonder what possessed me to agree to take this on," said Gus.

Gus and Alex made their way outside. They walked in the sunshine to the car, and Gus stopped, looking at Alex over the roof of his beloved Ford Focus.

"You know the buzz you get when you've got the answer to a tough case, Alex?"

"Yes, guv, there's nothing to match it. Do you believe we're close to finding our killer?"

"Oh, I've known since yesterday afternoon. Today was useful in confirming my suspicions. What worries me is I'm not feeling any buzz."

Gus drove back through Devizes and parked behind the Old Police Station. Once they got upstairs to the office, Luke and Lydia wanted to know how things went.

"We chatted with Tammy Belafonte, who fancied Alex," said Gus. "After a pleasant lunch in Salisbury, we uncovered a dark secret that Clive Breakwell kept hidden for fourteen years."

The phone rang before he could continue.

"Gus Freeman speaking,"

"Hello, Gus, it's me, Bob. I've got bad news, mate. Carole Brown called ten minutes after you left us. Tony passed this morning."

"Ah, that's terrible news, Bob. Not unexpected, though. He was a good bloke. So what did you dig up for me?"

"Forensics did have a laptop entered into evidence. You know how things are. They collect everything, just in case, at a crime scene. When an accident is ruled, there's no point in wasting time seeing what's in it. It took me half an hour to find the box someone had stored it in. That laptop's been gathering dust for the past fifteen years."

"Thank goodness for that," said Gus, "hide it again where nobody will find it, Bob, or get it decommissioned. There's a pal."

"No problem. As for the weapons you mentioned, several guns, knives, and machetes were handed in during an amnesty period in '04. They destroyed the lot. I've got a list of the items. Shall I email that to you?"

"That will be great, Bob. Thanks. Oh, before you go, can you let me know when Tony Brown's funeral is, please? I want to attend and pay my respects to Carole."

"Will do, Gus. Take care now. Bye."

"DS Brown didn't last long then, guv," said Alex, "he was weak when we visited him, but it's still sudden."

Gus sighed.

"Let's catch up quickly, then get off home for the weekend. No doubt you'll want to watch the wedding on TV tomorrow. After that, Harry goes to Hollywood."

"Nobody does it better than us, guv," said Alex, "and with the weather we've got, it will be special."

"Yes," said Gus, "I'll have a quiet few hours at the allotment to tend to my vegetables and consider this case. But, right, who wants to go first?"

"I found nothing on Kayleigh, guv," said Lydia, "she's a brilliant nurse, a wonderful mother. The list goes on. She's made hundreds of friends worldwide through Raleigh International and MacMillan. She's worked with kids who benefited from her projects and families who lost a loved one to cancer. She's a superstar in their eyes."

"That's one thing Ruby Belafonte can be thankful for," said Gus.

"Kai Belafonte isn't as prolific on social media, guv," said Luke. "He's a reserved type, but no doubt he's a do-gooder who never feels the need to broadcast it."

"Understandable," said Gus.

"Do you want to let us into the secret, guv?" asked Alex.

"What do you mean?" asked Lydia.

"Gus told me he'd known the killer's identity since yesterday afternoon," said Alex.

"Another day, another collar," said Lydia as Neil Davis was still absent.

"Perhaps," said Gus, "but some cases should remain unsolved. I must think things over during the weekend and report back to Geoff Mercer and the ACC on Monday morning."

"Does that mean you won't tell us, guv?" asked Luke.

"Alex can give you everything but the final piece of the jigsaw once the Freeman Files get updated with our conversations with Tammy Belafonte, Clive Breakwell and DS Martin at Salisbury police station."

With that, Gus updated his copy of the Freeman Files. The three CRT members realised they had heard his last word for today.

Gus switched off his computer at a quarter to five, grabbed his jacket, and wished them goodbye.

Saturday, 19 May to Sunday, 20 May 2018

WHILE THE WORLD turned its attention to the capital, Gus Freeman sat outside his shed on the allotment. Birdsong was his sole companion.

He reviewed the information he and the team gathered in the past forty-eight hours.

Ruby Davenport found religion after her second son, Michael, died on the tenth of January 2003.

Police found his body lying next to those of his two cousins. The three young men were addicted to drugs and committed crimes to feed their habit.

Clive Breakwell told Gus about the break-in at the lab. The burglars stole McGuire's laptop containing a deadly formula for crystal meth. The break-in fitted with the timing of the subsequent deaths. Those deaths were not so much from an overdose as from the extraordinarily high purity of the batch achieved by Ian McGuire.

The late Tony Brown frequently mentioned Vince and his mate. Tammy Belafonte had identified him as Jax, and Bob Martin added a surname yesterday.

Jax Jackson was the missing link. Ricardo Jackson left Ruby with three kids under the age of ten. If he checked, Gus thought he would uncover several more Jackson children across the South of England. Whatever name Jax received at birth was irrelevant. He was Tammy, Kai and Kayleigh's half-brother.

Gus didn't think Tammy and Kayleigh knew that fact, nor were they involved in Ian McGuire's killing. But, Kai, well, blood will out.

Gus wondered how it had gone after Michael died. It triggered Ruby's religious conversion. Kai was unaware of how Michael and the cousins met their end. He sought

Tammy out to see if she knew who had sold Michael the drugs. Of course, Tammy didn't know, but she knew a man who might. Tammy sent Kai to Jax. When they stood face-to-face, did they realise there was more to their likeness than the colour of their skin?

Gus imagined the conversation.

"How did they get the drugs, Jax?"

"Nothing to do with me, mate. They told me they had broken into a laboratory. The guy who knew about this was a Saints supporter who works in Salisbury. He's a scientist."

Kai wasn't a genius, but he worked it out in a few days. After that, he returned to see Jax.

"I want to do something, Jax. It ain't right."

"I can get you a gun, Kai. But you have to bring it back. It will be more than my life's worth if my bosses find it missing."

Jax supplied the pump-action shotgun and the ammunition. He showed the fourteen-year-old Kai how to use it and reminded him to collect the spent cartridges. Kai waited until his fifteenth birthday, the anniversary of Michael's death. Then, he climbed over the fence, crept to the patio, and blasted Ian McGuire through the window. His first shot blazed high and wide, and the second hammered into McGuire's chest. Kai knew it was a lucky shot.

Kai gathered the cartridges and high-tailed it over the fence, and disappeared. Later that day, or in the morning, he returned the gun to Jax. Safely stored away in the gang's stash of weapons, there it sat until Jax saw an opportunity to dispose of it. The amnesty provided the perfect cover.

Kayleigh benefited from Ruby's born-again faith and became the first Belafonte to stick to her schooling and become a credit to her mother.

Tammy believed her mother brainwashed Saint Kai,

but he was crafty, just like several others with the same surname before him. Kai went along with everything Ruby told him to do. He studied hard, searched for charity work overseas, took revenge for his brother's death, and fled the country. Kai came back to visit her on rare occasions. Maybe it was a guilty conscience. More likely, he wished to check the police no longer sought McGuire's killer.

Ian McGuire died on Kai's fifteenth birthday. Fourteen years on, which sentencing guidelines would apply? If the police caught Kai at the time, he might have been 'Held at Her Majesty's Pleasure.' But, on the other hand, after spending half his life on the run doing missionary work, was there a realistic chance of a conviction?

When Gus finished his gardening and thinking for the day, he'd come to a decision with which he could live.

ON SUNDAY, Gus took Vera to lunch. They spent the afternoon chatting about everything except the cold case, her ex-husband Monty, and Terry Davis's murder.

"This must be what life is like for normal people," said Vera as Gus dropped her at home. The 'Sold' sign on her cottage was a welcome sight. Her new home was over a mile closer to Urchfont.

Every little helps.

Epilogue

Monday, 21 May 2018

NEIL DAVIS WAS first in the Crime Review team office. He was glad to be back. His father's death was still fresh in his mind, but at least now, he knew the name of his killer. Gus Freeman would ensure Ricky Gardiner paid in full for his crime.

Neil looked up to see Gus walking from the lift.

"Morning, guv," said Neil, "are you OK?"

"Hardly, Neil. John Ferris called just as I was leaving home. DI Ferris has been attending a management course for the past two weeks. Her parents expected her back by yesterday evening. But, unfortunately, she didn't get home, and her phone's unresponsive."

Alex, Luke and Lydia arrived together and caught the end of the conversation.

"Who's missing, guv?" asked Alex.

"Suzie Ferris," said Gus, "I'm heading straight to London Road."

Gus fretted as the traffic lights, the school run and the general Monday blues slowed his progress to Devizes to a crawl. He scolded himself for not following up on the last pair of words on the scrap of paper he'd filled in on Thursday evening.

He should have gotten in touch with Suzie on Friday evening. The trail was cold already.

GUS HAD RECEIVED an email on his phone from Bob Martin late on Friday evening. The last piece of the jigsaw. A pump-action shotgun handed in by an unknown person was on the list of items destroyed.

As soon as Gus parked the Ford Focus, he dashed inside to sign in at Reception.

"Mr Freeman, perfect timing," said the young officer on the desk, "this call is for you."

Gus took the phone from him.

"Freeman, speaking, who's this?"

"Suzie Ferris dies if you open your mouth."

Gus stopped breathing. He could hear nothing but the dialling tone.

The voice belonged to Ricky Gardiner.

Geoff Mercer met him at the top of the stairs.

"The ACC is back in harness, looking refreshed. Shall we go in, and you can bring us up to speed?"

Kenneth Truelove was standing by his window. He returned to his desk and took his seat.

"Come on then, Freeman, tell us the good news."

"The McGuire investigation has stalled. No matter what we do, we can't find a way forward. Maybe someone can look at it again in another ten years."

Gus thought it best not to suggest they at least wait until

Ruby Belafonte dies. She'd suffered enough. It would be cruel to risk Tammy's recovery and the twin's salvation.

"The Chief Constable won't like that," said the ACC, "it will add weight to her campaign to get rid of you."

"Until a few minutes ago, I was ready to charge Ricky Gardiner with Terry Davis's murder and start proceedings against Her Ladyship and Dominic Culverhouse. Once Neil Davis has spent an hour or two chasing evidence of management course attendees and hotel accommodation and then taken witness statements, we will be ready to proceed."

"What's changed?" asked Geoff Mercer.

"Gardiner has kidnapped Suzie and threatened to kill her if I tell you everything I know."

Next in The Freeman Files series

vinci-books.com/finaldeal

A team member kidnapped, and a cold case that refuses to stay buried.

When DI Suzie Ferris is kidnapped, Gus Freeman's team faces off against a corrupt ex-officer. Their investigation links past crimes and deadly threats in a race against time to save Suzie.

Turn the page for a free preview…

Final Deal: Chapter One

Friday, 18 May 2018

DI Suzie Ferris woke to the sound of her alarm.

Today was her last day at the College of Policing before returning to Devizes. The call she received from the Chief Constable ten days ago came as a complete surprise. Suzie was about to drive into the London Road HQ to start the week after the Bank Holiday.

Her thoughts at the time centred on Gus Freeman and whether she would see him later. Suzie expected Gus to report to the ACC and Geoff Mercer about his team's progress in Swindon. She prayed things wouldn't be awkward if they bumped into one another.

The events of the fourth of May, followed by a passionate Saturday morning, meant Gus remained conflicted, but Suzie's feelings were crystal clear. She wanted Gus in her life, no matter what problems it raised.

Back in the real world on Tuesday, Sandra Plunkett informed Suzie she had enrolled her on a Digital and

Cyber-crime course at Ryton-on-Dunsmore, near Coventry. The Chief Constable also gave strict instructions that mobile phones and laptops were not permitted. She told Suzie to leave her communication devices at home.

On her two-hour drive to the Midlands on the A429, Suzie split the journey time between thoughts of Gus and wondering why this course at the College of Policing had never surfaced before today.

Geoff Mercer was her immediate superior. Her career improvement initiatives came through him in the usual scheme of things. Perhaps the Chief Constable knew about her and Gus and wanted to keep them at arm's length.

Suzie had told herself not to be daft. It was their secret, and that's the way it stayed.

After a tiring day at College last Friday, Suzie called her mother from her hotel room in the evening and said she decided to stay in Coventry over the weekend. There were several course attendees from the West Midlands force, and with plenty of live music venues, party bars and nightclubs available, it offered a chance to relax with her colleagues.

The aim of a hedonist weekend was not to get Gus Freeman out of her system; far from it, Suzie needed to keep active to stop pining for him.

On Saturday morning, after a boozy night, Suzie wished she was back home to take her usual horse ride across the fields near Worton. Fresh air always helped clear a thick head. She spent the morning in recovery mode.

After a light lunch, Suzie drove to King's Norton for the Farmer's Market. She'd spotted an advert online weeks ago, and this course offered a perfect opportunity to fit in a visit. Two dozen producers displayed their wares on brightly coloured stalls. The site soon filled with families and couples wandering from stall to stall, enjoying the sights and sounds of rural England.

Everything reminded her of the community spirit that flourished in the Wiltshire countryside she called home. The walk did her good. Suzie prepared for another night on the town.

Most of Sunday, Suzie spent in bed, under the covers. Even with the curtains drawn, the bright sunlight hurt her eyes. Suzie had recovered by Monday morning when she returned to the College to start the final five days of the course.

Now, on this overcast Friday morning, only a half-day wrap-up session remained before everyone said their farewells and headed home for the weekend. Time ticked on, so Suzie jumped out of bed and took a shower.

There hadn't been many opportunities to use her car since she'd been in the Midlands. Still, a glance at her petrol gauge yesterday evening suggested a visit to a garage for petrol would be best before embarking on the two-hour journey home.

Suzie wondered what Gus was doing this morning as she towelled herself dry. She wanted to call him. It was so frustrating not having her mobile phone. Everyone else had access to theirs in the evenings and weekends when she met them. It made no sense.

During the day, the busy schedule left little spare time for checking messages or social media, and every guest speaker reminded people of the ban on mobiles in the lecture halls. What the heck, thought Suzie. The course will be over by lunchtime, and I can get back to Wiltshire and call Gus as soon as I get home.

With her bags packed and dressed to impress for her last day, Suzie checked out and left the hotel for the last time.

She drove towards Ryton-on-Dunsmore, stopping at a garage to fill her Golf GTI's tank with petrol. She glanced at the pump number and crossed the forecourt to pay.

The garage's mini-supermarket had several customers in the queue, and Suzie waited her turn to reach the counter. She spotted a Costa Coffee franchise in the far corner with a tall, angular man with his back to her.

Suzie resisted the temptation to dash over to buy a large latte. She couldn't stand those people who wandered into work carrying a giant container of overpriced liquid. Why didn't they get out of bed earlier and have a decent breakfast before they left home?

The queue moved forward, and Suzie forgot the man lingering on the far side of the shop. Once she'd paid for her petrol, she left and walked to her car. As she pulled off the forecourt into traffic, she spotted a black van forcing its way into the queue behind her.

How inconsiderate, Suzie thought. What can they hope to gain? Everyone has to wait for a gap in heavy rush-hour traffic. There's no panic. Fifteen minutes later, she pulled into the College entrance. The black van followed her two cars back. Suzie slowed as she turned left into the car park and glanced across at the driver's cab. She should have guessed. The driver was that tall angular-looking guy, maybe in his fifties, who had stood by the coffee machine earlier. Suzie thought he stared straight at her.

As she parked in a bay reserved for course attendees, she recognised a girl she'd befriended over the weekend. Suzie gathered her things from the passenger seat, hopped out and locked her car.

"Hi, Josie," she called.

"Not long before we can get back to the humdrum life of crime we've missed so much," grinned Josie Bennett.

"This cyber-crime stuff is so different from the reality I face on the streets surrounding the old nick in Bordesley Green."

"I guess they staff that relic of Victorian grandeur with community police these days?" asked Suzie.

"A uniformed Sergeant, a handful of Constables and the rest are PCSOs," said Josie, "everything major gets organised from Snow Hill."

"Did you grow up around Bordesley Green?" asked Suzie, keeping a weather eye on the black van.

The vehicle was stationary, engine idling and not yet sited in a parking bay.

"Growing up isn't the word I would use. My parents dragged me up, more like it. My experience in an inner-city borough wasn't idyllic. Not like you in the rolling countryside."

"You mean for us soft Southerners? It was different growing up on a farm, I grant you, but not a bed of roses. Unless you've worked on a large farm and realise how much work goes into keeping your head above water daily, it's hard to compare. You had to grow up fast because you lived on an estate of so-called mean streets. So my brothers and I grew up fast, watching calves and lambs struggle to survive in the first few hours after we'd help deliver them into the world. Every lost animal became an emotional punch in the gut. We soon learned that clothes, the toy we craved, and a replacement for the clapped-out tractor our father coaxed into daily life relied on us to salvage all the little mites we could."

"Alright, keep your hair on. We never had a Pony Club on our doorstep, though. Let's change the subject. How have you got on with your new Chief Constable?" asked Josie as they reached the front door.

"She's as hard as nails," said Suzie, "which is understandable. It's the only way a woman can be if she wants to reach the top."

"You don't want to get on the wrong side of her," said Josie, "Sandra can be a right bitch. It goes with the territory, I guess, although her partner is a pussy cat. When they socialised with us, which wasn't often, the guys called them Butch and Sundance."

The two DIs paused inside the building as Josie nodded towards a group of male course attendees trotting across the car park towards them.

"Cutting it fine, as usual," she laughed, "and yet they'll still get further than you and I with the promotion boards."

"Not if I can help it," said Suzie. "Did you see that black van in the car park?"

"I never noticed one. Why?" said Josie.

"A van followed me here. I'm sure of it. The driver was alone at the garage, where I filled up, getting a coffee. I'd never seen him before."

"Either he fancied you, or he lost his way. You would need some nerve to enter this car park if you weren't a copper unless you had a good reason to be here. The signs are big enough. He's gone now, hasn't he? Why worry?"

Suzie shrugged. Josie was probably right.

Three hours later, the course ended, and groups gathered to say their goodbyes and make empty promises to keep in touch. Suzie collected a few phone numbers in her notebook.

"Did you leave your phone in the car?" asked Josie as they swapped numbers.

"I was told not to bring any communication devices; no mobiles or laptops permitted, according to my Chief Constable."

"No way," said Josie, pulling a face, "none of us got that message. Perhaps she fancies you. Or are you sleeping with one of your ACCs, and she wanted to put a spoke in your wheel?"

Suzie hoped the heat she felt at that remark didn't show on her face.

"I thought my behaviour over the weekend convinced you I enjoy a good time as much as the next single girl," she replied. "I'm thirty-three. There are no women in my life, and I've had fun without wanting to marry any of the men I've dated yet."

"Sandra Plunkett may have the right idea for reaching the top in this game," said Josie. "Somehow, I don't see her needing children to complete the family unit. I'm two years younger than you and want to get married and have kids. But, when I look at the men I come into contact with, it doesn't fill me with optimism."

"I made the mistake of trying to turn the clock back a few weeks ago," said Suzie as she and Josie stood by Suzie's car. "An old boyfriend moved back into the area and got in touch. He played professional rugby for several years. Now he's a player-coach with a local club. He's not a copper nor a criminal, but it was a disaster."

"Can you remember his number? I'll stick it on my phone. If you don't have any further use for him, I enjoy a scrum-down now and again."

"I can't recall it at the minute," said Suzie, "when I get home and get reunited with my mobile, I'll forward his details."

Josie gave Suzie a quick hug and headed towards her car. Suzie called after her.

"Just make sure you never forget his name."

Suzie was already motoring out of the car park. Josie

stood with her hand on her door handle with a bemused look.

"I wonder what that was about?" she thought, jumping into the driver's seat and looking forward to another hectic weekend.

As Suzie Ferris negotiated the early afternoon traffic between the College and the quickest route south to Wiltshire, Gus Freeman and DS Alex Hardy were going to Salisbury. They met with Clive Breakwell at the research establishment where Dr Ian McGuire used to work. Breakwell and McGuire were friends and colleagues.

Gus knew Suzie was attending a course in the Midlands, but his lack of success in getting a reply to his text messages troubled him more than he wanted to admit. He hated not being able to give total concentration to a meeting. Gus hoped Alex Hardy picked up any crumbs of valuable information he missed this afternoon.

Clive Breakwell told them of a break-in at the lab between Christmas and New Year 2003. The burglars stole McGuire's laptop containing a deadly formula for crystal meth. The break-in fitted with the subsequent deaths of two of Kai Belafonte's cousins. Those deaths resulted from the high purity of a batch of crystal meth achieved by Ian McGuire. The scientist was proving to himself that his genius was undiminished. He destroyed the test batch and forgot about the experiment. However, the laptop retained details of the formula, and the thieves were unaware of the price they would pay for playing with fire.

Kai's half-brother Jax Jackson supplied the weapon and ammunition the fourteen-year-old used to get his revenge. He climbed over the fence behind McGuire's home, crept to the patio, and shot the scientist through the window.

When Gus left Salisbury later that afternoon, he knew the identity of McGuire's killer. Finally, another open cold case could close after a fourteen-year gap. But, even as he left the research lab, Gus Freeman wondered whether unmasking the killer was the right thing to do.

While Alex and Gus returned to the CRT office, Suzie was nearing Royal Leamington Spa, the Regency town famed for its wide boulevards, Georgian architecture and beautiful parks. She'd tuned her car radio to the local station to catch traffic alerts when she travelled from her hotel daily. Suzie thanked her lucky stars she'd forgotten to switch channels. There was a fifteen-mile tailback on the M5 below Junction 6 near Worcester. That was where she planned to join the motorway, with her ultimate destination being the Bath junction on the M4. There weren't many better places to shop when you had a spare afternoon.

Suzie did a quick re-jig of her trip home. She could take advantage of the opportunity to shop here in the Spa town. The place had a reputation for excellent food, and with Royal Priors and Regent Court shopping centres within a stone's throw of a large car park, it was ideal. If the tailback eased by three o'clock, she'd join the M5 as planned. If not, she'd take the more leisurely A429 route as she had when she came north.

She forgot the unwanted attention of the stranger this morning. Suzie saw plenty of black vans on the roads, but none gave her cause for concern. She spent two pleasant hours eating a light lunch and strolling through various department stores. It was impossible to avoid making a few purchases.

A girl can never have too many shoes. Suzie also bought more underwear. Her mother always warned her never to go out without a clean pair in case she was in an accident.

Suzie would have returned to her car twenty minutes earlier if it wasn't for a handbag dilemma. She eyed it in the shop window of a famous brand, and it was just the right size and colour—something she'd wanted for ages. Inside the shop, Suzie held it, hung it over her shoulder and admired the look in the mirror. It was expensive. Should she splash out and buy it? There was just one tiny niggle. The strap wasn't adjustable. If Suzie were six feet tall, it would be perfect. Any attempt to shorten the strap would be apparent. The design only worked with the strap as it was. In the end, Suzie admitted defeat.

Suzie hurried back to the multi-storey car park. She wanted to check the traffic situation before deciding which road to take out of town. She darted up the stairwell to the First Floor and strode towards her Golf GTI.

Car parks aren't the safest places for women alone, but Suzie felt secure enough in the middle of the afternoon. The low ceilings would make this place much scarier late in the evening. Suzie looked to her left and right. She could see nobody close by her.

It was eerily quiet, and Suzie sighed with relief when she saw the boot of her car in the bay beyond the next pillar. She was thankful the architect opted for wider bays than average. Suzie rummaged in her handbag for her keys and gathered her purchases into the same hand while she opened the door.

She sensed movement behind her and froze. Her feet swept from under her, and a firm shove pitched Suzie forward onto her knees. Her shopping slid under the rear of the GTI. On the floor, Suzie realised she was dealing with a single attacker. The man dragged her to her feet and frog-marched her towards a vehicle opposite. The rear doors were open, and her attacker bundled her into the back of a black van.

It had to be the man from the garage. She'd not spotted him all afternoon. Despite her training, Suzie realised resistance was pointless.

Inside the van, the man placed a cloth bag loosely over her head, holding her in a tight headlock face down, making it hard to breathe. He flipped her onto her back like a rag doll, and she felt the cold steel of a handcuff clamped onto her right wrist.

Her instinct was to kick out and punch her attacker with her left arm, but she encountered nothing but fresh air. He had moved out of reach. Suzie realised the other handcuff was now securing her to the side of the van. There was no escape. She heard the back doors slam shut. At first, there was silence, and then a minute later, they were on the move.

Who was he, and what did he want? Where was he taking her?

Suzie tried to think as she sat on the floor of the van. They were out of the car park and in traffic within a minute. What time was it when he kidnapped her? She thought it must have been three o'clock. Suzie listened to the van's engine sound and the frequency with which they slowed or stopped.

The way the van was travelling, they were still in a built-up area. That meant there were traffic lights, roundabouts, and a pedestrian crossing. She could hear the beeps indicating it was safe to cross. Suzie yelled for help, but nobody could hear her cries. The van was on the move again.

Progress was smoother now, and they were travelling at speed. Did that mean they were on a major road, dual carriageway, or motorway? Suzie cursed. If only this had happened near her home. She might recognise where they were. She had planned to head for the M5 near Worcester when her captor struck. He could take her in any direction now.

The van slowed and turned left. Was this their destination? The engine died. Everything was quiet. Suzie shouted for help at the top of her voice. She could hear nothing. The cloth bag was slowly suffocating her; she felt lethargic. Suzie willed the adrenaline needed to attack her captor when the time came. She had to throw off this stupor and find the courage to escape. To sit and wait for what he planned for her was not an option.

The van's rear doors opened, and the man removed the handcuff from the metal framework on the interior wall. He soon secured both of Suzie's wrists in front of her. He dragged her to the doorway. Suzie felt a warm breeze on her bare arms as she felt the edge of the van floor under her feet. She caught him unawares. Suzie ripped the bag off her head and, clasping her hands together, swung hard across the man's face as she sprang forward.

Suzie landed on her feet and stumbled but soon ran for her life.

At last, she could see the lay of the land. The van sat in front of a 1930s detached house. Mature trees screened the driveway from the road. She glanced left as she reached the pavement. Her captor was already in pursuit. Wherever she was, there were no other houses within a hundred yards in that direction. She had to go to her right. Suzie prayed they were on the outskirts of a small town. Surely she could outrun a guy twenty years her senior? She sprinted to her right, looking for signs of life, another property, and a vehicle to flag down. There had to be something. Where was everyone?

The man was closing. It was her fault. She was doing

what every woman does when chased in a horror film. They trip and fall or run into a blind alley. Suzie knew that with each frantic attempt to locate an escape route, she slowed in anticipation of the need for a sudden change of direction.

The road surface was dreadful, with potholes everywhere. Suzie could feel the man's breath on her neck. Her right foot caught a hole's edge and turned her ankle. Pain screamed through her leg, and she sprawled forward onto the tarmac. The handcuffs prevented her from making a comfortable landing. Her arms were torn and bleeding after scraping along the rough surface.

The man jumped on top of her. Suzie screamed as his knee rammed into the small of her back. Two minutes, Suzie thought. He chased me for two minutes, and nobody saw or heard a thing. So much for her dash for freedom.

Suzie struggled in vain as her captor led her towards the house. The fall had winded her, and he was too strong. Her heart sank when she saw her purse, shopping bags and suitcase on the van's front seat. That explained the delay in leaving the car park.

Nothing remained to show anything untoward, let alone evidence of a kidnapping. Suzie's parking ticket expired after four hours. Someone would slip a note beneath a windscreen wiper to say she would receive a fine through the post. It could be ages before anyone thought to check for her car hidden away in Leamington Spa. The town had never been on her list of destinations. Without that tailback on the M5, she could have been safe at home in Worton.

Once inside the house, the man pushed her towards the first room off the hallway. It was small and dark. Everything smelled musty as if the house had been empty for ages. The door closed, and Suzie heard the snap of a padlock. She ran to the bay window, but a lock secured every exit point.

Suzie checked her surroundings. She had visited several similar properties in her time. This room was the sitting room that families kept for high days and holidays in the decade following the war. The dining room and kitchen lay at the back of the house, where the family spent most of their time. There was no central heating, but the kitchen was always warm.

Few homes had a television in those days, so everyone crowded around the radio in the dining room. The large table offered plenty of space for games of cards, board games and jigsaws. Suzie realised she was rambling. It was hard to concentrate.

Why was someone holding her prisoner, anyway? The man hadn't attempted to touch her. Thank God. He hadn't spoken one word to her throughout the ordeal. There had to be something she was missing.

Suzie listened for movement inside the house. Where was he? She hadn't heard the front door since they came indoors. Was she alone in the dark with nobody coming to rescue her? Suzie bit her bottom lip. She refused to cry. There was nothing to do but wait and worry about what followed. Suzie sank into the nearest comfortable chair.

It was morning when she awoke. Suzie blinked hard to clear her head. The events of yesterday afternoon came rushing back. Her elbows, forearms and knees stung from the cuts and scratches she had suffered. Her mouth was dry.

"Is there anyone there?" she croaked.

Suzie heard heavy footsteps on the stairs, and a kettle whistled behind her in the kitchen. She could hear a faint clicking of china and cutlery. Was this breakfast for one or two, Suzie wondered. The padlock scraped against the wooden door, and the man opened it just enough to slide in a tray. The door closed again, and the lock snapped shut at once.

"What do you want?" cried Suzie, "why are you keeping me here?"

There was no reply.

The breakfast tea was drinkable, and Suzie devoured the two slices of toasted white bread. She wouldn't recommend wearing handcuffs while breakfasting, but she coped. There was no cutlery. What an idiot to think he might have left a knife or spoon for her to unscrew the window locks. Suzie wondered what Gus was doing this Saturday morning. She missed him.

Stop thinking of Gus, she scolded herself. Don't get emotional. Keep learning what you can about the man who's taken you and where this house is. You have to believe that your parents will raise the alarm.

Suzie brushed her teeth with her finger. She needed to use the bathroom. She called out and sighed with relief when she heard the padlock opening. Her captor led her across the hallway to a downstairs cloakroom with no toilet paper. She longed to climb to the shower or bath she imagined was behind the door she could see at the top of the stairs.

He never offered her the chance to get washed. So far, the small front room with shuttered windows and the loo were the only rooms she could describe to her colleagues.

If she ever got out of here alive.

There was nothing in either room to show who lived there. The décor was dated, and the furniture was sparse but functional. Perhaps that was why the man brought her here. It might have been his parent's home, even if the shiny stainless steel padlock was a recent addition.

To pass the hours until the next visit from her captor,

Suzie imagined what lay behind the wall. Did they have comfortable chairs next door and dining chairs? Were there French windows leading into the garden? Could you access a conservatory from the kitchen? How many bedrooms were upstairs? She thought it was three rather than two. Did her captor have a brother or sister? What was it like growing up here?

In his formative years, what turned him into a predator who collected women off the streets and imprisoned them? Suzie was determined not to think of herself as a victim. She was a survivor.

Final Deal: Chapter Two

Monday, 21 May 2018

Neil Davis was first in the Crime Review team office and was glad to be back. His father's death was still fresh in his mind, but now Neil knew the name of Terry's killer. Gus Freeman would make sure Ricky Gardiner paid in full for his crime.

Neil looked up to see Gus walking from the lift.

"Morning, guv," said Neil, "are you OK?"

"Hardly, Neil. John Ferris rang me just as I was leaving home. DI Ferris attended a digital and cyber-crime course for the last ten days. Her parents expected her home on Friday. Suzie spent the previous weekend in the Midlands, so it was always possible she would stay there longer. John said they began to wonder when Suzie didn't get in touch by last night, and he phoned her. There was no response."

Alex Hardy, Luke Sherman and Lydia Logan Barre arrived together and caught the end of the conversation.

"Who's missing, guv?" asked Alex.

"Suzie Ferris," said Gus, "I'm heading straight to London Road for a meeting on our last case, but this matter will get priority."

"What can we be getting on with while you're gone, guv?" asked Alex.

"Alex, you can ensure everything we uncovered on the McGuire case gets included in the Freeman Files. Lydia, clear the decks ready for action. Despite everything that's blown up in our faces this morning, I expect to bring another cold case back for us to unravel. Luke, your stint ends with us on Friday. Perhaps you could help Neil with what he's doing."

"Do I need to get him to sign the Official Secrets Act, guv?" asked Neil.

Neil was hunting details of the other course members when Dominic Culverhouse and Sandra Plunkett attended the old Bramshill House Training College together. A young man died in a hit-and-run accident late one night six years ago. Gus Freeman believed those two were attempting to cover up their involvement in his death.

"Not on this occasion, Neil, but that task *is* confidential, Luke. For our eyes only. Do you understand?"

"I get it, guv. You can rely on me."

Gus hurried to the lift.

"Right then, Luke," said Neil, "the hunt begins. We need the names and addresses of those officers on the same course in 2012. We're looking for hotels in the Basingstoke area that the various police forces used to house those senior officers during their stay. Gus wants to interview as many people as possible to confirm the events leading to the hit-and-run accident on the B3400 Andover Road. Jason Whitworth was cycling home after work on the twenty-second of September when a car struck him from behind. The following morning, a passing motorist spotted his body and broken bicycle in the ditch.

"Nasty," said Luke, "and they never found the driver?"

"No, but once we've found the other police officers in the area, our next task will be to locate the car involved."

"That might be difficult," said Luke, "unless they found evidence from the car at the scene."

"Oh, we don't need that," said Neil, "Gus knows who the driver was, so we need to check which car he drove at the time."

Luke looked puzzled.

"I know, mate," said Neil, "now you can see why it's confidential."

Luke started whistling. ♫ There could be trouble ahead♫.

Alex and Lydia shared a glance. Luke was a round peg in a round hole. What a shame he had to return to his old job.

Gus dashed into Reception at London Road. Before John Ferris's call, his original plan was to sign in, get upstairs to see the ACC and collect the murder file for his next case. Gus planned to stall the ACC on the McGuire business and hoped to get away with promising to have the data with him later today. However, the call meant that a search for Suzie needed to begin as soon as possible. What lay behind her uncharacteristic disappearance?

The young officer at Reception was speaking to him, but his thoughts were on Suzie. Gus realised the lad was holding a phone towards him. He grabbed it impatiently and answered.

Gus stopped breathing as he heard the sinister voice.

"Suzie Ferris dies if you open your mouth."

Ricky Gardiner rang off before Gus could reply. Gus reached the top of the stairs and found DS Geoff Mercer smiling at him without a care in the world. Gus blanked out the small talk. He was thinking about Gardiner and why he had taken Suzie.

Geoff finished speaking and tapped on the ACC's door. Gus followed his friend inside the office. The ACC looked in better form than before his few days' holiday.

There was no preliminary chat this morning. It was straight to business.

The ACC's first request was for an update on the McGuire case. Gus decided to wing it. He admitted the investigation was going nowhere. He suggested sticking the file back in the box until someone else had nothing better to do. Gus expected a chilly reaction to that news.

Gus reckoned if they pursued Ian McGuire's killer and the case reached the courts, it would create a bigger mess than if they drew a veil over it here and now. Kenneth Truelove prattled on about the Chief Constable not liking that Gus now had something in the Loss column after three straight Wins.

The three men knew Dominic Culverhouse and Sandra Plunkett wanted the Crime Review Team out of business. They'd known that before Terry Davis ventured home from Marbella for the first time in five years. What hadn't been clear was how far the duo would go to protect the secret Terry held.

They had paid Ricky Gardiner to keep tabs on Gus and his activities. Who knows how many of his friends and colleagues were under surveillance? Gus could only speculate on what they planned to do. However, Terry's arrival in Devizes increased the pace and scale of things altogether. Culverhouse and Plunkett panicked and ordered

Gardiner to remove the perceived threat posed by Terry Davis.

Last week, besides attending to the McGuire cold case review, Gus secured extra resources to investigate Terry Davis's murder. They now knew Gardiner was their man. On Friday, when Suzie was supposed to be driving home from the Midlands, Neil gathered the final pieces of the Bramshill and Oakley jigsaw. Gus shared none of that information with Geoff and the ACC last week.

Was there nothing he could do without the Chief Constable and her cronies hearing about it? Who could have known how far his team had reached?

Gus was ticking names off the list in his head.

He believed it was time to show his hand.

"Until a few minutes ago, I was ready to tell you to charge Ricky Gardiner with Terry Davis's murder and start proceedings against Her Ladyship and Dominic Culverhouse. Neil has a few hours of work to do chasing evidence and getting witness statements, and we will be ready to go ahead."

"What's changed?" asked Geoff Mercer.

"Gardiner has kidnapped Suzie Ferris and threatened to kill her if we use everything we know against them."

"What?" said Geoff Mercer, "I hadn't seen Suzie this morning, but I had no idea she was missing. What on earth happened?"

Gus explained the phone call from John Ferris. Failing to contact her parents was out of character. Whatever caused her to change her plans to return home on Friday afternoon meant Suzie had been missing for sixty hours. However, the phone call from Gardiner just before Gus came upstairs solved one problem. They now knew Suzie had been taken against her will by a known killer.

"I don't like the sound of that one bit," said the ACC.

"Don't lose your nerve now, Sir," said Geoff Mercer.

"I don't intend to, Mercer," said the ACC, "modern policing shouldn't be represented this way. These people are worse than criminals. They're supposed to be setting an example. Right, Freeman, what can we do to help?"

"I want to keep DS Luke Sherman on the team for the time being, Sir. The sooner we can close the net on Culverhouse and Plunkett, the better, regardless of the threat Gardiner issued."

"He killed Terry Davis," said Geoff, "We can't risk him getting a taste for it. I'll call his handlers in the Met to check whether he has a history of excessive force in any other cases. I can't allow DI Ferris to get sacrificed. Even if saving her derails our attempt to bring down two corrupt high-flying officers."

"I'll hold the fort here, Mercer," said the ACC, "you get over to the CRT office. Grab the young WPC you borrowed last week. She acquitted herself well. I'll square it with her, Sergeant; he owes me a favour. We must keep a lid on what we're doing, loose lips and all that. Her Ladyship won't hear a peep from me, and unless she visits the CRT office, she won't know who's working there and on what. Your office is on the first floor, Freeman. The only access is by lift, yes? Don't bloody let her inside the office. Is that understood?"

"Yes, Sir," said Gus.

"Start the lads in the Hub on a search for Ferris's car. Concentrate on the area between the College for Policing and her most likely route home. Does she have a GPS tracker on her vehicle? What about her mobile phone?"

"I don't know the answer to the first question, but her father told me her mobile is unresponsive Sir," said Gus.

"That's unusual, isn't it? Ferris and others like her

carry a charger with them wherever they go. They run their lives through a blessed smartphone. If she was at Ryton-on-Dunsmore for ten days, it needed regular re-charging. Who was on the same course? Identify them, and discover the last person to see her. Which way did she travel home? Let me think. Credit card, yes, check for that too. A modern girl, like Ferris, probably uses this tap-and-go business and never needs to scrabble through her pockets for loose change. If there's anything else that narrows the field for her whereabouts, add them to the list."

"I think that's enough to be going on with, Sir," said Geoff Mercer.

"One thing, Freeman, before you dash off," said the ACC.

"Yes, Sir?"

"What was it you discovered in the past couple of days you intended to enlighten us with this morning?"

"Culverhouse and the Chief Constable attended a course at Bramshill in 2012. A twenty-six-year-old cyclist from Basingstoke died in a hit-and-run. Nobody found the body until the following morning, and they never traced the driver."

"You're sure one of our mutual friends hit him? I assume the other person was in the car at the time?"

"Yes, Sir. Terry Davis discovered the truth and believed it was one of his 'get out of jail free' cards. But, unfortunately, they couldn't risk Terry letting me in on the secret, so Gardiner silenced him."

"How did you learn of their involvement if Davis hadn't told you yet?" asked the ACC.

"Terry left a cryptic clue with Donna, one of his confidential informants. He passed it to her in a pub he visited on Sunday night. A little detective work unlocked the clue, and now we need to fill in the finer details."

"When will I receive the files on the McGuire case? I hoped you would nail someone for that. I wanted to keep the Chief Constable off our backs, not just because I wanted Tony Brown to learn we'd caught the killer. It played on his mind, you know, he put everything into that case and got nowhere. He was never the same man after that."

"You'll have the files by this afternoon, Sir," said Gus, "You'll see that we did our best. Someone much cleverer than me said you can't win them all."

"That chap Kierkegaard again, I bet," said the ACC, "I can't say I've ever read any of his books. I sense his philosophy wouldn't fit with my religious beliefs. You set great store by him. Each to his own."

"I believe it was Connie Mack, an American businessman who said you can't win them all," said Gus, "but don't quote me on that."

"Another wise man said that," said Geoff Mercer, "time we left."

Geoff and Gus left the ACC in his chair.

"That's the most I've heard him say since I've known him," said Geoff.

"He was on the money with his list of priorities, Geoff. It's a pity he's retiring a year from now. We could make a decent copper out of him, given time."

"Kenneth's always been one of the good guys," said Geoff, "sometimes, a promotion takes an officer out of the action too soon. The ACC got the job done when he was an Inspector. His uniformed officers spoke highly of him; I can guarantee that. He loved being in the thick of it. Once he made ACC, the job became meetings, budgets, targets and initiatives. He can cope with anything anyone throws at him, but times like this are his forte. Although, like us, he'd rather not have to face up to one of our female officers getting kidnapped."

"I'll drive to the CRT office," said Gus, "and inform Luke Sherman that he's staying. I'll brief the team on what's required."

"Thanks. My first task is to round up WPC Cranston, and then I'll visit the Hub to set the wheels in motion there. Amelia and I should be with you in an hour."

"Fair enough," said Gus, "see you later."

Gus sensed movement to his right. It was Vera.

"How much can you tell me?" she asked.

"What have you heard?" asked Gus.

"Suzie's not returned to work as planned. We've received no phone call to say she's ill. You and Geoff Mercer seem stressed. Are the two related?"

"Try not to worry," said Gus, "we're on top of things. I can't say more at present. Keep the ACC calm if you can. This morning, he might need a drop of Scotch in his cup of tea."

"Keep us in the loop, Gus," said Vera.

"You can count on it," said Gus. He pushed through the main door and made for his trusty Ford Focus. What a start to the week.

Grab your copy....
vinci-books.com/finaldeal